THE SUPERNATURALIST

EOIN COLFER

SCHOLASTIC INC.

New York   Toronto   London   Auckland   Sydney
Mexico City   New Delhi   Hong Kong   Buenos Aires

ISBN 0-439-69988-6

Published by Scholastic Inc., 557 Broadway, New York, NY 10012,
by arrangement with Hyperion Books for Children,
an imprint of Disney Children's Book Group, LLC.
SCHOLASTIC and associated logos are trademarks and/or
registered trademarks of Scholastic Inc.

12 11 10 9 8 7 6 5 4 3 2 1   4 5 6 7 8 9/0

Printed in the U.S.A.   40

First Scholastic printing, October 2004

This book is set in 11-point Scala.

CHAPTER 1
COSMONAUT HILL

Satellite City, Northern Hemisphere. Soon

SATELLITE CITY: THE CITY OF THE FUTURE, proclaimed the billboards. A metropolis completely controlled by the Myishi 9 Satellite hovering overhead like a floating man-of-war. An entire city custom constructed for the third millennium. Everything the body wanted, and nothing the soul needed. Three hundred square miles of gray steel and automobiles.

Satellite City. A supercity of twenty-five million souls, each one with a story more heartbreaking than the last. If it's happy-ever-afters you want, stay away from the city of the future.

Take Cosmo Hill, for example, a nice-enough boy who had never done anything wrong in his short existence. Unfortunately, this was not enough to guarantee him a happy life, because Cosmo Hill did not have a sponsor. And in Satellite City, if you didn't have a sponsor and they couldn't trace your natural parents through public-record DNA files, then you were sent to an orphanage until you reached adulthood. And by that time you were either dead, or the orphanage had fabricated a criminal record for you so you could be sold to one of the private labor prisons.

Fourteen years before we take up the thread of this story, baby Cosmo was discovered swaddled in an insulated Cheery Pizza envelope on Cosmonaut Hill in Moscowtown. The state police swabbed him for DNA, searched for a match in the Satellite mainframe, and came up blank. Nothing unusual about that—orphans turn up every day in the city. So the newly christened Cosmo Hill was dipped in a vaccine vat and sent on a tube to the Clarissa Frayne Institute for Parentally Challenged Boys. Freight class.

Satellite City was not part of any welfare state, so its institutions had to raise funds in any way they could. Clarissa Frayne's speciality was product testing. Whenever a new modified food or untested pharmaceutical product was being developed, the orphanage volunteered its "no-sponsor" charges as guinea pigs. It made perfect financial sense. The orphans got fed and cleaned, and the Frayne Institute got paid for the privilege.

Cosmo received his schooling from education software, his teeth were whiter than white, and his hair was lustrous and flake-free; but his insides felt like they were being scoured with a radioactive wire brush. Eventually, Cosmo realized that the orphanage was slowly killing him. It was time to get out.

There were only three ways out of Clarissa Frayne:

adoption, death, or escape. There was zero chance that he'd actually be adopted—not at his age. Truculent teenagers were not very popular with the childless middle classes. For years, he had cherished the dream that someone would want him; now it was time to face facts. Death was much easier to achieve. All he had to do was keep on doing what he was told, and his body would give up in a matter of years. The average life expectancy of an institutionalized orphan was fifteen years. Cosmo was fourteen. That left him with less than twelve months before the statistics said his time was up. Twelve months to plan for the final option. There was only one way he would get out of Clarissa Frayne alive: *escape*.

At the Clarissa Frayne Institute for Parentally Challenged Boys, every day was basically the same. Toil by day, fitful sleep by night. There were no days off, no juvenile rights. Every day was a work day. The marshals worked the orphans so hard that by eight P.M. most of the boys were asleep standing up, dreaming of their beds.

Cosmo Hill was the exception. He spent every moment of his waking life watching for that one chance. That split second when his freedom would beckon to him from outside an unlocked door or an unguarded fence. He must be ready to seize that moment and run with it.

It wasn't likely that his chance would come on this particular day. And even if it did, Cosmo didn't think he would have the energy to run anywhere.

The no-sponsors had spent the afternoon testing a new

series of antiperspirants. Their legs had been shaved and sectioned with rings of tape. The flesh between the bands was sprayed with five varieties of antiperspirant, and then the boys were set on treadmills and told to run. Sensors attached to their legs monitored their sweat glands, determining which spray was most effective. By the end of the day, Cosmo had run ten miles, and the pores on his legs were inflamed and scalded. He was almost glad to be cuffed to a moving partner and begin the long walk back to the dormitory.

Marshal Redwood ushered the boys into the dorm. Redwood resembled a waxed gorilla, with the exception of a red cowlick, which he toyed with constantly.

"Now, boys," said Redwood, unlocking one pair of cuffs at a time. "There's a game on tonight that I am very interested in seeing. As a matter of fact, I bet a few dinars on the outcome. So if you know what's good for you . . ."

Redwood didn't have to finish his threat. The boys knew that the marshal had a hundred legal ways of making a no-sponsor's life miserable. And a thousand illegal ones.

"Sleep well, young princes," said the marshal, grinning, keying his code into the dorm door. "Tomorrow, as usual, is a busy day. Jam-packed full of fun."

The no-sponsors relaxed once Redwood had gone, and the silence of discipline was replaced by the groans and sobs of boys in pain. Cosmo touched his leg gingerly where a particularly acidic spray had actually burned the skin.

"Five minutes to lights-out," said Redwood's voice over a network of speakers. "Climb the ladders, boys."

Three hundred orphans turned immediately to the dozen or so steel ladders, and began climbing. Nobody wanted to be stranded on the dorm floor once the ladders were retracted. If the marshals caught a no-sponsor on the ground after lights out, a ten-mile run would seem like a Sunday stroll compared to the punishment they would dish out.

Each boy had an assigned space in the dorm, where he ate, slept, and passed whatever leisure time the no-sponsors had. These rooms were actually sections of cardboard utility pipe that had been sawed into six-foot lengths. The pipes were suspended from a network of wires almost fifty feet off the ground. Once the pipes were occupied by orphans, the entire contraption swayed like an ocean liner.

Cosmo climbed quickly, ignoring the pain in his leg muscles. His pipe was near the top. If the lights went out before he reached it, he could be stranded on the ladder. Each step brought fresh stabs of pain to his tendons, but he climbed on, pressing against the boy ahead with his head, feeling the boy behind closing in.

After a few minutes of feverish climbing, Cosmo reached his level. A narrow walkway, barely the width of his hand, serviced each pipe. Cosmo slid across carefully, gripping a rail on the underside of the walkway above him. His pipe was four columns across. Cosmo swung inside, landing on the foam-rubber mattress. Ten seconds later, the lights went out.

A sick yellow glow lit the interior of each pipe. Dinner. The meal had been thrown in earlier by a marshal in a cherry picker. The meal packs had been tested a few years previously by the no-sponsors for use by soldiers in the field. The trays and water bottles were luminous, and also edible, which meant that the orphans could eat after lights-out, saving the management a few dinars. The tray was made from a rough, unleavened crispbread, and the water bottle from a semirigid gum. The army had discontinued use of the meal packs following several lawsuits by soldiers, claiming that the luminous packs caused internal bleeding. The orphanage bought up the surplus and fed them to the orphans every single day.

Cosmo ate slowly, not bothering to wonder what was in the meal. Wondering about it would only add one more worry to his list. He had to believe that he would escape Clarissa Frayne before the meal packs could do him any lasting damage.

Cosmo saved the water for last, using most of it to wash down the crispbread tray. Then he turned the gum bottle inside out, laying it across his head like a facecloth. There must be a better life, he thought glumly. Somewhere, at this very moment, people were talking openly. Surely people were laughing. Real laughter too, not just the spiteful kind that so often echoed around the orphanage halls.

Cosmo lay back, feeling the gum bottle's moisture seeping into his forehead. He didn't want to think tonight. He didn't want to play the parent game, but the sleep that he had yearned for was proving elusive. His own parents. Who were they? Why had they abandoned him on Cosmonaut Hill? Maybe he was Russian. It was impossible to tell from his features. Brown curly hair; brown eyes; light skin, freckled brown. He could be from anywhere.

Why had they abandoned him?

Cosmo transferred the gum bottle to a red strip on his leg. Shut up, he told his brain. Not tonight. No living in the past. Look to the future.

Someone knocked gently from the pipe above. It was Ziplock Murphy. The network was opening up. Cosmo answered the knock with one of his own, then pulled back his mattress, signaling Fence in the pipe below. The no-sponsors had developed a system of communication that allowed them to converse without angering the marshals. Clarissa Frayne discouraged actual face-to-face communication between the boys, on the grounds that friendships might develop. And friendships could lead to unity, maybe even revolt.

Cosmo dug his nails into a seam in the cardboard pipe and pulled out two small tubes. Both had been fashioned from mashed gum bottles and crispbread, then baked on a windowsill. Cosmo screwed one into a small hole in the lower surface of his pipe, and the other into a hole overhead.

Ziplock's voice wafted through from above. "Hey, Cosmo. How are your legs?"

"Burning," grunted Cosmo. "I put my gum bottle on one, but it's not helping."

"I tried that too," said Fence from below. "Antiperspirants. This is nearly as bad as the time they had us testing those Creeper slugs. I was throwing up for a week."

Comments and suggestions snuck through the holes from all over the pipe construct. The fact that the pipes were all touching, along with the acoustics of the hall, meant that voices traveled amazing distances through the network. Cosmo could hear no-sponsors whispering a hundred yards away.

"What does the Chemist say?" asked Cosmo. "About our legs?"

The Chemist was the orphanage name for a boy three columns across. He loved to watch medical programs on TV, and was the closest the no-sponsors had to a consultant.

Word came back in under a minute. "The Chemist says spit on your hands and rub it in. The spit has some kind of salve in it. Don't lick your fingers, though, or the antiperspirant will make you sicker than those Creeper slugs."

The sound of boys spitting echoed through the hall. The entire lattice of pipes shook with their efforts. Cosmo followed the Chemist's advice, then lay back, letting a hundred different conversations wash over him. Sometimes he would join in, or at least listen to one of Ziplock's yarns. But tonight all he could think about was that moment when freedom would beckon to him. And being ready when it arrived.

Cosmo's chance at freedom came the very next day during a routine transfer. Forty no-sponsors, Cosmo among them, had just spent the day at a music company watching proposed TV spots for computer-generated pop groups, followed by a sixty-kilobyte questionnaire. Which sim-singer did you prefer? Which sim-performer was cool? Cool? Even the company's computers were out of touch. Kids rarely said *cool* anymore. Cosmo barely read the questions before checking a box with his digi-pen. He preferred music made by real people to pixel-generated pop. But nobody complained. A day watching music videos was infinitely preferable to more chemical tests.

Frayne marshals loaded the no-sponsors into a truck after the session. The vehicle must have been a hundred years old, with actual rubber tires instead of plastic treads. Cosmo was paired with Ziplock Murphy as a cuff partner. Ziplock was okay, except that he talked too much. This was how he had earned his orphanage name. Once, the Irish boy had *talked too much* to the wrong person and got the ziplock from a food baggie superglued over his mouth. It took weeks for the blisters to heal. Not only did Ziplock not learn his lesson, but now he had something else to talk about.

"They don't call it superglue for nothing," Ziplock said animatedly, as one of the marshals threaded the cuffs through the restraining ring on the seat. "Medics use that stuff in war zones to seal up the wounded. They pour it straight onto the wounds."

Cosmo nodded without much enthusiasm. Ziplock seemed to forget that he had told this story about a million times, maybe because Cosmo was the only one who even pretended to listen while he talked.

"They had to use boiling water to get the bag off my face," continued Ziplock. "I didn't feel anything, in case you're worried. One of the marshals shot my entire head full of anaesthetic first. They could have been banging six-inch nails into my skull and I wouldn't have minded."

Cosmo rubbed the flesh beneath the cuffs. All the no-sponsors had a ring of red flesh around their wrists. A mark of shame.

"You ever try breathing only through your nose for an entire day? I panicked a few times, I'll admit it."

In the cab, the pilot was uplinking the truck to the navigation section of the Satellite. But there had been trouble with the Satellite lately. Too many add-ons, the TV brains said. Myishi 9 was simply getting too heavy for its engines to support such a low orbit. There was even talk of some companies' aerials snapping off and burning up.

"What's the delay?" shouted Marshal Redwood. The bulky redhead had bad breath today and a worse attitude. Too many beers the night before. His pendulous belly spoke of too many beers almost ever night.

"If I'm late again tonight, Agnes swears she's moving to her sister's."

"It's the Satellite," shouted the pilot. "I can't get a line."

"Well, make a line, or my boot is going to make a line to your butt."

Ziplock snickered just loud enough for Redwood to hear.

"You think I'm joking, Francis?" shouted the man, boxing Ziplock on the ear. "You think I wouldn't do it?"

"No, sir. You'd do it, okay. You've got that look in your eyes. It isn't smart to mess with a man who's got that look."

Redwood lifted Ziplock's chin until their eyes met. "You

know something, Francis? That's the first clever thing I've ever heard you say. It isn't smart to mess with me, because I do whatever I please. The only reason I don't get rid of a dozen of you freaks every day is the paperwork. I hate paperwork."

Ziplock should have left it there, but he couldn't. His big mouth wouldn't let him. "I heard that about you, sir."

Redwood tugged harder on Ziplock's chin, cranking it up a few more notches. "What's that, Francis? What did you hear?"

Cosmo tugged on the cuff chain. A warning. Redwood was not a man to push over the edge. Even the psycho kids were afraid of Redwood. There were stories about him. No-sponsors had gone missing.

But Ziplock couldn't stop. The words were spewing out of him like agitated bees from a hive. "I heard you don't like the paperwork, on account of some of the words have more than three letters."

The sentence was followed by a high-pitched giggle. More hysteria than humor. Cosmo realized that Ziplock was headed for the psycho ward, if he lived that long.

Redwood transferred his fingers to Ziplock's throat, squeezing casually. "Morons like you never get it. Being a smartmouth doesn't win you any prizes in this city, it just gets you hurt, or worse."

The Satellite saved Ziplock's neck, beaming down a transportation plan before Redwood could tighten his fingers another notch. The truck lurched from its spot in the parking bay, rolling onto the main highway. A guiding rod extended from below the chassis, slotting into a corresponding groove in the highway.

"We're locked in," called the pilot. "Ten minutes to the Institute."

Redwood released Ziplock's neck. "You've got the luck of the Irish, Francis. I'm too happy to inflict pain on you now. But later, when I'm in a foul mood, you can count on it."

Ziplock drew a greedy breath. He knew from experience that soon his windpipe would shrink to the diameter of a straw and he would whistle when he spoke.

"Keep a lid on it, Ziplock," hissed Cosmo, watching the marshal continue down the aisle. "Redwood is crazy. We're not real people to him."

Ziplock nodded, rubbing his tender throat. "I can't help it," he rasped, tears in his eyes. "The junk just comes out of my mouth. This life just drives me crazy."

Cosmo knew that feeling well. It visited him most nights as he lay in his pipe listening to the cries around him.

"You must feel it too, Cosmo? You think anybody is going to adopt a borderline psycho kid, or a moody teenager like yourself?"

Cosmo looked away. He knew that neither of them fit the likely adoptee profile, but Ziplock had always managed to pretend that today was the day his new parents would show up. Denying that dream meant that Ziplock was teetering on the brink of crackup.

Cosmo rested his forehead against the window, watching the city beyond the glass. They were in the projects now, flashing past gray apartment blocks. Pig-iron buildings, which was why the locals referred to Satellite City as the Big Pig. Not that the material was actually pig iron. It was a superstrong steel-based polymer that was supposed to stay cool in summer and warm in winter, but managed to do exactly the opposite.

The truck shuddered violently. Something had rear-ended them. Redwood was thrown to the floor's plastic planks. "Hey, what's going on up there?" he said.

Cosmo raised himself to the cuff's limits, straining to see. The pilot was on his feet, repeatedly punching his code into the uplink unit. "The Satellite. We lost our link!"

No link! That meant they were out here on an overcrowded highway with no pattern to follow. Minnows in a sea of hammerheads. They were struck again: sideswiped this time. Cosmo glimpsed a delivery minivan careering off the highway, bumper mangled.

Redwood struggled to his feet. "Go to manual, you cretin. Use the steering wheel."

The pilot paled. Steering wheels were only used in rural zones or for illegal drag racing in the Booshka region. More than likely he had never wrestled with a steering wheel in his life. The choice was taken away from the unfortunate man when a revolving advertisement drone hit them head on, crushing the cab like a concertina. The pilot was lost in a haze of glass and wiring.

The impact was tremendous, lifting the truck from its groove and flipping it onto its side. Cosmo and Ziplock dangled from their chairs, saved by the restraining cuffs.

Redwood and the other marshals were scattered like so many leaves in a storm.

Cosmo could not tell how many times other vehicles collided with the truck. After a time the impacts blended together like the final notes of a frenetic drum solo. Huge dents appeared in the paneling, accompanied by resonating thunderclaps. Every window smashed, raining crystal rainbows.

Cosmo hung on—what else could he do? Beside him, Ziplock's hysterical laughter was almost as piercing as the shards of glass. "Oh, man, this is it!" shouted the Irish boy.

The truck revolved a half turn, slewing off the highway in a cascade of sparks. Chunks of asphalt collapsed beneath the onslaught, leaving a thirty-meter trench in the vehicle's wake. They eventually came to rest after smashing through the window of the Dragon's Beard Chinese Restaurant. The spicy odors of ginger and soy mingled with the smells of machine oil and blood.

Cosmo put one foot on a windowsill, taking the strain off his arms. "Ziplock! Francis, are you okay?"

"Yeah, still here." The boy sounded disappointed.

Throughout the bus, no-sponsors were groaning and yelling for help. Some were injured, a few were worse. The marshals were generally out for the count. Either that, or staring at whichever limb was pointing the wrong way. Redwood gingerly touched a swelling nose. "I think it's broken," he moaned. "Agnes is gonna love this."

"Oh, well," said Ziplock, dangling above Redwood's frame. "Every cloud has a silver lining."

Redwood froze, crouching on all fours like a pit bull. A fat drop of blood slipped from one nostril, falling through an empty window frame. "What did you say?" The marshal spoke slowly, making sure every word came out right.

Cosmo swung his foot across, catching his cuff partner in the ribs. "Shut up, Ziplock. What happens to you, happens to me!"

"Okay! Okay! I didn't say anything, Marshal. Nothing at all."

But it was too late. An invisible line had been crossed. In the midst of all the chaos, Redwood retreated into himself. When he came back out, he was an altogether more dangerous individual. "The way I see it," he said, standing slowly to face the dangling boys and running a pocket comb through his precious red locks, "is that your cuff ring snapped, and you tried to escape."

In spite of his quick mouth, Ziplock was a bit slow to catch on. "What are you talking about, Mr. Redwood? There's nothing wrong with our cuff ring. Look!" He tugged the cuff to demonstrate.

"I ordered you to stop, but you wouldn't listen." Redwood sighed dramatically, his nose whistling slightly. "I had no choice but to shrink-wrap you."

Shrink-wrap was security-speak for the cellophane-virus slugs that the marshals loaded their gas-powered rods with. Once the slug hit a solid object, the virus was released and coated the target with a restrictive layer of cellophane. The cellophane was porous enough to allow shallow breathing, but had been known to squeeze so tightly that it cracked ribs. Cosmo had been shrink-wrapped once before. He had spent a week in a body cast as a result.

Cosmo elbowed Ziplock aside. "Marshal Redwood, sir. Francis didn't mean anything. He's just an idiot. I'll teach him, sir. Let me take care of it. You get that nose fixed up."

Redwood patted Cosmo's cheek. "It's a pity, Hill, because I always liked you. You don't stand up for yourself. But unfortunately, all wars have collateral damage."

The marshal reached over, inserting his swipe card into the cuff ring. The boys dropped two meters, crumpling onto the carpet of glass.

Redwood drew his rod, checking the chamber. "I'm a reasonable man," he said. "You've got twenty seconds."

Cosmo shook the glass from his clothes, dragging Ziplock to his feet. This was it. His chance had come. Live or die. "Why don't you give us thirty seconds?"

Redwood laughed. "Now, why would I do that?"

Cosmo grabbed the marshal's nose, twisting almost ninety degrees. "That's why."

Redwood's eyes filled with tears and he collapsed, writhing in the broken glass.

"Let's go," said Cosmo, grabbing Ziplock by the elbow. "We have thirty seconds."

Ziplock stood his ground. "I want to spend my half a minute watching Redwood squirm."

Cosmo ran toward the rear window, dragging the Irish

boy behind him. "Use your imagination. I prefer to live."

They climbed through the broken window into the restaurant. Diners were hugging the walls, in case the truck decided to lurch another few feet. In a few more seconds the city police would arrive, and all avenues of escape would be shut off. The searchlights from TV birds were already poking through the decimated front wall.

Ziplock grabbed a couple of duck pancakes from a stunned diner's plate. The no-sponsors had heard of freshly prepared food, but never actually tasted any before.

Ziplock stuffed one into his own mouth, offering the other to his cuff partner. Cosmo was not stupid enough to refuse food, no matter what the circumstances. Who knew when they would get to eat again, if indeed they ever did? This could be the condemned boys' last meal.

He bit into the pancake, and the tangy sauce saturated his tongue. For a boy raised on prepackaged developmental food, it was an almost religious experience. But he could not pause to enjoy it. Sirens were already cutting through the engine hiss.

Cosmo ran toward the rear of the restaurant, dragging Ziplock behind him. A waiter blocked their path. He wore a striped jumpsuit, and his hair was exceptionally shiny even by product-tester standards. "Hey," he said vaguely, not sure if he wanted to get involved. The boys skipped around the man before he could make up his mind.

A back door led to a narrow stairway, winding out of sight. Possibly to freedom, possibly to a single-room dead end.

There was no time for conscious decision. Redwood would be coming soon, if he was not already on his way. They took the stairs, squeezed together shoulder to shoulder.

"We're never going to make it," panted Ziplock, plum sauce dribbling down his chin. "I hope he doesn't get us before I finish this pancake."

Cosmo increased the pace, the cuff digging into his wrist. "We will make it. We will."

The boys rounded a corner straight into a luxurious studio apartment. A man's face peered out from beneath a large double bed.

"The earthquake," the man squeaked. "Is it over?"

"Not yet," replied Ziplock. "The big shock is on the way."

"Heaven help us all," said the man, retreating behind the fringe of a chintz bedcover.

Ziplock giggled. "Let's go before he realizes that his reporters are runaway no-sponsors."

The apartment was decorated with ancient Chinese artifacts. Suits of battle armor stood in each corner, and jade dragons lined the shelves. The main room had several windows, but most were decorative plasma; only one led to Satellite City. Cosmo popped the clip, pulling open the triple-glazed react-to-light pane.

Ziplock stuck his face into the outside air. "Excellent," he said. "A fire escape. A way down."

Cosmo stepped through, onto a metal grille. "Down is what Redwood will expect. We go up."

Ziplock held back. "Up?"

Cosmo pulled him through. "Don't tell me the boy who irritates marshals for fun is afraid of heights?"

"No," replied Ziplock, pallor washing his gaunt face. "I'm afraid of the ground."

Marshal Redwood did not pass out. He wasn't that lucky. Instead, a block of pain battered him like a malignant glacier. He combated the agony using a trick from his army days. *Locate the white center of the pain and concentrate on it.* Redwood found to his surprise that the root of his pain was not his nose, but in the center of his forehead. He focused on the spot, sucking the pain in and containing it. He trapped it there long enough to pop a pain tab from its plastic bubble in his medi-kit. Barely a minute later the pain receded to a dull throb behind one ear. Under control. For now.

Back to business. Those no-sponsors had thrown his authority back in his face. Those two were getting shrink-wrapped for sure. Still, best to pretend to follow the rules. He unclipped a communicator from his belt. "Redwood to base."

"That you, Redwood? We thought you were dead."

Redwood scowled. Fred Allescanti was on duty back at base. That man made goldfish look smart. "Yeah, well, I'm alive. But I've got a couple of runners. I'm leaving now in pursuit."

"I don't know, Marshal Redwood. You're supposed to stay with the vehicle. Regulations. They're sending a truck for you. Five minutes, tops."

Redwood lifted a rod from one of his unconscious colleagues. "Negative. The no-sponsors are armed and have already fired cellophane slugs. Can you imagine the lawsuit Clarissa Frayne will be looking at if they wrap a civilian?"

Fred did not answer for a few moments. Doubtless he was checking protocol in the security manual.

"Okay, Redwood. Maybe you could knock them around a bit first, that way we get to test some of the new pharmaceuticals."

That was typical of the institute, always looking for the upside. A new batch of synthetic skin had just come in, but they needed people with wounds to test it.

Redwood hid the throw-down rod inside his jacket. "I'll see what I can do."

In the restaurant, patrons were escaping through a side door. Not that they were guilty of anything, but nobody wanted to spend their evening answering questions from private security, state police, insurance agents, and lawyers.

When Redwood clambered through the remains of the escape hatch, people instinctively stepped out of his way. The marshal's fierce eyes and pulped mass of a face made it seem not wise to obstruct him.

For a man in pursuit of fugitives, Redwood did not seem overly eager, or even anxious. And why would he be? Though the no-sponsors were not aware of it, escape was impossible. Every move they made was being tracked. And these were not the kind of trackers that could be discarded. They were in every pore. Whenever the no-sponsors took a shower, their skin was coated with micro beads of an electronegative halogen solution, which would show up on the Clarissa Frayne scanner. Even if the orphans stopped taking showers, the solution would take months to wear off.

Redwood keyed the talk button on his communicator. "Fred. Send the Hill C and Murphy F tracker patterns to my handset."

Fred cleared his throat into the mike. "Uh . . . the tracker patterns?"

Redwood ground his teeth. "Dammit, Fred, is Bruce there? Put Bruce on."

"Bruce got called out for a little situation in D Block. I'm all on my lonesome here."

"Okay, Fred. Listen to me carefully. Punch up Cosmo and Ziplock on the tracker file, then e-mail their patterns to my handset. Use the e-mail icon. My number is right there under Personnel. All you have to do is drag and drop the folders. Got it?"

Fred wiped his sweating brow. Over the radio it sounded like sandpaper on soft wood. "I got it. Drag the folders. No problem. Here it comes."

"It had better be coming. Or I'm coming for you."

It was Redwood's habit to turn statements into threats. In sim-coffee shops he was known to say, "It had better be hot, or I'll make it hot for you." Redwood thought this was extremely clever.

Five seconds later, two moving icons appeared on the

small screen on Redwood's communicator, placing the fugitives on a fire escape outside the building. Going up, too, the idiots. What were they going to do? Fly off the roof?

Redwood grinned, the action bringing tears of pain to his eyes. Fly off the roof. That wasn't such a bad idea.

In Satellite City, raindrops could take a person's eye out if he were foolish enough to look up during a storm. Reaction with certain toxic fumes caused the water molecules to bond more efficiently until they fell to earth like missiles. Traditional umbrellas were no longer sufficient, and new rigid-plastic models were becoming popular in the Big Pig.

Ziplock and Cosmo did not have the luxury of umbrellas to help them through the current downpour, and had to make do with keeping their eyes down and shoulders hunched. Raindrops battered their necks and backs, but the boys were so cold that they barely felt any pain.

Ziplock was thrown against the fire escape bars by a flurry of drops. "I can see the city. I always wanted to see the city without shackles on my wrist. Maybe we can do that soon, Cosmo. Just walk around without shackles."

Cosmo saved his energy for flight. The roof was still one floor up. After that they were banking on good fortune. Maybe they could make the jump to the next building. Maybe not.

They hugged the wall, avoiding the brunt of the rainstorm. Below, in the streets, car alarms were activated by the mutant drops. Security firms never responded to car call-outs during a rainstorm. They were always set off by weather conditions or very foolish car jackers.

Cosmo rounded the final corner onto the roof, a flat expanse of slick, tar-coated felt, punctuated by a stairwell box, like a submarine's conning tower. The box's corrugated roof was buckling under the rain's onslaught. And, suddenly, the downpour stopped, as though God had turned off the water. Another characteristic of Satellite City's freakish weather.

"Someone up there likes us," said Ziplock.

"It's a bit late for that," commented Cosmo, shaking the water from his hair. "Let's go."

They padded across the saturated felt. With every step the roof sagged alarmingly, and in several spots the support girders were visible through sparse strands of felt. The connecting building was one story down. As a landing pad, it left a lot to be desired. The rooftop was littered with the remains of a squatter camp. Breeze blocks lay like discarded dominos, and sparks spluttered from the cracked casing of a rooftop generator.

Cosmo hooked his toes over the edge, trying not to think about the drop. "You think we can make it?" he asked.

Ziplock's reply was to rear back from the brink.

Cosmo was undeterred. "I think we can make it. I really think we can."

"I don't think you will. Either of you," said someone in nasal tones. Anybody who spoke like that either had a bad cold, or a broken nose.

* * *

Cosmo and Ziplock turned slowly. Marshal Redwood stood in the rooftop doorway, lips stretched in a huge grin. Tears were streaming down his cheeks. "I took the elevator," he explained. "You two are dumber than recycled sewage. What did you think? Going up would fool me?"

Cosmo didn't answer. It wasn't really a question. Water was dripping from his hair, down between his shoulder blades. Perhaps that was what made him shiver.

"We surrender, Marshal. Don't we, Ziplock?"

Ziplock was too petrified to answer.

"Too late for surrender. You're armed fugitives now. I can't take any chances. You gotta be wrapped." Redwood took the throw-down from his vest, dropping it at their feet.

Cosmo's breath came in short gasps. "Please, Marshal. We're on a rooftop. It could be hours before they get us in the vat."

The vat contained an acidic compound used to dissolve the cellophane.

"I know," said Redwood, the craziness in his eyes shining through the tears.

Redwood marched over to Ziplock, gathering a bunch of his lapel in his fist. He leaned the terrified boy over the lip of the roof. "This is the last lesson, Francis. You'd better learn from this one."

Ziplock began to giggle, hysterical laughter that had nothing to do with happiness.

Redwood placed the rod against his forehead. "I'd advise you to shut your mouth, Francis. You don't want any plastic going in there."

"Do your worst, Redwood," shouted Ziplock, eyes wide. "I can't get any more scared than I am right now."

Redwood laughed, causing a fresh spurt from his tear ducts. "Oh, I don't know about—"

Then Ziplock's jumpsuit ripped. One too many cleanings had left it with the strength of wet cardboard. Redwood was left holding a rose-shaped bunch of material, and Ziplock was left at an angle he couldn't correct.

His final word was to Cosmo. "Sorry," he said, and slipped over the edge.

It wasn't a long way down. Schoolchildren have jumped from higher trees and escaped without so much as a twisted ankle. But when Ziplock went over, he went over backward, dragging Cosmo with him.

There was no time for prayer, or screams. Cosmo's life did not flash before his eyes. One moment he was pleading with Marshal Redwood; the next, land and sky flipped, and he was facedown in the next building's rooftop generator.

Alive, though. Definitely. In some considerable pain, but alive. Pain was proof of that. Cosmo's vision was filled with multicolored wires, sparks, ancient transformers, and rust chips that fluttered around his head like bloody snowflakes.

His arm jiggled. Ziplock was moving.

"No," Cosmo whispered, no air for shouting. "Don't move."

Ziplock moved again. Maybe he had heard, maybe he hadn't. Cosmo would never know. His partner's movement dragged the metal cuff across two exposed wires, diverting ten thousand volts from the supply wires and into the two boys.

The charge catapulted the boys from the generator, spinning them across the roof puddles like stones across a pond. They came to rest against a guardrail. On their backs. Looking up.

Redwood peered down from above. Both boys' patterns had disappeared from his tracker. The generator could have shorted out the electronegative halogen microbeads in their pores. But most likely they were dead.

It was obvious what could have happened. The fugitives had been knocked from the roof by the rainstorm. It was a simple lie, and believable, so long as he did not stick around here to get photographed by some snoop satellite. The marshal hurried to the stairwell. Better to let someone else find the bodies. He would be in the restaurant helping the injured when it happened.

Cosmo did not have the energy to speak. His entire body felt bleached by the electric shock. All he could hear was his own heartbeat, slowing with every breath. Missing beats. Shutting down.

His eyes played tricks on him. Hallucinations, he supposed. Strange inhuman creatures appeared on the walls of the surrounding buildings, crawling at amazing speeds with no regard for gravity. They hurtled over the lip of the building, veering sharply downward toward the crash site. Two split from the group, swerving toward the injured boys. One settled on Cosmo's chest. Weightless. Watching him with large, expressionless eyes. The creature was the size of an infant, with smooth, blue, translucent skin, four slender limbs, and an oval head. Its features were delicate and impassive. Hairless and smooth. Sparks rolled in its veins instead of blood.

The second creature flickered in the corner of his eye, settling beside Ziplock, cradling his smoking head. Cosmo felt his heart skip another beat. Maybe two. What were these creatures? Fear sent a shiver through his chest, like another blast from the generator.

His spine arched in shock and panic, bucking the creature on his chest, but it held on effortlessly. It reached out a blue hand. Four fingers, thought Cosmo, only four. The hand settled on his heart and sucked. Somehow the hand was pulling the pain from his body. The agony dipped, faded, and was gone. The more the creature sucked, the brighter its light became, until its blue glow morphed to sunset gold. Cosmo used the last of his energy to look down. Something was flowing from him in a starry stream. He knew what it was. Life. Cosmo felt his days and months slips from his body like water through a fractured dam. The creature was killing him. The panic rose in him again. He wanted to struggle—he tried to grab the creature, but his muscles had turned to jelly.

Then things happened very quickly. Three kids appeared on the rooftop. Two boys and a girl. They weren't medics of any kind—that much was clear from their clothing and their ages—but at least they were human.

"Two here," said the first, a tall older boy clothed from head to foot in black. "I'll take them. You check below."

His comrades scurried to the roof's edge, peering down to the street.

"They're looking, but they're not landing," said the second newcomer. A Latina girl, maybe fifteen, with a gang tattoo over one eyebrow. "Too much water. The fire brigade are hosing the truck."

The first youth drew what looked like a torch from his shoulder holster, twisting a ring on its base. White sparks flickered at the business end. He fired the device on the move: two blasts of pure electricity erupted from the barrel of his strange weapon. The effect was spectacular. The white bolts sank into the ghostly creatures' skin, branching into a million tendrils. Each one traced a vein, fusing with the sparks already in there. The creatures shuddered and convulsed, their skin swelling to bursting point. And past it. They both exploded into a dozen perfect spheres of light, which drifted away on the breeze.

"Wow," croaked Cosmo, wasting his last gasp of air.

"A live one!" said the group's third member, who seemed about six years old. Blond, with a child's disproportionately large head, he knelt beside Cosmo, checking his heartbeat and shining a light into one pupil. "No dilation and irregular heartbeat. He needs a defibrillator, Stefan. We need to kick-start his heart."

Hallucination. It must be an hallucination.

The tall youth, Stefan, loomed in Cosmo's fading vision. "What about the other one, Ditto?"

Ditto placed a hand on Ziplock's chest. For a second Cosmo thought he saw lifestream playing around his fingers. Then . . .

"The other one? No. He's gone. Not a peep."

Stefan adjusted his weapon. "Well, I don't have a defibrillator."

Ditto stepped away hurriedly. "You sure? This roof is wet."

Stefan pointed the weapon at Cosmo's chest. "No," he said, and fired.

Cosmo felt the charge going in like a sledgehammer through his ribs. Surely it must have broken every bone in his chest. Surely this was the last straw. His body could take no more. He felt his hair straightening, tugging at the pores in his scalp. His jumpsuit caught fire, dropping from his skin in burning clumps. Ditto doused him with the contents of a nearby fire bucket, but Cosmo did not feel the cold. Something else was happening.

Ba-doom . . .

His heart. Beating again. And again.

Ba-doom. Ba-doom.

"We got him!" crowed Ditto. "This guy's got the will to live of a hungry dog. But he needs serious medical attention. His head is cracked open like an egg."

Stefan sighed, relieved that his gamble had paid off. He holstered the lightning rod. "Okay. The lawyers will find him. I don't want them to find us too."

Cosmo drew his first breath in over a minute. "Please."

They couldn't just leave him here. Not after all this. "Take me."

Stefan did not look back. "Sorry. We have enough trouble looking after ourselves."

Cosmo knew that Redwood would never allow him to reach the institute alive. "Please."

The girl leaned over him. "You know, Stefan? Maybe he could make the sim-coffee or something."

Stefan sighed, holding the door open for his team. "Mona, we go through this every night."

Mona sighed. "Tough break, kid."

Cosmo's heart beat steadily now, sending blood pulsing to his brain. "If you leave me," he rasped, "they'll come back."

And suddenly Stefan was half interested. "Who'll come back?" he said, striding across the roof.

Cosmo struggled to stay conscious. "The creatures."

Ditto clapped his hands. "Did you hear that? The creatures, Stefan. He's a Spotter. Wrap me if he isn't."

Stefan shrugged. "It could be nothing. Maybe one of us mentioned the creatures. Maybe it was an hallucination."

Cosmo coughed up some smoke. "The blue creatures, with electricity in their veins. They were sucking the life out of me."

"Pretty accurate hallucination," noted Mona.

Stefan nodded at Ditto. "Okay, we take him. He's a Spotter."

The Spanish girl examined the cuffs. "Okay, Stefan. Gimme a minute."

"A second, Mona. We can spare a second."

Mona picked a clip from her hair, jiggling it expertly in the cuff's lock. In slightly more than a second, Ziplock's wrist was free, not that it was any good to him now.

Stefan hoisted Cosmo onto his shoulder. "Let's go. We can open the other cuff at the warehouse."

Cosmo hung there like a side of meat. He could have spoken then, asked a few more questions. But he didn't, afraid that if he pestered this tall young man, they would decide not to take him wherever it was that they were going. And anywhere was better than the Clarissa Frayne Institute for the Parentally Challenged.

Cosmo's brain decided that there was no room for this new feeling of relief and shut him down for repairs.

CHAPTER 2
SPOTTER

THE SMELL WOKE COSMO. The bitter pungent aroma of a nearby sim-coffee pot had set his nostrils twitching. And even though the smell was not unpleasant, it was too much for his raw senses. Everything made the headache worse. The rasp of material, the light hammering on his eyelids, and now this smell.

But even worse than the pain was the thirst.

Cosmo tried to open his mouth, but his lips were dry-gummed together. A frustrated moan escaped through his nose. Footsteps approached across a hard-sounding surface.

"Okay, *bueno*," said a voice. Female. "Welcome to Abracadabra Street."

A wet cloth brushed his lips, breaking the seal. Cosmo opened his mouth, squeezing the material between his teeth. The water tasted like life, trickling down his throat.

"Easy, not too much."

Cosmo opened his eyes a crack, squinting against the glare of sunlight. The girl was ringed by a corona of white light. For a second he thought . . . But no, it was the girl from the roof. The roof?

"Welcome back. Though the way you're gonna be feeling for a couple of days, maybe you'd rather be dead."

Cosmo remembered it all then. The crash, the climb, the fall. "Ziplock?" croaked Cosmo, his voice alien and distant.

The girl scratched her forehead, stretching the DNA strand tattooed on her forehead. Cosmo knew that the tattoo was the signature of one of the various Satellite City street gangs. The ink was probably loaded with an isotope that could be tested by a bar scanner. This prevented police infiltration.

"Ziplock?" she said. "You got the energy for one word, and that's the word you pick?"

Cosmo felt a single tear crawl down his cheek. Ziplock had been just about the closest thing he'd had to a friend.

The girl saw the tear, and made the connection. She winced at her own blunder. "I'm sorry. Ziplock, that was your friend's name?"

"Is he . . . ?"

"Sorry, kid. He was gone when we got there. We left him behind, remember?"

Cosmo raised his arm. The only thing around his wrist was a bandage.

"The electricity fused part of the cuff to your skin. Ditto had to peel it off. You were lucky the vein didn't pop."

Cosmo didn't feel so lucky, and it wasn't just his wrist.

"In fact, Ditto had to do quite a bit of work on you. You never would have made it to a hospital, so we had to use whatever was lying around. Your painkiller drip was a bit past the sell-by date, but hey, it didn't kill you."

Mona consulted a wall monitor over Cosmo's bed. "Ditto glued the Achilles tendon in your left heel and replaced your right kneecap with grown-bone."

Cosmo nodded, aghast.

"We also had to go into your chest and plasti-coat a few of your ribs. I took the staples out this morning. And, of course, I had to shave your head."

"What?"

Mona shrugged. "It was either that or let your brain fall out on the floor. Lucky for you Ditto had a couple of robotix plates lying around. He used one to patch your fractured skull. Those robotix plates are made of the same material used to armor assault tanks. When your skin heals up, Ditto says you'll be able to head-butt your way through a brick wall."

Cosmo remembered something. "Ditto? The little boy."

Mona glanced over her shoulder. "Shhh! Don't call him that. He's very touchy." The girl stepped closer, lowering her voice. "Ditto is a Bartoli baby. That *little boy* is twenty-eight years old."

Now it made sense. Doctor Ferdinand Bartoli's genetic experiments were an infamous chapter in modern history. The doctor had performed gene-splicing tests on a batch of infants in an attempt to create a superhuman. Instead, he

corrupted the babies' own DNA, resulting in a series of mutations. ESP was one side-effect, but the most common was
arrested physical development. The Bartoli scandal led to the
outlawing of gene experimentation for more than ten years.

Cosmo gingerly rubbed his bristling scalp. A section of his
forehead felt hard and stippled.

"There are pressure-release pores in that plate, so don't
poke anything through the skin."

Robotix plates in his head and Bartoli babies. It was
almost too much to take in. "Anything else?"

"That's about it. Of course there are still a hundred or so
staples in various cuts and bruises, but I disguised them with
skin-spray. All in all, you're a lot worse than you look."

But not worse than I feel, thought Cosmo.

Mona peeled the foil from a patch and stuck it to his arm.
"The best thing for you is rest and recuperation. This sedative
patch should keep you out for a while. The next time you
wake, you might even be able to walk around a bit."

"No," protested Cosmo, but it was too late. The sedative
was already seeping into his bloodstream.

"'Nighty night," said Mona gently.

Cosmo's limbs felt weightless. His head wobbled like a toy
dog's. "'Nighty night," he echoed.

Or maybe he only thought it, because the world was dripping down his eyeballs like wet oil paint down a canvas.

Cosmo woke again about five seconds later, or so it seemed.
But that couldn't be right, because the halogen strip lights

were on, and muffled stars poked through the smog beyond old-fashioned hanging curtains. Not many people used curtains anymore, generally react-to-light glass came with the building.

Cosmo ran through his memories as if they were files on a computer screen. Who was he? Cosmo Hill, fourteen years old. Fugitive no-sponsor. Where was he? A warehouse maybe, rescued by a band of creature hunters. A tall teenager, a Latina girl, and a Bartoli baby. Could that be true? It seemed impossible. Could he become part of this strange band? Was that what he wanted?

Cosmo's brain stuttered to a halt. What did he want? This was a question that nobody had ever asked him. He rarely asked it of himself. The only thing he had ever wanted was to escape from Clarissa, and now that he was out, he had no idea what to do next. But Cosmo did know one thing with absolute certainty. He was never going back to Clarissa Frayne. Never.

Cosmo checked his injuries. The pain was still there—muted, but there. Like a troll under the bridge, ready to pounce if he moved too quickly. The bandage was gone from his wrist, and his entire forearm was covered with skin-spray.

After several minutes of basic breathing and blinking, Cosmo decided to put his limbs to the test. He sat slowly, dizzy from the sedative patch stuck to his arm. He peeled it off, checking the sponge. White. No more juice. That explained why he was awake.

His new knee was covered with a plexi-cast. The transparent cast was filled with an anti-inflammatory that would accelerate the healing process. A green LED over the cast's x-ray panel told him that the leg was safe to walk on.

Cosmo tested the ground like a swimmer testing arctic waters. His knee twinged, but nothing more. He must have been out for at least forty-eight hours for the cast to have done its job. His forehead was a different story. Every movement, however slight, sent a steel nail of pain hammering into his skull. Almost as bad as the pain was the itch of new skin growing over the robotix plate in his forehead.

He gritted his teeth and began walking, his initial target being the jug of filtered water on the table five yards away. Not exactly a marathon, but not bad, considering what he'd been through.

Cosmo almost reached the table. He would have made it, if it hadn't been for one thing. A steel mirror bolted to the wall. Cosmo caught sight of his own reflection and, for a moment, thought there was someone else in the room. His dry lips parted to form a single syllable. "Oh."

The figure in the glass reminded him of a war child from those history vids. Battered and thin, haggard and hangdog. He looked like a miniature Frankenstein's monster. Cobbled together from various parts. None of them the right size, some of them not even intended for humans. His head was especially grotesque. Completely shaven, with a dozen staple scars crisscrossing the scalp. The robotix plate in his forehead bulged slightly beneath the swollen skin, the pressure pores clearly outlined against the pink tissue. The only things that he recognized were the wide-spaced round brown eyes.

Cosmo completed his journey shakily, grasped the jug with both hands, and drank from the neck. Most of the water splashed down his front, but some went in. Everything was being fixed, he told himself. It was all temporary.

But not for Ziplock. It was too late to fix him.

Ziplock. His friend should have been here with him. But where was *here* exactly? Cosmo looked around for the first time. He was in a large open warehouse constructed from pig-iron polymer. The windows were tall and thin, church style, with blackout curtains hanging on each side. Workbenches and electronic equipment littered the concrete floor, and power cables flowed from every wall socket like multicolored snakes. Various cubicles were sectioned off by mobile dividers, and a dozen hard drives hummed inside the makeshift rooms. But no people. Besides him, the warehouse was completely deserted.

Cosmo moved slowly, getting used to his new knee. There was a kitchen area in one corner. Nothing cozy. Just a two-ring burner, molded garden furniture, and a pot of sim-coffee. A bunch of lilies lay on the table, cellophane wrapped, with a bubble of water at the base. Real flowers. Expensive. There was a card stuck between two of the lilies. *Mother*, it read. *I miss you more than ever.*

A set of steel cuffs lay on the bench beside the simulator. Cosmo felt a lump in his throat. The last remaining evidence that Francis Murphy had ever lived, and they didn't even know his real name.

"Let's go, Francis," he said, picking up the cuffs. "It's time you saw the city."

One of the warehouse windows faced across the river toward Satellite City's famous downtown skyline, dominated by the cylindrical Myishi Tower. The Cuzzy Cola building fizzed from across the bay, its walls animated by computer-generated rising bubbles. And a red light winked in the Statue of Endeavor's stone hand, an eight-hundred-foot colossus, pointing at the Satellite overhead.

Cosmo climbed through the window onto a balcony, trying to get his bearings. Judging by the position of the Journey River, he was somewhere on the Westside. The piercing wail of sirens, and the overhead *whup-whup* of police birds confirmed this theory.

Cosmo dangled the cuffs over the edge. There should be something to say. Something special to mark Ziplock's passing. Cosmo thought for several moments, but he couldn't find any words to describe how desolate he felt. Maybe that was the point. How could any words capture feelings like these? He knew how he felt, and that's what was important.

Cosmo tossed the cuffs into the Satellite City air, and they twinkled through the neon like shooting stars.

Cosmo's hosts seemed to go from one crisis to the next. He had barely latched the window behind him when they burst through the elevator's grille, bearing a shopping trolley before them. Mona was folded into the trolley. Her skin had a greenish tinge and she was shivering violently.

Cosmo hobbled after them. "What happened?"

Stefan did not answer, clearing a laminated work surface with a sweep of one arm. "Close the curtains!" he shouted.

Cosmo pointed at the react-to-light control panel beside a window. "But the glass. Why don't I adjust . . . ?"

"Because the police birds see right through react-to-light. That's why it comes with the building. Get it?"

Cosmo hauled the sackcloth curtains across the windows. Seconds after he had finished, a government bird swept past the building. Cosmo heard an electronic crackle as the windows were remotely depolarized. With the curtains open, the room would have been exposed. Which was fine, so long as nobody was fleeing the scene of a crime. Which they obviously were.

Stefan was bent over Mona. Her slim frame was racked with pain, every muscle and tendon stretched tight. Long streams of Spanish fluttered from her bloodless lips, and her black, sweat-drenched hair slapped the table like strands of seaweed.

Ditto hopped up on the table, pulling a screwdriver from his belt. He jammed the tool's handle into Mona's mouth, to stop her swallowing her tongue. "I don't know what this is," he admitted. "This is a new one on me. I've never seen this strain before." He peeled the adhesive back from a thermostrip, sticking it to her forehead.

"She's on fire," he said, reading the temperature off the strip. "Going critical."

"Get a bucket of ice," said Stefan to Cosmo. "Whatever you can carry."

Cosmo lurched to the refrigerator, emptying a fire bucket of sand on the floor. He jammed the rim against the fridge's ice-dispenser toggle, watching while the cubes rattled out with infuriating slowness.

"Come on, come on!"

It took almost a minute to fill the bucket halfway. That would have to do. Ignoring the pain in his knee, Cosmo hurried back to the table.

Stefan grabbed the bucket and began packing the ice inside Mona's clothing. Ditto's gaze remained fixed on the thermostrip. "It's not working. A hundred and twelve, and still rising."

"No!" shouted Stefan. His features tight with worry. "We need to take her to a hospital."

"What hospital?" snorted Ditto. "I've worked in every hospital in the city, remember? There's nothing but General on the Westside, and believe me, if I don't know how to fix something, they don't know how to fix it either."

Cosmo peered in around Stefan's frame. Mona's convulsions grew more violent. Green tendrils spread across her eyeballs.

"Should we give her an antibiotic?" wondered Stefan aloud. "We have to try something."

"No!" Cosmo blurted. The word was out before he could stop it.

Ditto hopped down from the table. "No? What do you know, kid?"

Cosmo's aches and pains picked that moment to come back. "I don't know. Something, maybe. I've seen this before at the institute. What happened to her?"

"We don't have time for this," said Stefan. "We have to take her to General. Take our chances."

Ditto stood up to the tall boy. A molehill facing down a mountain.

"Take our chances? By the time we get processed, she's dead. You know it as well as I do. Let's hear what the boy has to say. Now, kid, what do you need to know?"

Cosmo avoided Stefan's gaze. "Just what happened. How did she get this way?"

Stefan kneaded his brow. "There was an explosion at Komposite chemical plant. We were doing a sweep for Parasites. Some of the local marshals caught us, and one got a dart into Mona. She's been getting worse ever since."

Cosmo racked his brain. By law, private marshals were not licensed to carry guns. They got around the problem by arming themselves with nonlethal lightning rods that fired cellophane slugs or various chemical darts. The darts were clever because they were technically nonlethal, so long as you stayed around for the antidote.

"What color was the dart's casing?"

Ditto frowned. "Casing? I'm not sure. Green, maybe."

"With a white stripe along the side?"

"Maybe. I can't swear."

"Yes," said Stefan. "A white stripe. I remember pulling it out of Vasquez's leg. Green and white."

Cosmo closed his eyes, remembering the institute. "Those Komposite darts were tested at Clarissa Frayne. I remember. The green-and-white ones were the worst. We called them Creepers. Guys were sick for hours, even after they got the antidote. The institute's plumbing got all backed up. One guy found a cure, though. He ate a moldy sandwich, and felt better. It wasn't the bread, it was—"

"The mold," completed Ditto. "Of course. This is a flora virus. Cellulose would shut it down. We need some plants."

Cosmo limped to the cellophane-wrapped flowers. "Here. Right here."

He pulled a single flower from the bunch and ripped the lily's stem and leaves into bite-size pieces, cramming some into his own mouth. The rest he handed to Ditto, who did the same. Stefan grabbed another bloom, folding the stem into his mouth.

They chewed furiously, ignoring the acrid taste seeping down their throats. The stems were tough, splitting into stringy lengths, refusing to be broken down. But Cosmo and the others persisted, grinding the strings between their molars. Green juice dribbled over their chins. Finally they spat wads of green paste into their palms.

"Do the wound," Cosmo instructed.

The Bartoli baby ripped Mona's trousers apart, spitting the goo directly onto the puncture mark on the girl's thigh. Stefan added his wad of paste to the wound, kneading it into the inflamed hole.

Cosmo removed the screwdriver from Mona's mouth, force-feeding the paste between chattering teeth. Mona gagged, shuddering, her body naturally rejecting the plant, but Cosmo rubbed her windpipe until she swallowed. Gradually, more and more green ooze slipped down the girl's throat. By the time he was finished, Cosmo's fingers were chewed bloody. For what seemed like an eternity, there was no change in Mona's condition. Then . . .

"A hundred and eleven," said Ditto. "She's peaked."

Mona's eyes continued rolling, but the green tendrils pulsed gently, then disappeared.

Ditto checked the thermostrip. "One hundred and eight. It's working, wrap me if it isn't."

Something flickered in Mona's eyes. Recognition?

"One hundred. Ninety-nine."

The girl's slight frame slumped onto the table. Gradually, tension lost its grip on her muscles.

"Ninety-eight. Normal. She's going to be all right."

Mona turned on her side, throwing up green sludge onto the tiles.

Ditto grinned an angelic baby grin. "That's what happens when you eat cow food."

They cleaned Mona off and put her on a cot.

"Sleep is what she needs now," said Ditto. "Better than any medicine."

Cosmo could have done with a few hours himself. A lot had happened in the minutes he'd been awake, but there were a few things he had to know. "Who are you people?" he asked. "What's going on here?"

Stefan was repairing what was left of his bouquet with tape. "We live here. So I think the question is, who are you?"

Fair enough. "Cosmo Hill. When you found me I was escaping from the Clarissa Frayne Institute for the Parentally Challenged."

Ditto laughed. "Cosmo Hill. You were found on Cosmonaut Hill, right?"

"Yes. That's right."

"The orphanages have been using that tired old trick for centuries. I once knew a man from San Francisco called Holden Gate. Guess where they found him?"

"Marshal Redwood will come looking for me and Ziplock."

Ditto shook his head. "No. As far as the authorities are concerned, you're as dead as your friend, Cosmo. I worked in an orphanage sick bay for a couple of months, before I found out what goes on there. All the orphanages, and the other human trade institutes, use micro trackers in your pores to keep an eye on their residents. That rooftop generator would have fried any tracers in your skin. You're clean and clear, a nonperson."

Cosmo felt the worry lift from his shoulders like a physical weight. "Now, it's my turn. Who are you?"

"Who are we?" Ditto pointed dramatically at Stefan. "This is Stefan Bashkir. A second-generation Satellite City native, of Russian descent. I am Lucien Bonn, also known as Ditto, due to my annoying habit of repeating whatever people say. And Mona Vasquez, I believe you already know."

"So we know each other's names. But what do you do?"

Ditto spread his arms wide. "We, Cosmo Hill, are the world's only Supernaturalists."

Cosmo grinned weakly. "What? You don't like clothes?"

Stefan couldn't help smiling. "That's *naturists*, Cosmo. And nobody does that anymore, not with the ozone layer spread thinner than cellophane. We call ourselves Supernaturalists because we hunt supernatural creatures."

"Not me," interrupted Ditto. "I'm a medic. I try to heal people, that's all. I leave the hunting to Stefan. He's the one with police academy training."

Cosmo glanced at the sleeping girl. "What about Mona? She's not police. Not with that tattoo."

"No," agreed Stefan. "Mona takes care of transport. She's had some . . . eh . . . training in that area."

Cosmo nodded. So far everything had been straightforward enough, but he felt that his next question would open up an entirely new world. "These supernatural creatures. What are they? I suppose you mean the blue ones on the rooftop."

A frown cut a slash between Stefan's eyes. "Exactly. The Parasites have been preying on us since god knows when. Sucking the very life from our bodies. You know. You've seen it. Not everyone does."

"You called me a Spotter?"

Stefan took a seat opposite Cosmo. He was a charismatic

figure. About eighteen, with haunted features. His jet-black hair stood in unruly spikes, and a pink scar stretched from the corner of his mouth, giving the impression of an impish grin, an impression that did not match the pain in his eyes. Eyes that were probably blue, but to Cosmo seemed blacker than outer space. It was obvious that Stefan was the leader of this little group. It was in his nature. The way he slouched in his chair, the way Ditto automatically turned to him, even though the Bartoli baby was several years older.

"There aren't many of us," said Stefan, looking Cosmo straight in the eyes. Cosmo made an effort not to look away. "Not enough to be believed. It doesn't help that most Spotters are kids. Maybe our minds are more open. Ditto is the only adult Spotter I've come across, if you can count Ditto as an adult."

"Oh? Did Stefan make an actual joke?" said Ditto, reaching up to punch Stefan in the side. "Not actually funny, but not bad for a first attempt."

Stefan grasped his side in mock agony. "You've never seen the creatures before that night on the rooftop, have you, Cosmo?"

Cosmo shook his head. He would have remembered.

"The sight usually comes after a near-death experience, and I think what happened to you qualifies as a near-death experience."

"About as near as you can get," added Ditto, rapping the plate in Cosmo's head.

"Usually the sight goes again just as quickly," continued

Stefan. "But sometimes when the new spectrum is opened it stays open. Sometimes for a week, sometimes for good. You could lose the sight tomorrow, or in ten years, or never. You're a rarity, Cosmo. Your choice is to be a rarity with us, where it will do some good, or go back to Clarissa Frayne."

What choice? Cosmo would take his chances with a thousand Parasites before returning to the orphanage. A person can only take so many medical experiments.

"I'd like to stay."

"Good," said Stefan. "You'll need courage and determination to be part of this little family."

Family, thought Cosmo—I'm part of a family. Stefan used the word lightly, but to Cosmo this was a very big deal.

"We're a family?"

Stefan hoisted Ditto off the ground. "Yes, this grumpy little man is Granddad. And Mona is our kid sister. It's a dysfunctional group, but we're all we have. We're all anybody has. Sometimes it seems that we can never win, but we save who we can. You, for example. If it hadn't been for us, that Parasite would have sucked you dry, and no one would have ever known."

"They can suck us dry?"

"Of course—it's what they live for."

Cosmo shifted on the stool. "Then, they could be here, any minute."

Stefan's good humor disappeared. "No, this is the one place you're safe. We insulated the walls with hydro-gel. Parasites don't like water. There's even gel between the glazing."

"But as soon as we step outside?"

Stefan shrugged. "Then we're fair game."

"Things have changed over the past year," explained Ditto, opening a bottle of beer. He drank deeply and belched. A little blond boy drinking beer. It was a bizarre sight.

"Ditto's right," said Stefan. "It used to be that the Parasites would only show up at night. At the scenes of accidents or at hospitals. They would find someone on death's door and leech the remaining life force right out of them. The doctors never suspect a thing. It's how they've stayed hidden for so long. That monster you had on your chest the other night probably sucked five years off your life before we popped him."

Cosmo rubbed his chest instinctively. "But now?"

"But now, nobody is safe," said Stefan bitterly. "For some reason there seems to be even more of them. The rules have changed. They can strike anytime, anywhere, at anyone. The Parasites come calling if they sense even the slightest injury."

Cosmo swallowed. "So how do you fight something like that? How do you kill ghosts?"

Stefan pulled a lightning rod from inside his jacket, spinning it between his fingers like a cheerleader's baton. "With one of these. They want energy, I give it to them."

Ditto snatched the rod. "Show-off," he said. "There are various projectile options on this thing, depending on which cartridge you choose. A certain kind of slug sends the Parasites into overload. You saw the results. These are called Shockers, a slug initially developed by a weapons company as an alternative to the Taser. Even if we do miss, the charge isn't enough to injure the smallest person. Unlike the shot Stefan gave you, which could have barbecued a wild boar."

Cosmo remembered the creature on his chest exploding into a cloud of blue bubbles.

"Or you can choose regular nonlethals—gumballs, shrink-wrappers, and so on," continued Ditto. "The last thing anyone wants to do is hurt someone. But sometimes we need to buy a little time, and nonlethals can really help us out."

Cosmo blinked. "I understood about sixty percent of that."

Stefan stood, buttoning his coat. "That's more than most people understand. Ditto, would you give Cosmo the tour. I have to go out for a while." He tucked the bouquet inside his overcoat, heading for the elevator.

Cosmo called after him. "One question."

Stefan did not turn around. "Make it quick, Cosmo."

"I know what you're doing, but why are you doing it?"

"Because we're the only ones who can," said Stefan, tugging the cord on the elevator grille.

I'm inside a cartoon, thought Cosmo. This is all a graphic novel. Someone is turning the pages right now and saying, *This is too weird, who could believe something like this?*

"Stefan was a police cadet three years ago," said Ditto, tossing his beer bottle in the recycler. "His mother was on the force too. She was one of the city's chief trauma surgeons. After she died, he spent a year in the widows-and-orphans' home. When he got out, he spent every dinar of the insurance settlement on this place."

Cosmo glanced around. The building was not luxurious, even by an orphan's standards. The cots were army issue, the paint was bubbled with damp, and the windows hadn't seen a cloth in years.

"Not exactly the Batcave."

"The what cave?"

"Never mind."

The blond boy pointed to a bank of mongrel computers stacked on a workbench. The latest crystal screens sat side-by-side with last-century monitors.

"Most of this stuff is black market. We observe Satellite sites, waiting for disasters."

"What? You hack the state police site?"

Ditto chuckled. "The state police site? No, thank you. We're in too much of a hurry to wait around for the police. We hack the law firms."

It made sense. With lawsuits being so costly, most corporations hired private teams of rapid-response combat-lawyers to beat the police to accident sites.

Ditto turned his attention back to the room.

"We all have a bunk. Basic stuff, but it's a place to lay your head."

"And you just happen to have a spare one for me?"

Ditto sighed. "A spare one for you? Well, no. That was Splinter's. He used to be one of us. He couldn't take the visions anymore. He left the city six months ago. He lives out of town now. He wears blue-lensed sunglasses, never takes 'em off."

"Are you a Spotter, Ditto?"

"A Spotter? Yes, we all are. But with me, it's a Bartoli side effect. Mona told you about me, right?"

"Yes. And how did you find Stefan?"

Ditto frowned. "Stefan had an . . . accident a few years ago. I was in the ambulance that picked him up. The world's shortest paramedic. That particular hospital made a big deal of hiring a Bartoli baby. Maybe you read about me on the Sat-net?"

Cosmo shook his head.

"Well, anyway, when we picked up Stefan, he was babbling about blue creatures sucking the life out of his chest. I couldn't believe it. Until that moment I'd thought I was crazy. So I visited him at the hospital, and we took it from there. When Stefan decided to set up our little group, I quit my job without a second thought. Ever since then, we've been saving the world together."

"One more question."

Ditto shook his child's head. "One more question. With you kids, it's all questions."

"What's Stefan doing with real flowers?"

"The flowers? Stefan will tell you when he's ready."

Cosmo's heart sank. He was almost part of a group. Almost, but not quite.

The LED on his plexi-cast switched to red, and an alert began beeping gently.

"That's enough walking around for you today. The cast needs another eight hours to do its job. Are you in pain?"

Cosmo nodded.

Ditto pulled a pain plaster from his pocket. The rumpled tab looked about ten years past its sell-by date. "Here. There's still a bit of juice in this."

He peeled off the adhesive backing, slapping the pad onto Cosmo's forehead. "How's the heartbeat? Your ticker took quite a hammering." Ditto placed his hand on Cosmo's heart, and suddenly the pain disappeared.

"It's gone. The pain. How'd you do that?"

"Not me. The pad. One of my own concoctions. I get plenty of opportunities to put my medical training to use in this job."

"And Stefan trained at the police academy?"

Ditto grinned a grin far too cynical from one of his apparent years. "Yes, he specialized in demolition."

"Tomorrow, do I get to be a Spotter?" asked Cosmo.

Ditto nodded at Mona Vasquez, who was snoring gently, in a deep but untroubled sleep. "No one can teach you how to be a Spotter, kid. That's what you are. But that little innocent-looking girl there will teach you what to do when it's time to put your natural talent to work."

Stefan Bashkir left the warehouse on Abracadabra Street through what looked like a little-used side door. In fact the door was well oiled and alarmed, but to the casual observer the creeping rust and stacks of rubbish made the entrance seem obsolete. Outsiders were not to know that the rust was carefully cultivated and the rubbish stacks were on casters. With the simple push of a button, the entire mound slid aside, revealing an entrance wide enough to admit a large truck. Not very high-tech, but sufficient so long as no one tried to recycle the rubbish.

Stefan opened the door a crack, slipping into the Satellite City dawn. Sunrise used to be orange. But now sunrises were a multicolored affair, as the sun's light illuminated whatever chemicals were in the smog that particular day. Today the smog was deep purple, so that probably meant pesticides. The air would stink by noon. Still it was better than red. Nobody ventured outdoors without a mask when the smog was red.

The street vendors were busy even at this hour, firing up their mobile braisiers and barbecues, ready for the breakfast trade. It was too early for the gangs though. Hoodlums tended to keep vampires' hours. The streets would be relatively safe until late afternoon.

Stefan bought a pazza from Carlo's Kitchen and made his way toward the crematorium. Pazzas were a new fast-food craze—calzone stuffed with pasta shells and various sauces. The perfect food for a person on the move.

Stefan walked along Journey Avenue, keeping his eyes on the pazza. In Westside, people would steal the food right out of your mouth. It was a sorry state of affairs. If this was the City of the Future, Stefan would take the past any day of the week.

Stefan was in a bad mood, and it wasn't just the smog. In spite of all his efforts, the group had taken on another stray. Okay, so the kid was a Spotter. But he couldn't be more than fourteen years old, and he had absolutely no experience of surviving in the city. Mona was young too, but she was streetwise and gutsy. Cosmo looked like the streets would eat him alive in minutes. Stefan already felt responsible for the boy, though he had no desire to be. He was barely old enough to be responsible for himself. It was one thing to risk his own life in pursuit of the Parasites, but to put someone else in danger was something else entirely. Especially someone as green as Cosmo Hill.

Five city blocks down, he arrived at the Solace Crematorium. The building was inevitably pig-iron gray, but the manager had made an effort to cheer up the place by having computer graphic angels flit up and down the façade.

Stefan went around back to the Hall of Eternal Rest. He swiped his resident's card, and passed through the turnstile. His card activated what appeared to be a wall of mirrors but was in fact a ten-story carousel of small glass boxes. The magnetic strip in his swipe card summoned a box from the top level. He followed its progress through the rows, twinkling down the levels to a vacant booth on ground level.

Stefan selected the no-music option on the touch-sensitive screen and entered the booth. The box slid from its compartment onto a velvet cushion.

"I don't like all this, Mom," muttered Stefan, abashed. "Velvet and fairies. But believe it or not, there are a lot worse places than here."

The box was six inches square, transparent, with a brass plate on the front. The inscription was short and simple. Seven words: DEAREST MOTHER. MUCH LOVED. GONE TOO SOON.

Stefan pulled the bunch of flowers from beneath his overcoat, laying them on the cushion before his mother's ashes.

"Lilies, Mom. Your favorites."

Stefan's spiky hair had fallen over his eyes. It made him look years younger.

"We picked up another Spotter, Mom. He's a good boy. Sharp. He saved Mona tonight. A quick thinker. Definitely Supernaturalist material. But he's just a kid, a no-sponsor right out of Clarissa Frayne."

Stefan rested his head in his hands. "But even with Cosmo, there are too many of them. Every day, more and more. They come out in the daytime now, you know. Even if you have the smallest cut on your arm, you'd better watch out. Nobody is safe. Every night we pop a hundred, and the next day there are a thousand new blue demons to take their place."

Stefan's young brow creased with the worry lines of a man three times his age. "Am I crazy, Mom? Are we all crazy? Are the Parasites really there at all? And if they are, how can a bunch of kids ever hope to fight them? The others think I'm their leader. I see the way they turn to me, as though I have all the answers. Even the new boy, Cosmo, is looking up to me already, and he's only been awake for a few hours. Well, I don't have any answers. There are more Parasites every day, and all we can do is save a few people at a time."

Stefan rested his head in his arms. He knew what his mother would say. *Everyone you save is someone's son, or someone's mother. When you save them, you save me.*

If only, thought Stefan. If only I could have saved you. Then everything could have been different.

CHAPTER 3
BLOWING BUBBLES

MONA VASQUEZ FELT AS THOUGH her insides were trying to punch their way out of her stomach. She lay on her cot, sweat pumping from every pore in her body. Mona could remember everything that had happened the previous night, but the images were blurry, as though viewed from underwater. The private police had tagged her with a dart. Stefan and Ditto had managed to cart her back here. Literally. And then what?

Then the new kid had saved her. After that she had puked for six hours straight. And if the intestinal gymnastics in her stomach were anything to go by, she wasn't finished yet. Mona lay still as a statue. Perhaps if she didn't move, the jitters would go away.

This kind of thing was happening more and more lately. You couldn't expect to go charging around Satellite City shooting off lightning rods without repercussions. In the past eighteen months, she had accumulated sixty-seven stitches, three broken bones, a slipped disk, and now a puncture wound in her leg. She was lucky to be alive, though she didn't feel particularly lucky at this moment. The cold truth was that the odds were against her, and were stacking higher all the time.

But what choice did she have? Stefan's quest was her quest. Someone had to put a stop to the Parasites. Her own parents had died young. Maybe the Parasites had stolen their last few years from them. And the creatures were becoming more brazen by the day. They were attracted to any illness or injury however small, and stalked their victims in broad daylight.

Mona did not share Stefan's driven hatred of the Parasites. After a night of creature blasting with the Supernaturalists, she had no problem sleeping for eight hours solid. But Stefan could be heard puttering around the workbench, repairing weaponry or rigging climbing equipment. Often his obsession kept him awake for forty-eight hours straight.

The girl sat up slowly, waiting for her stomach to lurch. It didn't happen. Perhaps she was finally on the mend. She studied her face in the bedside mirror. She was green, no doubt about it. Not a deep green, but there was a definite hue. There were even a few green tendrils in her eyeballs. What kind of poison had been in that dart? If it hadn't been for Cosmo, she'd be nothing more than a shrub now, with a couple of shriveled leaves.

Mona sighed, stretching the skin on her cheek between finger and thumb. There was a time when she used to worry about being pretty. Her mother used to say she was beautiful like an exotic flower. Mona had always remembered the phrase. *Exotic flower*. Even if sometimes she couldn't remember her mother and father anymore. They had been lost in a food riot in Booshka.

Mona wandered out into the common room, scratching her head. Stefan, of course, was already at a workbench, pouring cleaning solution on the lenses of his night-vision goggles. His dark eyes were completely focussed on the job. Mona took a moment to study him. Stefan would be a big hit with the girls, if he ever stopped working long enough to bring one out on a date. He had all the right ingredients. Tall, dark, handsome in a *beaten-up-once-too-often* way. But Mona knew that Stefan did not have time for himself, let alone anyone else. He only had time for the Parasites.

Stefan noticed her standing there, and a genuine smile brightened his face. "Hey, Vasquez, you're back on your feet."

Mona nodded, the motion causing her stomach to flip. "Just about. Thanks to the new kid."

"Are you up for some business?"

"Always ready for business, Stefan," replied Mona, trying to summon some enthusiasm.

Ditto tossed her a lightning rod. "Good. Show Cosmo how to use this. We have an alert three blocks away."

"Do you think the Parasites will show up?"

Stefan looked at her through the lenses of his night-vision goggles.

"What do you think?" he said.

Cosmo was halfway through a particularly nasty dream involving two Parasites, Ziplock, and a hair dryer, when Mona shook him from his sleep. He opened his eyes, expecting to see the Clarissa Frayne dorm marshal looming over him. Instead, he saw Mona Vasquez. Incredibly, she managed to look pretty in spite of her pasty, green complexion. "You look pretty," he sleep mumbled.

Mona thrust out her bottom lip. "Excuse me?"

Cosmo groaned. Had he said that aloud?

"You look pretty . . . green. Pretty green. It's the virus. Don't worry, it passes."

Mona smiled. "I hear you're quite the medical expert."

The smile woke Cosmo quicker than an adrenaline patch. "Not an expert, exactly. I was lucky."

"Me too." Mona straightened. "Okay. Sentimental moment over. Get your bald head out of bed. We've got work to do."

Cosmo threw back the worn blanket. "I know. Training."

"Training? You wish. We got an alarm three blocks away."

She handed Cosmo a lightning rod. "Green button, prime. Red button, fire. Make sure the narrow end is pointing at the spooky blue creature. Got it?"

Cosmo held the rod gingerly. "Green, red, narrow end. Got it."

Mona smiled once more. "Good. Consider yourself trained."

* * *

The Supernaturalists were strapping on their kits—weird combinations of police and mining equipment. Some instruments seemed like they were held together with duct tape and prayers. Everything looked out of date.

Stefan was shouting as he worked. "The Stromberg Building. Mostly residential units. The Satellite feeds the rotation times to the units. Apparently two apartments got rotated south at the same time. One hell of a collision."

Mona explained to Cosmo while strapping an extendable bridge on his back. "The Big Pig is a twenty-four-hour city, so factories revolve their buildings just as they revolve their shifts. Everybody gets eight hours quiet and eight hours south facing. For the other eight, you're working, so you don't care where your apartment is. The Satellite tried to squeeze two apartments into one space. Nasty."

Cosmo shuddered. The Satellite had messed up again. This was becoming a regular occurrence.

Ditto handed him large plastic night-vision goggles that covered most of his face and crown. "We all wear these fuzz plates. X-rays bounce off them. If the privates get a shot of your skull, they can computer generate your face. It's accepted as evidence in court these days."

"Uh . . . okay," mumbled Cosmo. He felt as though he were walking toward the edge of a cliff, with every intention of jumping. In the orphanage everything had been predictable as day following night. With the Supernaturalists, every moment brought fresh adventure. Was this the life he wanted? Did he have a choice?

"Everybody strapped?" shouted Stefan. "Then let's go."

They squeezed into the elevator, tense and excited. Cosmo could not believe that he was on his way to shoot supernatural creatures. The rest of the crew were performing their pre-engagement rituals. Ditto daubed his arms with camouflage paint, Mona cracked every knuckle in her fingers, and Stefan burned a hole in the shaft wall with his gaze.

Cosmo noticed that they were going up.

"Do we have a helicopter?" he asked hopefully.

"A helicopter? Oh sure," chuckled Ditto. "Two helicopters and a Transformer."

"So why are we going up?"

"Because the lawyers are on the ground," said Mona. "And up is where the Parasites are."

"Oh," said Cosmo, not in the least reassured. He hadn't had a lot of luck on rooftops recently.

The Supernaturalists' warehouse was in a relatively low building by international standards. A mere one hundred and forty stories high. They emerged on the rooftop into a cloud of grim green smog.

In Westside, all the buildings were roughly the same height, give or take a floor or two. This ensured a clear signal from the Satellite to the rooftop dishes. It also made it easier for vigilantes to move between buildings, provided they were prepared to risk life and limb doing so.

Westside stretched before them like a box of upright dominoes, with only building graphics and neon signs to distinguish between skyscrapers. Overhead, police and TV birds jockeyed for airspace, buffeted by the winds that squeezed through the pig-iron columns.

Stefan unhooked an extendable bridge from his back. Cosmo paid close attention—obviously there wasn't going to be time to practice this. He had seen the window cleaners at Clarissa Frayne operate these contraptions, running between buildings with suicidal nonchalance, and had always thought, *Never in a million years*. Things change. Circumstances change.

The bridge, in its collapsed state, resembled a steel tray with twin rows of semicircular holes. The was a cable reel attached to one end of the tray. Stefan placed the other end firmly beneath his heel, wrapping his fingers around the reel's grip. He let out a few feet of cable, then pressed the fire button on the reel's thumb-pad. The bridge unfolded instantly, powered by a small canister of gas, shooting across the divide. Stefan played the reel expertly, keeping the bridge's nose aloft until it cleared the lip of the other building. "Go!" he ordered, standing to one side.

Mona and Ditto ran across, careful, yet confident.

"Don't look down," advised Ditto, from the other side.

Cosmo took a deep breath and crossed, holding his breath as though he were under water. Crossing a bridge at this altitude is not as easy as it would seem. The wind calls you to jump, the metal creaks below your feet, and time teases you, stretching every second to an hour. Cosmo focused on Mona smiling at him.

He was across, stepping eagerly from the lip. Stefan came behind him, stowing his bridge with the press of another button. It slotted back into its reduced size, hopping into Stefan's hand like a yo-yo.

On the building's southern edge, Ditto had already laid down another bridge. No time to think, no time to make decisions. Just time to follow the pack and be scared.

"Keep up!" Stefan advised over his shoulder. "We don't have a spare second. The Parasites will already be there."

The Parasites! Cosmo had almost forgotten about them. Would they be waiting? How would he react when they came face to face again?

He trotted across the second bridge; already the fear had diminished. Cosmo didn't think he would ever be comfortable scooting around the rooftops, but at least he wasn't paralyzed by terror.

Mona jogged beside him. "Look," she said, between breaths. "All around us. Can you see, Cosmo?"

Cosmo did see. Dozens of the blue creatures were scurrying across the rooftops, being drawn to a single point like dirt down a plughole. There are so many. His thoughts seemed as breathless as his lungs. There must be thousands. But he kept going forward, in spite of the instinct to turn and flee.

One block south, two penthouse apartments were skewed off vertical, both still attempting to occupy the same slot of the Stromberg Building. Gigantic gears groaned, and electrical fires licked the side of the building. The Parasites leaped effortlessly across the divide, crawling into the residential units.

"We're going over there?" said Cosmo incredulously.

Stefan nodded brusquely. "Yes. And quickly. The TV birds are closing in, and I hear sirens."

Cosmo heard the sirens too. The steady *woo-woo* of the police, and the strident *bips* of the legal firms. The *bips* were louder. They had a couple of minutes at the most.

Mona laid down a bridge, stepping to one side.

Stefan drew his lightning rod, priming it. "Okay, everybody, we go in through the roof box. We take one apartment only. Thirty seconds and we're out of there. I want us all miles away by the time the Stromberg Privates get on this roof. Clear?"

"Clear!" shouted Cosmo, having seen it on TV. Mona and Ditto simply nodded, priming their own weapons.

Stefan laid a hand on his shoulder. "Calm down, Cosmo. Remember, don't worry about the Parasites, they don't fight back, so long as you're not injured. Worry about the lawyers and private police. They fight dirty."

"Okay."

Mona punched him on the shoulder. "You'll be okay, Cosmo. I'll look out for you."

They crossed the final bridge. Cosmo could feel his ribcage shudder as his heart beat against it. The only thing that kept him going was a feeling that none of this was actually happening. In reality he was probably lying in a hospital somewhere, heavily sedated, with Marshal Redwood looming over him. Might as well enjoy this dreamworld while it lasted. Think of it as a video game. Go in, blast a few aliens, and compare scores later.

The rooftop's surface was irregular, buckled by mammoth gear cogs. Steam and hot-oil geysers spouted from rents in the concrete. The stairwell was blocked by mangled steps. Stefan wrapped a length of burn tape around the metal struts. Burn tape had been developed for logging companies in South America before it became illegal to use wood as a building material. "Cover your eyes."

Cosmo obeyed, a split second too late. Stefan snapped the fuse, igniting a magnesium strip that glowed brilliant white and fuelled an oxyacetylene balloon. The tape cut through the metal struts like a wire through cheese, and Cosmo would have the image burnt into his retinas for several minutes. A section of stairs dropped into the shaft, blocking the lower levels.

"Bridges," said Stefan.

The team members hooked the instruments over sections of banister, and expertly steered them down to the chaos below. One by one they descended into the unstable penthouse. Cosmo climbed down last on Mona's ladder, blinking stars from his eyes.

He stepped into pandemonium. People fled in panicked droves to the fire escape, oblivious to the blue creatures clinging curiously to the walls. Not everybody was oblivious. Stefan drew his lightning rod and started blasting. Parasites exploded in azure bubbles, bouncing around the confined space like pinballs. They made no sound and showed no surprise, simply swelled and popped.

Mona began firing with deadly accuracy, also with a stream of Spanish words that Cosmo suspected were not taught in kindergarten. She quickly cleared one wall of any remaining creatures, then shouldered her way through the melee to the displaced apartments.

Cosmo drew his own rod, primed it, aimed, and hesitated. The Parasites regarded him through round eyes, heads cocked. Alive. He couldn't do it. Not even the memory of the blue creature crouched on his chest, sucking his very life force, could make him push the button.

At the corridor's end, the apartment hadn't managed to lock into place. A six-foot gap yawned between it and the main structure. Stefan cast a bridge across, using it to winch in the wayward apartment. Parasites flowed around him, eager to reach the wounded.

The youth looked back.

"Thirty seconds, remember?" he said. His eyes were wide, possessed. Only one thing was important to him now.

He ran across the bridge, blasting as he went. His team followed into the lion's den. The apartment had obviously been struck with considerable force. Every stick of furniture was piled up against one wall. TVs, chairs, and domestic robots were reduced to little more than wires and sticks.

The people hadn't fared much better. At least a dozen assorted men, women, and children were heaped in one corner of the room, limbs entangled. The Parasites were all over them like flies on meat, hungrily devouring their life force.

Cosmo's doubt disappeared. He pointed his lightning rod at the nearest blue creature and pressed the red button. There was surprisingly little kick from the rod—it was almost like a toy. But the effect was anything but playful. The charge scorched the air as it passed, sinking into the Parasite's mid-section. The creature absorbed every volt, conducting not a spark to its victim. Its greed for energy was its undoing. The blast pumped it up beyond its limit, shattering the creature into a dozen spark-filled orbs.

Ditto was not shooting. He was the medic, doing what he could for the injured. He pulled gashes together with staples, doused open wounds with antiseptic disinfectant, and poured liquid painkiller down the throats of the conscious. For some it was too late.

Ditto placed his hand over the heart of an elderly man. "Shock," he said sadly. "Just shock."

Mona was half ninja, half gunslinger, popping off charge after charge into the blue creatures. She never missed. In moments the swaying room was filled with blue bubbles, like party balloons. They rose to the ceiling and melted through with an electric fizz.

Cosmo fired again, and again. The Supernaturalists were right. The creatures were sucking the life from these unfortunate people. And he had never known. Never seen. How could they beat adversaries like these?

Mona appeared at his shoulder, her chin sunburned by muzzle flash. "Chin up, Cosmo. You just saved a life."

That was the way to keep going. Save one life at a time. Cosmo took aim at a creature glowing silver from absorbed life force. He fired. The creature dissolved into bubbles.

The floor beneath their feet suddenly began heating up. Cosmo's rubber-soled boots left melting strings where he stepped. "The floor is burning!" he yelled.

Stefan laid a palm on the carpet. "Lawyers," he pronounced. "They're coming through the floor. We blocked the stairwell. Time to go."

"But the Parasites! There are more."

Stefan grabbed Cosmo by the lapel. "We've done what we can. If you get arrested, you can't help anybody."

An orange cutter beam erupted through the flooring, an inch from Cosmo's foot, carving out a small circle in the surface. The beam withdrew, to be replaced by a fiber-optic camera.

Mona grabbed the cable, yanking it repeatedly until the cable separated from its box. "Wrap it up. It's time to leave!"

The cutter beam reappeared, this time glowing blue for a quick burn. The harsh clicks of several guns being loaded emanated from the hole.

Stefan lead the retreat, shooting as he went. To the residents the Supernaturalists must have seemed crazed. Shooting at nothing, into the air, when there were people to be helped.

They traversed the retractable bridge into the main building. Cosmo glanced down through the gap. A dozen rapid-response lawyers were huddled on a raised platform below, the Scales of Justice logo plastered across their helmets, waiting for the cutter beam to finish making a hole. One spotted Cosmo.

"You there!" he shouted. "Do not flee the scene of an accident. There are waivers to be signed."

"Keep going," urged Ditto. "These guys have better equipment than we do."

The lawyer ripped a Velcro patch from his combat vest, revealing a rappelling spike and coil.

"It is illegal to flee the scene of an accident!" he called. "Freeze! Or the Stromberg Corporation will not be responsible for your injuries."

The lawyer ducked under the platform's safety rail and fired the spike through a gap in the twisted stairwell bars. Cosmo ducked, and the spike buried itself in the ceiling overhead. The lawyer smacked a button in the rig, and the spike's cable reeled him up at high speed. He crashed through two layers of plasterboard, landing in the corridor behind Ditto.

"Freeze, defendant," he said, leveling a lightning rod. "You have the right to get seriously messed up if you attempt to flee."

Ditto's eyes were wide. A perfect imitation of an innocent six-year-old. "Seriously messed up? But, sir, I'm a minor."

The lawyer snickered. "Not by the time your case gets to court."

"I object," said Ditto, head-butting his adversary in the stomach. The stunned lawyer tumbled through the hole in the floor; only his rappelling cord prevented him from plummeting to earth.

Stefan and Mona were already on the roof. "Move it, you two. We've got choppers coming in."

It was a kaleidoscope of chaos. Different crises swirled into Cosmo's vision and out again before he could deal with any of them. Lethal lawyers and a belligerent Bartoli baby. Life-sucking Parasites and now helicopters. All because they were trying to help people. Wasn't there someone they could tell?

Cosmo scrambled up the bridge onto the rooftop. The night sky was alive with converging choppers. Dozens of searchlights strobed the building. Most were TV birds. Disasters were big news. Even small ones like this would be sure to headline every bulletin.

Mona and Stefan were crouched by the lip of the Stromberg Building. Stefan took a shockproof walkie-talkie from his belt, switching the volume setting to high. He threw the radio onto an adjacent building. "We need a bridge," said Stefan. "Mona?"

"Not me. I already put down three. I'm almost out of gas."

"Ditto?"

"Same here."

Stefan kneaded his forehead. "Cosmo. Bridge. Now."

"Me?"

"No time like the present. No one else has enough juice for a big gap. And there isn't time to switch cannisters."

The rookie Supernaturalist lifted his bridge from its rack on his back. It seemed simple enough: stand on the bar, shoot the nose out and guide it with the cable. Not as easy as falling off a building, but easier than threading a needle with spaghetti.

He stood on the bar.

"Put your heel behind it," advised Mona. "Use your weight as an anchor."

He shifted his foot.

"Keep the nose up, better to overshoot."

Nose up. Okay.

Noises from below. Shouted commands and the thud of boots running.

"They're coming."

Cosmo wrapped his fingers around the reel, and fired. The bridge recoiled against his foot, sending tremors through his new kneecap. He ignored the pain, concentrating on steering the nose. It was heavier than it looked, and wilder. Twisting in the high-altitude wind. Cosmo leaned back on the cord, hauling the nose up. Then it was over, two feet clear of the next building. Cosmo relaxed, and the bridge touched down with a clang, two hooked grippers sprouting from the far end.

The team did not waste time on congratulations, bolting across to the safety of the next rooftop. Cosmo followed, stowing the bridge with the touch of a button.

Mona's smile shone from the shadows. "Not too bad for your first time, Cosmo."

Ditto smiled too. "Not too bad? The first time Mona laid down a bridge, we had to cut the cord, or it would have dragged her over the edge."

Mona frowned. "Yes, well at least I'm tall enough to steer a ladder across a big gap."

"Quiet!" ordered Stefan. "Company."

The legal team was rappelling onto the adjacent roof, sliding through the wrecked roof box. Shoulder-mounted lights poked through the hole like wartime searchlights. Several lawyers were switching their shrink-wrap cartridges for illegal lethal ammunition belts.

The squadron assembled in a loose circle, searching for signs of their quarry.

Stefan whispered into a second walkie-talkie.

"Everybody down: lawyers on the roof." The sentence was picked up by the first radio, two roofs away, and amplified so that it was clearly audible.

"This way," barked the legal leader. "Don't interrogate anyone until they've signed a waiver."

The lawyers rappelled after the sound of Stefan's voice. They were gung-ho now, but would shortly feel very stupid.

Ditto chuckled. "The oldest trick in the book. We have a crate of those walkie-talkies in the warehouse. I remember when lawyers were smarter."

Mona peeped over the rim. "Some of them still are."

Two of the lawyers were coming their way, lightning-rod rifles drawn tight against their shoulders.

"Beautiful equipment," said Ditto. "Those rappelling rigs are hands-free. And the rods can shoot forever. Nothing short of an electro magnetic pulse will stop those weapons firing."

Cosmo was too busy being scared to admire their equipment. "They're coming. What are we going to do?"

Stefan unhooked his backpack, placing his lightning rod on the roof. "We surrender."

Mona grinned. "Watch this, Cosmo. A thing of beauty."

Cosmo noticed that both Mona and Ditto were switching cartridges in their weapons.

Stefan rose slowly to his feet, hands raised high above his head. "Don't shoot!" he cried. "I'm unarmed."

The lawyers split apart, becoming two targets. Both guns were pointed at Stefan's head. "You fled the scene!" one shouted across the divide. "We're legally entitled to wrap you."

"I know, but come on, guys. I just wanted to see the show. I didn't touch anything. Anyway, my Dad's an ambassador. We have diplomatic immunity."

The lawyers started. Diplomatic immunity had become more or less redundant since the One World treaty, but there was still the odd remote republic that held on to its rights. If you wrapped a genuine diplomat, you'd spend the next five years in court and the twenty after that in prison.

"If you have diplomatic immunity, why are you wearing that fuzz plate?" Fuzz plate was the slang for the night-vision masks Stefan and his team were wearing. The low-level radiation in the plastic meant that they could not only repel X-rays but also wipe video. Even if the Supernaturalists were caught on camera, their heads would show up as static fuzz.

"Ultraviolet protection, that's all. I swear. I don't want to get my brain fried."

One of the lawyers cocked his weapon. "UV? At night? Okay, Mister Diplomatic Immunity. Let's see some diplomatic identification. And it had better not be fake, or you won't see a vat until morning."

Stefan reached inside his overcoat and, using two fingers only, withdrew an ID card. "I'm going to throw it across. Ready? Don't get trigger-happy. My Dad knows Mayor Shine."

"One hand. Put the other one on top of your head."

Stefan did as he was told, flicking the ID card high into to air. The wind caught it, spinning the plastic rectangle another twenty yards up.

"Moron," said lawyer number one, his eyes tracking the card.

"I got it," said number two.

At that moment, while both lawyers were watching the card, Ditto and Mona popped up simultaneously, squeezing off one round from their new cartridges.

Two green slugs sped across to the Stromberg Building, viscous trails in their wake. They splatted onto the lawyers' visors, spreading green goo across the lawyers' heads and shoulders. The two rapid-response lawyers keeled over, clawing at the blinding gunk on their visors.

"Gumballs," explained Mona, smiling her dazzling smile. "The most disgusting substance on the planet. Those helmets are history. I got clipped with a gumball one time, ruined my favorite flak jacket. Those guys are out of the game until their squad shows up."

Stefan watched the blank plastic card spiral toward the streets of Satellite City. Then his phone pulsed gently in his pocket. He pulled it out, consulting the small screen.

"A message from the computer. A citizen has pressed her panic button down on Journey and Eighth. Let's go. We'll take the street."

"One second," said Ditto. He laid down a bridge and quickly relieved the struggling lawyers of their rapelling rigs and weapons. The Supernaturalists were on a budget, and this equipment was too good to pass up. In seconds, the Bartoli baby was back with the rest.

"I thought you were out of gas," Cosmo said accusingly.

Ditto shrugged. "Out of gas? Me? I did say that, didn't I? Well, you learned, didn't you? And nobody got killed."

The Supernaturalists packed up, stowing bridges and holstering their lightning rods. Cosmo followed suit, his heart somewhere between his stomach and throat. The others seemed completely calm, oblivious to the insanity of their nighttime pursuits. Maybe they had been hunting the Parasites for so long that this was a normal night for them. Or maybe, and much more likely, they were all crazy.

Cosmo tightened the belt on his backpack, following Ditto through the roof-box door.

That meant he was crazy, too.

CHAPTER 4
THE BIG PIG

THE SUPERNATURALISTS STUMBLED back to the warehouse at five A.M. The panic button on Journey Avenue had been a false alarm. Some old guy had stuck his hand in the microwave while it was still on, setting off his personal alarm. Many citizens carried personal alarms that could be activated in the event of danger or illness, summoning a protection or medical team. It was expensive, but private teams arrived on average two minutes ahead of the city police. And that two minutes could mean the difference between life and death.

On the way back from Journey, the warehouse computer had notified them of a shootout outside a bank on the expensive end of Journey. The Supernaturalists camped on a rooftop and took potshots at Parasites that flocked to the scene.

The sun was poking through rainbow smog when they

finally arrived home. Even Ditto was too tired for jokes, his small face drawn, his kid's trousers spattered with the blood of those he'd tended to.

They sat around the table, chewing on processed dinners from flash-food packs. Cosmo pulled the tab on his food pack, waiting ten seconds for the heat to spread through his rations.

"I thought we did okay tonight," he said. "No one got hurt, and we blasted a hundred of those creatures."

Stefan threw down his army-issue spoon. "And tomorrow night there'll be two hundred to take their place."

Cosmo finished his food in silence, chewing slowly. "You know what I think?"

Stefan leaned back in his chair, arms crossed. His body language should have told Cosmo to shut up. "No, Cosmo— what do you think?"

Mona shot Cosmo a warning look, but he forged on.

"I think that if we could find out where they lived, then we could do some real damage."

Stefan laughed sharply, rubbing his face with both hands. "For nearly three years I've been doing this, and I never thought of that. Wow, you must be some kind of genius, Cosmo. Find out where they live. Amazing."

Cosmo's new knee suddenly began to itch. "I just thought . . ."

Stefan stood abruptly, his chair sliding across the floor. He reined his temper in, but it was an effort. "I know what you thought, Cosmo. I've thought about it too. Find the nest, and take them all out at the same time. It's a perfectly good idea, except for one thing. We can't find it.

"Suddenly I'm not hungry," he finished. "I'm going to bed." The tall boy dragged his feet into his cubicle, pulling the curtain behind him.

Ditto managed a chuckle. "Well done on the sucking up to the boss, new boy."

"Leave him alone, Ditto," said Mona. "Or I'll make you stand in the corner."

Ditto laughed, raising his tiny fists. "I know I'm a pacifist, Mona, but I'll make an exception for you."

Cosmo pushed his own food away. "I didn't mean to upset him."

Mona scooped the unfinished meals into her own carton. "It's not your fault, Cosmo. This is Stefan's whole life. Awake and asleep. It's what he lives for. And every night he has to face the fact that we're not making a dent."

"I keep thinking that there's something I don't know. Some other reason we're doing this."

Ditto opened a beer, draining half the bottle in one gulp. "We're helping people, isn't that enough?"

"We're helping people? No other reason."

Mona and Ditto shared a look. Cosmo caught it. "I get it. I'm not part of the group yet."

Mona draped an arm over his shoulder. "You know what, Cosmo? You're too tense. You need to get out for a walk."

Cosmo thought of Ziplock suddenly. "I haven't been out for a walk in fourteen years."

"No time like the present," said Mona, grabbing her jacket. "I can stay awake for a few more hours if you can. *Vamos.*"

Cosmo followed her to the elevator. "Where are we going?"

"Wait and see."

"Ditto, you coming?"

The tiny Bartoli baby settled back in his chair, flicking on the TV. "Am I coming? No, thanks. I went for a walk with Mona once—I was lucky to make it back with all my fingers."

Cosmo grinned weakly. "He's joking? Right?"

Mona pushed him into the elevator cage. "No, Cosmo," she said closing the grille. "He's not joking. But hey, who needs ten fingers?"

Mona led Cosmo through the maze of supply pipes and abandoned assembly lines to a large loading bay on the ground floor. A hulking panel truck sat heavy on its suspension on the parking ramp.

Mona slapped the fender, scattering a swarm of rust mites. Rust mites were a new breed of insect that had evolved in Satellite City. The TV brains said that they were nature's new superbug and would outlive even the cockroaches.

"The Pigmobile. This old heap has saved our hides more than once."

Cosmo kicked one of the tires. "We're not actually going to ride in this, are we?"

Mona popped the bonnet. "Don't be fooled by the exterior.

I prefer drab to stolen. But we're not riding today, Cosmo. The engine's manifold is shot. We need a new one, or at least one that's not too secondhand."

"I thought we were just going for a walk."

"We are walking," grunted Mona, yanking the tubular manifold from its clips. "No choice in the matter. I just need to do some business on the way."

"So, what do you need me for?" asked Cosmo, although in truth he was more than happy to accompany Mona anywhere she wanted to go. After all, he was fourteen years old, and Mona was the first girl he had ever spoken to unsupervised.

Mona wrapped the manifold in a rag. "Cosmo, I need you for backup."

Booshka was Big Pig slang for car theft. There were so many stolen automobiles in this region of Westside that the entire area was nicknamed after the pastime.

Teenage booshka pirates popped BMWs, Kroms, and Benzes right out of their racks in the uptown parking lots and refitted them for off-road racing. Every night, groups of youths gathered in abandoned warehouses for illegal drag races.

Booshka. Mona Vasquez's home turf.

It took almost an hour for the pair to walk from Abracadabra Street down to Booshka. South along Journey, then across the river to the old police blockade. Once past the line of burned-out cars, the pair were living on their wits. No police would respond to an alert from Booshka.

Cosmo tried to make himself invisible. It was a trick he'd learned in Clarissa Frayne. Shoulders hunched, small steps, and don't make eye contact with anybody. Mona did not subscribe to the invisibility theory.

"Down here, Cosmo. You gotta walk tall. Any of these vultures smell weakness, and they'll mess you up faster than sugar in a gas tank."

The vultures in question were groups of adolescents on their way home from a night's drag racing. They lounged on the sidewalk, or bounced their automobiles along the street on enhanced suspensions. There was no Satellite guidance down here; everything was manual.

Most of the vultures seemed to know Mona. "Hey, *chiquita*," shouted one of a large group, a muscular youth with a bandanna tied over one eye. "When are you coming racing again, Mona? We miss you."

Mona grinned. "*Hola*, Miguel. Maybe I'll come race when you build something worth racing against. I could walk faster than that last piece of junk."

Miguel moaned, placing one hand over his heart as though he'd been shot. "You got me, Vasquez. But someday I'll get you."

Mona kept grinning, but also kept walking. "In your dreams, Miguel. In your dreams."

When they had rounded a corner, Mona shuddered. Her bravado was all for show; beneath it, the girl was worried. "I thought they might ask me to come back. Miguel is a Sweetheart."

Cosmo blinked. "You think so?"

Mona punched him on the shoulder. "No, *estúpido*, not that kind of sweetheart. The Sweethearts are the biggest gang in Booshka. I used to run with them. I was their mech girl, looking after the hot rods. You check under those bandannas they wear, and you'll find a tattoo just like mine." Mona pointed to the DNA strand over her eyebrow.

"That's a gang tattoo, isn't it? What does it mean?"

Mona leaned close so Cosmo could get a better look at the ink over her eye. "It's a DNA strand made from car parts. You see the wheels and the pistons? It means that deep down all Sweethearts are the same. We live to race."

They walked on for several blocks, past the rows of pig-iron housing and barricaded shops. Vendors were warming up their street burners, protecting their wares with large dogs or visible sidearms. Several other gang members called out to Mona. And not just Sweethearts: they passed Celtic, Anglo, Slav, African, and Asian groups. Mona explained as they went along.

"Those are the Irish I's. They specialize in truckjacking from the docks across the bridge." She pointed at a pair of Africans in black suits. "Those tall guys are the Zools. Bodyguards mostly, they all learn some kind of African martial arts. One of those guys throws something sharp at you, and it's all over."

Cosmo tried to make himself look even more invisible.

"Those men with the piercings are the Bulldogs. They can strip a bike down in seconds. You turn away to tie your bootlace and when you turn back, your bike is just a skeleton."

"How did you get out of the Sweethearts?" asked Cosmo. "I thought gang membership was a for-life kind of thing."

"Stefan saved me. Eighteen months ago I was in a drag crash, a bad one. One of my lungs had collapsed and I was bleeding to death. The Parasites were settling in to suck me dry, and of course my brother Sweethearts scattered as soon as I hit that pylon. Stefan was out on a night patrol and heard the explosion. He came down here and blasted those monsters right off my chest. Ditto inflated my lung and they dropped me at General. On the way I was babbling about blue creatures sucking my life away, so a week later Stefan showed up at the hospital and offered me a new life. I took it. There was nothing to stay in Booshka for. My parents are gone and Stefan is eighteen, so he sponsors me. You can't believe how good it feels to be a legal citizen. I don't have to spend my life waiting for the state police to toss me in some institution."

"And the Sweethearts just let you go? Their best mechanic?"

Mona stopped at a stall and bought a couple of fresh rolls. They sat on upturned trash cans, eating the hot bread.

"It wasn't that easy. Miguel turned up at Abracadabra Street one night with a bunch of muscle. Stefan let them get into the loading bay, then he turned on the spotlights. He told Miguel that the Sweethearts had forfeited their right to my services when they left me to die."

"And the Sweethearts left it at that?" said Cosmo skeptically.

"No," admitted Mona. "Stefan offered them a Myishi

Z-twelve prototype nitrous racer in return for my ticket out of the gang."

"Stefan bought you?"

Mona punched him on the shoulder again. "No, Cosmo. He bought my freedom. That's why we're riding in the Pigmobile these days. And that's why we're down here looking for an ancient manifold." Mona finished her lunch, throwing the wrapper in a street incinerator. "Let's go. We have some negotiating to do."

Cosmo followed Mona down a narrow alley that reeked of raw sewage and motor oil. Rats tussled over food scraps, and rust mites burrowed into exposed patches of girder on the pig-iron walls. Mona pulled aside a lank oil-stained cloth, stepping through the entrance behind it. Behind the cloth was a steel door with security camera. Mona tapped on the safety screen. "*Hola*, Jean-Pierre, open up."

Nothing for a moment, then a crackle of static. "Mona Vasquez, you're still alive. Who's the kid?"

"Cosmo is with me. I can vouch for him."

The locking bars were remote opened, and the door swung aside. "Come on in, but don't touch anything."

They stepped into a mechanic's dream. The very walls appeared to be constructed from car parts. Everything from the latest plasma converters to ancient combustion engine components. They passed a maze of auto-parts walls and several cars in various stages of repair.

A tall slender man was buried to his waist in the engine of a Krom six-wheel-drive. His fine blond hair was tied back in a ponytail and every exposed inch of his skin was blackened by oil and exhaust fumes.

"Hey, Jean-Pierre, what's happening?"

The man extricated himself from the engine, pulling off magnifier goggles. "Vasquez, *ça va?* What's happening is that you are about to pay me the hundred dinars that you owe me for that exhaust box."

Mona laughed. "*Vaya al infierno,* Jean-Pierre. Go to hell. That exhaust box was full of filler. It blew up after a hundred miles. What I should do is kick your French behind all over this shop."

Jean-Pierre shrugged. "*Très bien.* Okay, you can't blame a man for trying."

"You owe me one and I've come to collect." Mona threw the manifold on a workbench. "You get me one of these and we'll call it even."

"Even? You're kidding me, Mona. These aren't easy to come by. Eighty dinars, if I can find one."

Mona folded her arms. "Thirty dinars, *hombre.* And you already know whether you have one or not."

Jean-Pierre smiled broadly, his teeth bright against the oil. "Mona, I have missed you. Okay, thirty, but only because you make me laugh."

Jean-Pierre disappeared between two metal-lined aisles.

"He's the only half-reliable parts man in Booshka," Mona told Cosmo. "Whatever you need, Jean-Pierre can get it or make it. The gangs leave him alone, because without him their rides would fall apart."

Jean-Pierre returned, twirling a replacement manifold like a baton. There was a Parasite perched on his shoulder. Cosmo reared backward, knocking over a tower of hubcaps. "Mona! Look! Can't you see it?"

The Frenchman frowned. "Hey, *mon ami*, watch the merchandise. What's the matter with you?"

Mona didn't bat an eyelid. "Ignore him, Jean-Pierre. He's crazy. He swallowed too many fumes at the drag meets. Sometimes he sees things."

Cosmo couldn't take his eyes off the creature, crouched there, waiting. "Can't we do something? Kill it?"

Mona picked up the hubcaps, glaring at him. "Shut up, Cosmo. There's nothing there! Nothing, get it?"

Cosmo tried to read her brown eyes. She saw the creature, he was certain of it. "Nothing. I get it."

"Good." She counted out the dinar chips onto the workbench. Outside the blockade, most people used credit cards, but in Booshka, cash was king. "Here, thirty dinars."

Jean-Pierre flicked the chips into a drawer. "The full thirty? Are you going soft on me, Vasquez?"

Mona took the manifold, resolutely ignoring the wide-eyed Parasite on Jean-Pierre's shoulder. "No, I just know a deal when I see it." She paused, eyes on the floor. "How have you been feeling lately?"

Jean-Pierre started. "Funny you should mention it. My chest feels tight. Just for the past few weeks. It's probably nothing. I should go to a doctor in the city, but who trusts doctors, *n'est ce pas?*"

Mona looked the Frenchman in the eyes. "Get it seen to, Jean-Pierre. We'd all be lost without you."

"*Certainement*. The customer is always right." He pulled open a basket drawer on the wall. "Here, a set of plugs on the house, for my favorite customer."

Mona pocketed the plugs, then kissed Jean-Pierre on the cheek. The Parasite casually moved out of her way. "Goodbye, Jean-Pierre. And thank you."

The Frenchman rubbed his cheek. "A kiss? From Mona Vasquez? You're not sick, are you?"

Mona glared malevolently at the Parasite. "No, Jean-Pierre. *I'm* not sick."

Mona refused to say another word until she and Cosmo had put two blocks between them and Jean-Pierre's workshop.

"Those monsters. Sometimes they know when a person is in harm's way."

"Why didn't we do something?"

"Do what? Blast a hole in the air in broad daylight? Jean-Pierre would have shot us himself. There's nothing we can do here, no more than we can go shooting up hospitals. Maybe Jean-Pierre will have a heart attack and the Parasite will push him over the edge. Natural causes, you see. Or maybe the Parasite will just siphon off a few years. That's the beauty of their race, no one ever knows. No crime, no foul, no suspect, no victim. You know, only a year ago, you would never see a Parasite out during the day. But now it's happening more and more."

Cosmo studied the growing crowds on the street. It was

harder to see the Parasites in the daylight, but they were there, squatting on their targets' shoulders or shadowing them from overhead.

Mona saw him watching. "That's right. They don't like the light much, but they're here. They don't like water either. It won't kill them, but a good soaking can suck the energy right out of them. That's why every day I pray for rain."

"Is that it, then? Once a Parasite selects you, it's all over?"

"Not necessarily. You can be saved by paramedics, or beat the odds, or like us, not go out on patrol that night. Parasites don't generally show up until the incident occurs, but sometimes the smell of death is too strong to resist."

They hurried through Booshka, toward the blockade. Cosmo kept his head down, terrified to draw attention from the Parasites. Scared that his gaze would attract one of them down to perch on his shoulder.

"Leaving so soon?" said a voice.

Miguel and the Sweethearts were hanging over a rail, three stories up.

"Gotta go," replied Mona. "I got work to do."

"You should stick around, *chiquita*. There's something big happening tonight. We're unveiling the Myishi Z-twelve. We're going to clean up."

"Really? Maybe you should give it a miss. I hear the smog is bad later."

Miguel laughed. "What are you talking about, girl? The Sweethearts don't care about no smog. Tonight we have business to take care of."

Cosmo glanced upward, from the corner of one eye. Half a dozen Parasites had adhered to the wall above the Sweethearts' heads, round eyes staring almost fondly at their targets.

Mona continued walking. "Looks like we're going to be busy tonight too."

CHAPTER 5
SWEETHEARTS &
BULLDOGS

TWELVE HOURS LATER COSMO was back down in Booshka; this time in the back of the Pigmobile with the other Supernaturalists. Mona parked in the shadow of a corrugated sheet-metal awning opposite the Sweethearts' headquarters, an abandoned police station inside the blockade. Outside, everything was locked down for the night, and the streets were deserted, apart from roving groups of youths and homeless wanderers.

Stefan was not happy with the situation. "The Parasites can be wrong. We could be wasting this entire night."

"There were too many, Stefan," responded Mona. "One could be a mistake, but the creatures were waiting for a major disaster. Miguel said the Sweethearts were bringing out the Myishi Z-twelve tonight. They're bound to win, and the other gangs are going to go ballistic."

Stefan shrugged. "The gangs are always going ballistic."

Mona's eyes flashed. "Those guys were my family for a long time, Stefan. You have to look out for your family, you should understand that."

"Okay," said Stefan grudgingly. "We tail them for a couple of hours, but then we're back on the computer."

"Thanks, Stefan."

Ditto turned away from the window. "All right, everybody. We're on."

The Sweethearts were leaving the police station's underground parking lot in a parade of souped-up Kroms, led by Miguel in a heavily camouflaged Myishi Z-twelve.

"There she is," said Mona. "The price of my freedom."

Cosmo rubbed a peephole through the dirty window. "It doesn't look like much."

Mona started the Pigmobile's engine. It was surprisingly quiet in spite of its size. "That's the clever part. If the Sweethearts arrived with the Myishi Z-twelve, nobody would bet against them. This way, they stand to make more money." She pulled onto the road, staying well behind the Sweetheart convoy. "You never did tell me the story of how you got that car, Stefan."

Stefan grinned. "I liberated it from the Myishi experimental division. They were testing a couple and one didn't make the curve. Ran straight into a fuel dump. I followed a swarm of Parasites into the facility and started blasting. The lawyers got a bit close to me, so I took the other car. That thing's amazing, years ahead of the competition. It's even got wing slots, if you want to upgrade. It really pained me to part with it."

Mona thumped him on the chest. A fond gesture for her. "Okay, Stefan. Thank you. How many times do you want me to say it?"

"Another couple of thousand should do it."

The Sweethearts paraded down the avenue, honking personalized horns to wake up the street. Soon crowds of people were gathered on the balconies, fluttering bandannas. Miguel waved royally out of the window.

Mona hung back in the Pigmobile until they had cleared Red Square. The convoy swung east.

"Okay. East. That's Bulldog country. They're racing in the old Krom factory."

Ditto typed this information into the onboard computer, and in seconds the warehouse server sent back a schematic of the factory. "It's perfect. If they use the assembly lines, you have two five-mile lanes set above solid asphalt."

"Access?" asked Stefan.

"Six doors on the ground level, which I presume we won't be using."

"Correct."

"Then I recommend the lines of solar panels on the roof. No doubt the locals have long since made off with the panels, so we should be able to climb into the upper gantry."

Cosmo groaned. More rooftops. But he didn't say anything aloud.

Stefan seemed to read his thoughts. "Don't worry, Cosmo," he said. "You did well last night. You laid down that bridge like a fireman. Not too bad with the lightning rod either, although you did hit more wall than Parasites."

"A compliment from Stefan Bashkir?" said Mona, in mock surprise. "You should record that and play it back every night, because you probably won't get another one."

Cosmo laughed. But Stefan's words had meant something to him. For the first time, he felt almost a part of the group.

Mona squeezed the Pigmobile down several narrow alleys, knocking the side mirrors flat to the doors. The Krom factory loomed ahead, orange firelight flickering from empty panels in the roof.

"This must be the place," said Mona, cutting the engine. She climbed into the back. "There'll be at least fifty Bulldogs inside. All armed with gunpowder antiques and maybe some shrink-wrappers or Shockers. My guess is that there's going to be some kind of accident, either that or a gang fight."

Stefan nodded. "Okay. We don't get involved until whatever is going to happen happens. Then we take care of our spirit friends."

Mona didn't like the plan. "Shouldn't we try to break the whole thing up? Prevent the disaster?"

"No. We can't tell the future. Maybe when we try to break things up, we actually cause the disaster."

It made sense, even if Mona wasn't happy about it. Stefan put a hand on her shoulder. "Are you okay, Mona? Will you be able to do the job?"

Mona snapped a power cell into her lightning rod. "Don't worry about me, Stefan. I know what we came here for."

"Good. We go up the fire escape, through the roof and onto the gantry inside. Stay sharp. The gangs could have grown some brains and posted sentries on the roof."

Ditto Velcroed a first-aid kit to his chest. "And pigs will fly."

The alley was so narrow, that they had to disembark from the rear of the Pigmobile, then climb over the roof to reach the Krom fire escape. The sounds of roaring engines and cheering were only slightly dulled by the factory walls. The fire escape's bottom rung was a meter above Stefan's reach. Rather than deploy a ladder, he grabbed Ditto by the belt.

"Ready?"

Ditto nodded. "Going up."

Stefan hefted the tiny boy-man straight up, until he could grab the bottom rung. His weight dragged the fire escape ladder to ground level. They climbed one by one, with Stefan taking up the rear. If anyone was likely to break a rung, it was the tall youth.

The fire escape bore their weight, and minutes later the Supernaturalists were facedown on the gently sloped roof, peering through an empty solar panel frame. Stretched out below them were the cannibalized remains of a megafactory that had once employed more than twenty thousand Satellite City residents.

The raised assembly lanes were bolstered by welded lengths of girder. Builder androids had been stripped of any useful components, and hung limply in their cradles like robot skeletons. Complicated-looking overhead gantries and magnetic monorail systems hung in the air, with hooks, clamps, and lighting rigs draped from them like mechanical jewelry.

The Bulldogs and the Sweethearts were facing off in classic tribal fashion. At least a hundred gang members postured around their vehicles, chests out, chins up, sucking in their guts. The vehicles themselves were the automobile equivelant of peacocks' tails—huge spoilers inset with digitized graphics, old-fashioned rubber tires and hoods stripped away to reveal throbbing engines. Only the Myishi Z-twelve was unadorned—a panther at rest.

The racing had already begun. Two cars at a time were ramped onto the assembly line, burning down the five-mile strip in an afterburn of gasoline and nitrous. The rules were simple. An electrified gate sat on each lane. When that gate was lifted, the driver put his foot down. Go too late and the race was over; too early, and the gate's charge would blow car and driver clean off the track. First past the post took the honors, and the winner's purse.

The Supernaturalists weren't the only beings in the upper regions. Several dozen Parasites clung spiderlike to the infrastructure, dropping down to suck a few drops of life from any injured drivers. As always, they were oblivious to the group's attentions.

Cosmo drew his lightning rod.

"Wait," instructed Stefan. "This is not the main event. You don't get this many Parasites for a few minor injuries. We have to hold back until something big happens." Stefan's fingers were twitching over his own lightning rod. It was obvious that allowing the Parasites to steal even one drop of life essence was killing him. Sometimes leaders have to make tough choices, Cosmo thought.

Ditto studied the altimeter on his watch. "We're at least two hundred feet off the ground here. If something does happen, I'm not going to be able to help anybody. And the only reason I'm here is to cure people. You know how I feel about blasting Parasites. So if I'm not allowed to heal, then I may as well go back to the old job. The pay is better and I don't have to put up with your teenage moods."

Stefan's gaze could have drilled holes in titanium. "Ditto. Now is not the time."

Ditto glared right back. "Not the time? Now we only save lives when you say so? Well, if I had known that, I would have stayed home in our palace and had a few beers."

Stefan ground his teeth, both in frustration and to stop himself from smiling. "Ditto, one of these days I'm going to sign you up for kindergarten, so help me. Okay, take Mona, get down near ground level. No risks though. These are not the type of people we generally deal with. These are armed killers. If you can help someone, then help them, but my advice is to tranquilize them first. And wear your fuzz plates. You never know."

Ditto grinned. "Stefan, you're a sweetheart." The Bartoli baby trotted down a connecting stairwell, surefooted as a goat. Mona ran after him, swearing in Spanish. They made their way across pipes and down rails until they straddled a cable conduit directly above the assembly line. In the event of a disaster, it would be a simple matter to lay down a bridge to ground level.

Stefan followed their progress through field glasses. "They're safe."

Cosmo lay beside him on the gantry. "Shouldn't we go down with her . . . them?"

Stefan kept his eyes on the scene below. "A bit of advice, Cosmo. Don't get too attached to Mona. She is the best Spotter I've ever seen, but some day she'll move on. And to answer your question, we can cover them from here. If they get in trouble we can create a diversion, draw fire away."

Cosmo sighed. Drawing fire sounded even more dangerous than everything else they had done so far.

Stefan misinterpreted the sigh. "Don't worry about it, kid," he said, rapping Cosmo playfully on his robotix plate. "I don't suppose they teach military tactics in Clarissa Frayne."

The rap reminded Cosmo that parts of his body were not the originals. How much had changed in a week. New knee, new forehead, new friends, new life. Cosmo gazed down at the hundred armed gang members. New life—for how long?

Ditto balanced easily on the cable conduit. He was a natural gymnast in spite of his size. Maybe you got used to your body when it hadn't changed in decades. "So you like the kid?" he said, in a teasing tone that belied his angelic face. "Your little *chico*?"

"Yes, sure, I like Cosmo. He's a good kid. Learns fast."

Mona lay flat on the conduit, scanning the crowd below

her for Miguel. If she had a chance to save anyone, it would be Miguel. He'd taken her in off the street when a couple of his boys had caught her trying a little booshka on a Sweetheart auto. Instead of punishing her, Miguel had put her to work.

Ditto chuckled. "He's a good kid? Come on, Vasquez, it's me you're talking to. You've been marginally less grumpy since he got here."

"Company, okay? It's nice to have someone my own age around Abracadabra Street."

Ditto kept on needling. "It's not as if he's handsome. No hair yet to speak of, and that forehead looks like he's got a porcupine hiding under there."

"Well, at least he's tall," said Mona pointedly.

"Look who's getting protective? Do I sense a crack in the Vasquez armor?"

Mona would never admit it to the Bartoli baby, but in a way he was right. The orphan kid was interesting. He had made quite an entrance into their lives as he lay smoking on a rooftop. Then he had gone on to save her life. After that he would have to have the personality of a hungry bear for her not to like him. "He's just a friend. That's all. Maybe that concept is too *big* for you to understand."

Ditto grinned, delighted that his needling was having an effect. "Oh, *big* jokes now is it? I may be small, Vasquez, but I have more brains in my undersized head than the rest of the Supernaturalists put together."

Mona pointed her lightning rod at her pint-sized

companion. "Stop annoying me, Ditto. Do you think I wouldn't gumball you? Is that what you think? Because if it is, you'd be mistaken."

Ditto raised his palms. "Threats of violence? I didn't realize how serious this had become. So quick too: who would have guessed it?" He paused, smiling genuinely. "Seriously, though. He's okay, that Cosmo kid. I'm glad you found a friend."

Mona tutted. "You make him sound like a puppy."

"I'm trying to be serious. You're young, Mona. A teenager. You need somebody to talk to. I may not look it, but I'm too old. And Stefan—well, most of the time he's not in the mood for talking."

Ditto's phone vibrated in his pocket. "Text from above," he said, reading the screen. "'What are you two playing at? Keep your mouths shut and your eyes open.'" The Bartoli baby waved in Stefan's general direction. "You'd better keep your mind on the job, Mona, or I may have to pull rank."

Mona grinned. "You know something. If you weren't three feet high . . ."

"Three feet two," said Ditto, pouting.

On the factory floor beneath them, things were heating up. The minor races had been run, and now the prized cars were being ramped onto the assembly line. The Bulldogs were gathered around a six-wheel charger, hooting and loosing Shocker charges into the air. The charger had wide-profile tires, plasma decals, and twin double exhaust pipes vibrating at its tail. Like the Bulldogs themselves, the car was loud and rippling with muscle. The Bulldogs were obsessed with appearance. The victors in tonight's drag would probably use their winnings to have some saline muscle sacs inserted under their skin.

The Myishi racer appeared tame in comparison. Its bodywork was retrospectively curved, a single exhaust pipe poked from beneath the rear bumper, and there were only four wheels. Ridiculous. The Bulldogs were not impressed. They howled at the roof, their trademark method of expressing derision.

Mona rolled her eyes. "Bulldogs. Nature's leftovers."

Mona was not as calm as she sounded. Whatever was going to happen would happen soon. Death was gathering in the very oxygen. The Parasites could feel it too, and they clustered ever lower on the factory walls.

Ditto's phone vibrated again. "Another text," he groaned. "What does Stefan think? I'm his secretary?"

He pulled the phone from his pocket, reading the message. "You'd better read this," he said in strangled tones.

Mona reached for the phone, keeping one eye on the scene below. The letters stood out black against a green screen.

Pigs have flown, said the text. *The Bulldogs posted a sentry. He's behind you.*

Mona heard a power cell charging beside her ear.

Cosmo jumped to his feet. "We have to help them."

Stefan grabbed him by the lapels, dragging him back down. "Get down, Cosmo, you're making a nice target of yourself."

"But they'll be killed!" protested Cosmo.

Stefan rolled over, clamping a hand on Cosmo's mouth. "Listen to me carefully, Cosmo. I know what I'm doing. I've been doing it for the past three years. You have spent your entire life in an orphanage. All you know about combat missions could be written on Ditto's underpants. Get the idea?"

Cosmo nodded.

"Good. We watch and see how this develops. Mona and Ditto may have some ideas of their own."

He removed his hand. Cosmo drew a shaky breath. "What if they shoot them?"

Stefan turned his gaze to the scene below. He was blinking rapidly and his hands were clamped around the walkway bars. He was not as in control as he pretended. "If they shoot them, then they pay."

Maybe, thought Cosmo. *But not as much as we do.*

The Bulldog sentry was naked except for black shorts, and his skin was dark. Unnaturally so. Ditto realized after several seconds' scrutiny that the man's skin had been almost completely tattooed. Initially he couldn't see anything in the ink, but then strange hypnotic swirls and patterns suggested themselves. "You like it?" asked the sentry. "Full-body coverage with Jamaican hypno-patterns, only $399 in The Ink Blot tattoo parlor. Ask for Sasha."

"Wow," said Ditto. The patterns were all over. How had he missed them before?

Mona snapped her fingers before his eyes.

"Don't look at the ink, *estúpido*. Hypno-patterns will zone you out."

"It's true," said the sentry. "I had a cab driver once, staring at me in the mirror. Fell asleep at the wheel." He pointed the nozzle of his weapon at Mona. "Now to business. On your feet. You just have time to make your last appointment."

Ditto opened his mouth to pass comment, and Mona clamped a hand over it.

"No problem, *amigo*. Lead the way."

The tattooed sentry prodded them down a steep stairwell to the factory floor. The other Bulldogs seemed a lot taller up close. They jostled the intruders, brandishing weapons and baying for blood.

Their leader stepped forward. They could tell he was the leader because the words HEAD HONCHO flashed across his bare chest in subcutaneous lighting. "What did we find, Shadow?" he growled, his metallic mohawk quivering on his skull. And Head Honcho actually did growl. He'd probably had surgery on his vocal cords to achieve the effect.

Shadow pushed his prizes into the ring. "Two little rust mites hanging in the rafters."

Head Honcho sized the intruders up. "Okay. Strap them on the bonnets, they'll make nice hood ornaments."

Dozens of hands grabbed the pair, hoisting them roughly overhead.

"Wait," said Miguel, blocking the Bulldogs' path. "Nothing gets strapped on my hood, Honcho. This machine is aerodynamic. Bumps like that will mess with the speed. *¿Comprende?*"

Mona glared down at him from a sea of arms. "Thanks a bunch, Miguel. And I thought you cared."

Honcho's brain gears ground noisily, making the connection. "You know this kid?"

Miguel sighed deeply. Another night fouled up. "Yes, sure. She's my . . . little sister. I told her to stay home, but she likes the races. In the blood, I guess. Do me a favor and cut her loose."

Head Honcho's chest lights flashed faster, racing with his heartbeat.

"I don't know, mate. Rules are rules."

Miguel persisted. "Come on, *hombre*. I can't go home without the *niña*."

"Why not, mate? Teenagers are just a waste of space and air."

"True, but this girl is one of the best drivers we have. Almost as good as me. Be a shame to waste all the driving hours we invested. In a couple of years she'll be burning up the strip."

A nasty smile spread across Honcho's face. His steel mohawk vibrated as he laughed.

"Okay, mate. I got a deal for you. The girl drives the last race."

"*¡Qué no!*" protested Miguel. "No way. That car is my baby."

"It's your call. She's in the car, or she's on it."

Miguel pulled his bandanna off, wringing it between both hands. "Okay. She drives." He pointed a rigid finger at Mona. "You mess this up, Mona, and there'll be hell to pay."

On the car or in it? Not that Mona actually had a choice. Dozens of strange hands fed her overhead to the Myishi Z-twelve. She felt herself being folded almost in half and stuffed in the car's side window. Ditto was hustled into the passenger's seat.

"You can take your mascot too," said Honcho, strapping himself into the Bulldog's contender. "You need all the luck you can get."

"Mascot," said Ditto, between gritted teeth. "That moronic sack of implants. I'd like to punch his lights out. Literally." He checked his blond hair in the mirror. "You can drive this thing, right?"

Mona studied the confusing array of dials and meters. "Yeah. Maybe. In theory."

"Do you think they'll give us a practice run?"

Outside the car, groups of adrenalized gang members were bouncing with anticipation. A mob of souped-up, tattooed, testosterone-fueled young men with big money riding on this race. "No. No practice runs."

Mona's thing was engines, not driving. She could take a few curves if she had to, but this was a nitrous racer, not the Pigmobile. Generally drag racers fed a nitrous oxide mixture into the regular fuel for that extra burst of speed when it was needed. But this thing actually used heated nitrous oxide as the regular fuel. Because nitrous was used up so quickly, the entire car had been converted into a fuel tank. Every strut and panel was filled with the explosive mixture. Nobody really knew how to drive a car like this.

Miguel leaned in the window. "Tell Stefan he owes me a big favor."

"Tell him yourself," retorted Mona. "In ten seconds I'm gonna be a carbon stain on the asphalt."

"Just hold her steady, let the nitrous do the work. Standard pedals, but brake early. This car is a terror to stop. You lose this one, Vasquez, and you'd better leave town in shame."

Honcho sounded his horn impatiently.

"A couple of questions," said Miguel. "Where's Stefan, and why are you here?"

Mona placed a hand on his arm. "When it happens, you'll know. Just keep your head down and get ready to run."

Miguel settled his bandanna gangster style. "We're Sweethearts, baby. We never run." And with that tough-guy rejoinder, he was gone, down onto the factory floor with his boys.

Ditto's phone vibrated. He slipped it out surreptitiously. On the screen was a single question mark. Ditto composed a return message. *Stay put*, read his response. *Everything under control.*

Mona craned her neck to read the text. "Under control? Let me know when we're in trouble."

The gates were lowered on Krom robot arms, powered by a portable generator. One sparking grille settled in front of each car. Honcho was howling now. The digi-cals on his fenders showed running, slobbering bulldogs. The other

Bulldogs took up his canine call, until the entire factory echoed with the yelping of deranged gang members.

"I don't know which is healthier," said Ditto. "Winning or losing."

Mona pressed the ignition button, revving the car in neutral. "I'm not waiting around to find out."

Ditto gripped the dash nervously. "Don't do anything foolish, Mona. I'm just a baby."

"Just hold on. And buckle up."

The gates rose slowly, cascading sparks on the audience below. Honcho was punching the roof of his car, denting the paneling. If he got any more excited, he might just short out his bulbs.

Mona shifted into first gear. The manual gearbox would have been added by the Sweethearts. There would hardly be time to shift all the way to sixth; she would have to skip a few gears. The Z-twelve lunged forward like an eager panther. She held it with the clutch.

There was a three-foot-wide gap between the gate and the surface now. A waterfall of dancing white sparks obscured Mona's vision. Bulldogs fired rounds into the air. The Parasites were closing in, perhaps for her. Whatever was coming was on the way. Ridiculous as that sounded.

The gates jerked upward another notch.

"Go!" screamed the Sweethearts in one voice. "Go! Go!"

Mona revved, but did not go. "Not yet."

Honcho had no such reservations. He floored the accelerator and shot out under the gate. It was too soon. His rear spoiler caught the gates. But there was no explosion, no conduction of thousands of volts through his chassis. Instead the spoiler melted into black slop, half coating the rear window. Honcho raced on.

"Rubber," said Mona contemptuously. "That cheat."

"Go!" howled the Sweethearts almost tearfully. Honcho was already a mile down the track and he hadn't even fired his nitrous yet.

"Not just yet."

Ditto pounded her shoulder with tiny hands. "What are you doing, Vasquez? Are you insane?"

"One more second."

Honcho was two miles gone. Two and a half. Doing at least three hundred miles an hour, his tires billowing black smoke. The Sweethearts were converging on the car, drawing weapons from their pockets. Miguel's lips were drawn back from his teeth.

"Time to go," whispered Mona, dropping the accelerator and lifting the clutch. The Z-twelve shot forward like Thor's hammer across the sky. The nitrous injection slammed Mona and Ditto back into their seats. If the headrests hadn't been padded, their skulls would have cracked like eggshells. Vision was distorted, colors ran and blended. Nothing was clear, except the track.

Mona locked her wrists, keeping the wheel steady. Everything on either side dissolved into speed trails, but ahead the track was a solid black strip, with Honcho's charger growing ever larger in the crystal windscreen. Compared to the

Z-twelve, Honcho's car may as well have been in reverse, though the Bulldog could not have known that. He was already firing victory flares out the window.

Check your mirror, lamebrain, thought Mona. *See what's coming up on you.*

It seemed as though Honcho did just that, because his twin exhaust pipes flared blue as he injected the nitrous into his engine. The Bulldog charger lurched forward, another fifty mph added to its speed. It was too late; the Z-twelve was an automated bullet burning down the track like lightning from the belly of a storm cloud. "Amazing," said Mona, the word jittering between gritted teeth. "This thing is an animal."

Ditto grinned at Honcho as they cruised past. An irritating smug grin that would make anyone on the receiving end want to do him severe injury. Quite possibly Honcho couldn't see the other car, never mind the Bartoli baby's grinning head—but it made Ditto feel better.

They flashed across the finish line, activating victory fireworks. Five miles in under a minute. The factory wall loomed large before them,

"You forgot to brake!" shouted Ditto over the engine's roar. "Your old boyfriend said to brake early!"

Mona floored the accelerator, heading for a sonic boom.

"He's not my old boyfriend, and do you really want to stop for a chat with Honcho?"

"Ideally, no. But what choice do we have?"

"We can go through that gate."

Ditto held his nose and blew until his ears popped, just in case the pressure was interfering with his hearing. "Go through the . . . Are you completely insane?"

"Think about it. We go off the end of the ramp at about three hundred. The gate is only polymer, the car is toughened alloy. We have a good chance of making it."

"There must be another way."

"I'm all ears, you have three seconds."

"Mona, don't make me hit you."

"If you have a sledgehammer in your pocket, I'll start worrying."

Ditto adopted the crash position, head between legs.

"We're dead," he muttered.

The pig-iron wall loomed before them, seconds away. A speeding procession of gang autos raced up the factory floor. Overhead the Parasites scurried ever closer to ground level. And there was one more factor, something no one could have anticipated. Something rarely seen in Booshka: paralegals.

The Z-twelve cut out.

"What?" said Mona.

All four wheels locked simultaneously and two minibraking parachutes shot out of the rear spoiler. "Not good," muttered Mona, fighting the frozen steering wheel.

The Z-twelve's dash flipped to reveal a backlit readout. A message flashed up on the remote. REMOTE MYISHI Z-TWELVE LOCKOUT, the message read. STEP AWAY FROM THE VEHICLE. The car spun to a halt, one wheel dangling over the track's edge.

Ditto peeped up from his crash position. "Are we dead?"

"No, we're locked out."

Ditto sat up gingerly. "Thank God for that."

Mona climbed from the car, shaking the speed buzz from her head. The situation was fast approaching critical and could only get worse. The gangs would be here any second, and Miguel could not save them again even if he wanted to. She turned to the heavens. Stefan was their only chance, up there watching over them like their own private guardian angel. He would come, she knew he would.

But there was something else. Above Cosmo and Stefan's perch. Several somethings.

Ditto stumbled from the Z-twelve. "A thought, Vasquez. If we're locked out, who locked us out?"

Mona pointed to several dozen shadowy figures free-falling toward the solar panel frames. "They did."

Overhead in the Krom factory gantry, Cosmo and Stefan watched the race with a mixture of terror and fascination. At one point Stefan's phone vibrated. He checked the screen.

"What does it say?" asked Cosmo.

Stefan deleted the text. "Everything's fine. See you soon."

"Okay, I get it. Don't ask."

Stefan watched the race's conclusion through field glasses. "Strange."

"Strange?" asked Cosmo. "What's strange?"

Stefan passed across the binoculars. "They've stopped. An emergency stop, too. I was sure Mona would punch out through the gate. Why would she stop on the track like a sitting duck? Unless . . ."

Cosmo felt a chill across his brow as the blood drained from his face. Unless what? He waited for Stefan to complete the thought.

"Unless someone else stopped the car for her."

Through the field glasses, Cosmo saw Mona point to the ceiling above them. He flipped onto his back, squinting through the huge panels into the night sky beyond. Dozens of shadowy figures were hurtling through midair toward the holes in the roof. "Are those things real? Or are they some other creatures that only we can see?"

Stefan grabbed the glasses, pointing them toward the ceiling. Several black-clad figures swam into focus. Combat chutes trailed behind them, and directional gas jets were attached to each heel. Cradled in the figures' arms were chunky assault rifles. There was a company logo emblazoned across each helmet. The same logo that flashed from the Satellite.

"Myishi Corp," said Stefan. "Paralegals. They're here for the Z-twelve."

"What? All this for a car?"

Stefan clambered to his knees on the grating, hoisting his greatcoat over his head. "That car cost billions of dinars to develop. Losing it was a real kick in the teeth for Myishi. This is probably the first time it's been out from under a lead sheet long enough to trace."

Stefan lifted the flap of his coat. "Quickly, under here, and pray we're not spotted."

Cosmo crawled under the leather, beneath Stefan's armpit. The coat smelled of hard work and lightning-rod flash. Through a gap in the coat, he watched the paralegals swoop gracefully through the gaping slots in the roof. With guiding bursts of gas from their boot jets, they avoided being snared by jutting girders and descended toward the gangs assembled below.

One ripped a mini-woofer radio speaker from a Velcro patch on his arm and dropped it to the factory floor below. It bounced a full ten feet in its plastic casing before rolling along the track to settled at Honcho's feet. He picked it up quizzically.

The paralegal's voice blasted from the mesh. "The Z-twelve Nitro Charger is the property of the Myishi Corporation. Step away from the car or you will be sanctioned. This is your final warning. You have ten seconds to respond."

The gang members did not need ten seconds. Most spun their cars through a one-eighty skid, heading back toward the doors. Halfway there they noticed the three-story assault tanks blocking the exits. Myishi was pulling out all the stops on this one. The gang members began firing whatever they had at the descending paralegals.

By then the ten seconds were up, and the Myishi lawyers were legally entitled to open fire. Which they did, with the most advanced weapons in the world. The first phase was to lay down a cellophane blanket. Fleeing gang members were wrapped as they attempted to escape. Every second shell was a Shocker, the charge of which ran across the surface of the cellophane, blasting everything beneath the sticky surface into oblivion, or beyond.

The Parasites pounced like iridescent wolves, sinking through the cellophane cocoons to settle on gang members' chests. The charge from the Shockers was too dispersed to do them any real harm; in fact it seemed to add to their enthusiasm.

The paralegals fell like deadly missiles, spitting pain and death. They hooked onto stairwells and lower gantries, picking off their prey from above. The gang members never had a chance. Most were unconscious before they had time to draw a weapon. The rest were herded into corners by lumbering assault tanks and glued to the walls by cellophane slugs.

Stefan poked his head out from under the coat. "This is all my fault," he moaned. "The Parasites are feasting, and it's all my doing. I gave the Z-twelve to Miguel."

Cosmo peered down at the chaos below. "You couldn't have known. No one could."

Stefan's eyes flashed in the light of electric shells. "I should have known! For three years I've been running from Myishi police. I know how they operate." He pointed his lightning rod at a group of Parasites. "Too far. We don't have the range. We need to get down there."

Cosmo searched the melee of fleeing bodies. "I see them. They're going under the track. They'll be trapped."

"I need to get lower," Stefan muttered. "I can't help from here."

Cosmo smacked the grille with his fist. "Why can't it ever rain when you want it to?"

Stefan looked at him strangely. "Rain? Of course, we need water to drive away the Parasites. We can do that much at least."

"Now you're telling me you can make it rain?"

Stefan was on his feet, scrambling toward an access ladder. "I can't, but they can."

"They?" shouted Cosmo, racing after the Supernaturalist. "Who are they?"

"There. In the doorway. You get back to the Pigmobile, try to hook up with Mona and Ditto if they make it out."

Cosmo still didn't get it. The only thing in the doorway was a thirty-foot-high assault tank. Surely Stefan didn't intend to take on one of those. Surely not. Cosmo followed Stefan down a ladder. He had no intention of going back to the Pigmobile. If Stefan was going after an assault tank, Cosmo was going with him. He was, after all, one of the team.

"Paralegals," gasped Mona. "The baddest of the bad."

Paralegals were a three-way cross between lawyers, paratroopers, and pit bulls. They were a corporation's last resort, and were only unleashed when there was big money at stake.

Mona twigged immediately. "They're after the car." She grabbed Ditto by the collar, dragging him to the lip of the track.

"Myishi shut the car down. There must be some kind of tracker in the wiring. We need to take cover."

"Cover?" croaked Ditto, half strangled by his partner's grip. "They're only after the car."

"And anyone who's seen it or worked on it. They can't risk another corporation stealing Myishi ideas. Everyone here will be taken in for interrogation."

"Interrogation? A few polite questions and a cup of sim-coffee?"

Mona tutted. "Sure, *amigo*. A few Shockers and a cup of sodium Pentothal. We'll be lucky if we can count to ten by the time they've finished."

Ditto nodded. "Cover. Good idea."

They jumped from the assembly line, worming their way between the girders that propped up the line. The asphalt was littered with juice pouches and gum. The stink of generations of assorted garbage was sharp in their nostrils.

Ditto slapped his sleeve as though that could dislodge the smell. "This jacket is ruined. I'll never get the stink out."

Mona crawled deeper into the shadows. "At least you'll still have a nose to smell the stink."

The shooting started. Huge blobs of liquid cellophane spattered the gang members and their cars. These were followed by searing jolts of electricity.

"They're getting the tar-and-spark treatment," said Ditto. "I almost feel sorry for them."

Honcho pinwheeled past their hiding place, chest lights flashing furiously. A Shocker clipped his elbow, sending a charge jittering through his torso. The bulbs below his skin blew out like bullets. A Parasite was on him in under a second. Honcho fought on oblivious, screaming his rage at anyone in earshot. Eventually a paralegal casually plugged him with a cellophane slug. The Bulldog leader flapped weakly beneath a layer of rubbery liquid.

A low rumbling came from the back of the hall, like a wolf growling in a tunnel.

Mona knew every engine signature in the book. "Assault tanks. Here to mop up the mess. We have to get out of this place."

Ditto's head bobbed in mock happiness. "You don't say?"

They crawled through years of debris, looking for a crack in the Myishi forces. But the paralegals were efficient as well as deadly. Obviously they had taken a while to survey the building before attacking. Every square inch was covered by a Myishi soldier. They clipped themselves onto railings on the upper levels, triangulating their fire to secure the building. In minutes, most had made their way to ground level and were herding any conscious gang members into the tanks' holding pens.

Meanwhile the Parasites were sucking life force with horrifying gusto, glowing bright gold with swirling energy. It was almost too much to bear. A very large part of Mona wanted to crawl under a girder and go to sleep; she wanted to sleep and dream of peace and happiness. If I get out of here, she thought, I'm giving up for good. Maybe go to South America and earn a living diving for shells. Sure, she told herself, if there was an ounce of seawater left on the planet that wouldn't bleach her skin.

"I don't see a way out," puffed Ditto.

Mona noticed Miguel being carted away, his features

barely recognizable beneath a layer of cellophane. There was a Parasite clamped onto his chest. "Me neither. Stefan will do something. He wouldn't just leave us here. Or maybe Cosmo can pull another miracle out of the bag."

Ditto grimaced. "I like Cosmo, but he's a kid. The Creeper thing was a fluke, he's not going to save anyone."

Mona rubbed her brow with a knuckle. "You're wrong about him, Ditto. There's something about that kid. He's got guts, brains too. Cosmo will get us out of here. I know he will."

Cosmo followed Stefan down a metal ladder surrounded by a tubular cage. Stefan heard his footsteps clanging on the rungs. "I thought I told you to go back to the Pigmobile," he whispered, wary of the two paralegals forty feet below.

"Mona and Ditto are trapped down there," Cosmo replied simply. "I have to help. No one else is running away, so why should I?"

Stefan lifted his fuzz plate for a moment. Some of the tension seeped from his shoulders. He was glad to have Cosmo with him.

"Okay, good, you're a Supernaturalist. Pigheaded, just like the rest of us. I have to make it to that assault tank on the northeast corner. You can open a hole for me."

"Open a hole?"

"We get down to the next level and borrow a few Myishi rods. I'll make a run for the tank and you knock out anyone pointing a weapon at me."

Cosmo swallowed. This was war. Stefan was talking about war. "What about you?"

Stefan settled his mask over his face. "They'll probably get me, but you can go out the way we came in. A distraction is the only way to save Mona and Ditto."

Cosmo summoned resolve from somewhere. "Okay. I'll do my best. Let's go."

Stefan actually winked behind his red lenses. "Good. And if you happen to hit a few Parasites, I won't be too upset."

Cosmo swallowed, trying to dislodge his heart, which seemed to be jammed in his throat, and followed Stefan down the ladder. Stefan's feet seemed to make no sound as they descended, but to Cosmo's ears his own boots rang out like church bells on the rungs.

Below, the two paralegals were enjoying themselves, laying down a saturation cellophane blanket in one corner of the factory. Their rifles bucked as they sent cartridges arcing toward a group of Sweethearts.

"Fish in a barrel," said one.

"Candy from a baby," agreed the other.

Stefan dropped the final few feet, landing behind the lawyers. Without pause for a movie-hero quip, he bashed their heads together, and the two men slid to the stairwell without so much as a whimper.

"Lawyers," grunted Stefan, unclipping their rifles. "I liked them better when they fought with briefcases." He flipped one over, removing his rappelling rig. Stefan let the straps out to their limits, fastening the rig across his own chest.

"I'm going in as fast as possible. Hopefully by the time they realize I'm not Myishi Corp, it will be too late."

Cosmo dropped onto the walkway. His stomach felt as though it were still halfway up the ladder. Stefan thrust a hefty rod into his arms. "It's set on cellophane slugs. Aim higher than the target—these shells have a bit of drop on them. Two feet above the head should be fine. You have about twenty slugs in this rod, maybe thirty in the other."

Cosmo studied the mystifying array of valves, barrels, and buttons. "I can't work this."

Stefan spun the rod jamming the butt against Cosmo's shoulder. "Think of it like a computer; you don't have to know how it works, or even use all the functions. All you need are sights, barrel, and trigger." He pulled a circular optic from its niche in the barrel, using the suction pad to seal it to Cosmo's right eye socket. "The sight gives you distance to the target, wind condition, and number of slugs left in the clip. Lie on the walkway and wrap anyone who casts a crooked look in my direction."

Cosmo lay down. "But what if . . ."

"No time for what-ifs," interrupted Stefan, securing the rappelling spike to a girder. "Do your best. Remember, Mona and Ditto are depending on us."

No pressure, thought Cosmo glumly.

Stefan vaulted the safety rail, plummeting toward the factory floor a hundred feet below. Cosmo followed his progress with the rod's barrel, the electronic sights feeding magnified images to his right eye. Stefan was descending into a world of madness. Assault tanks rumbled across the floor, bagging any stray fugitives with cannon slugs. Parasites sucked life force from the injured, and gang members struggled in cellophane balloons like souls trapped in hell.

The rappelling rig slowed Stefan's drop, but the cord ran out when he was still twenty feet up. His weight popped the reel and the tall youth plummeted earthward. Fortunately a squad of paralegals broke his fall. Stefan was out of the rig and running before the moaning stopped.

One paralegal made it to his feet, staggering after Stefan. Cosmo moved the rod's barrel and the eyepiece's sight moved correspondingly. He centered the crosshairs on the paralegal's head, then remembered Stefan's advice and raised the barrel a couple of feet.

"Hey, you!" called the lawyer, and Cosmo fired.

A slug sped from the barrel, striking between the man's shoulder blades. A pool of gunk exploded from the tiny pellet, pinning the man to the factory floor.

Stefan continued his run, blasting a sea of Parasites from his path. Blue orbs rose like party balloons. He was headed directly for an assault tank. But why? What could he achieve?

No time for questions and less for answers. Two more paralegals had noticed Stefan, and shrugging off their parachutes, brought their weapons to bear.

Cosmo aimed and fired. Too low. The slugs splashed across the floor. Two feet above the head. Concentrate. Concentrate.

He fired again. Two shots in quick succession. The rod

jumped in his arms, and the paralegals found themselves entangled in a cellophane envelope.

One on the left. Down low. The paralegal got off a slug that hit Stefan between the shoulder blades, knocking him forward three stumbling steps. Cosmo couldn't take his eyes off the Supernaturalist. Experience saved him. Stefan shrugged off his greatcoat. In seconds the leather garment was sealed tighter than a football.

Lucky, thought Cosmo. Lucky. He fired five slugs at the marksman. Three found their target.

Stefan had almost reached his goal. Twenty yards to the tank. There was a cluster of troops on a gantry one floor up. The final hurdle, apart from the tank itself. Stefan fired a few Shockers into the gantry. Most of the paralegals were completely insulated, but two had removed their gloves and were holding the rail. They collapsed, smoking. Cosmo covered the rest with a cluster of slugs from his borrowed rod.

A red logo flashed in Cosmo's sights. An ammunition clip. He was out of slugs. Cosmo hefted the gun aside, dragging the second rod across by the strap. He quickly swapped eyepieces and focused on Stefan.

It was difficult to ignore the surrounding chaos. Parasites swarming, gang members struggling, chargers circling the factory floor in a futile attempt to find an exit. Cellophane coating the floor and walls.

Focus, Cosmo ordered himself. One emergency at a time.

The tank gunner noticed the Supernaturalist, revolving the main turret in his direction. Stefan tried weaving, but the gun barrel was locked on and tracked his movements with fluid ease. Stefan appeared to give up, standing stock-still with his hands raised. Through his rod's eyepiece, Cosmo saw the index finger of Stefan's right hand. It was pointing at the tank's barrel. A message. Shoot the barrel! It was a shot in a million, even with the eyepiece.

Cosmo stood for a better angle, resting the rod on the upper bar. Two feet above the barrel's nozzle. No point in being delicate about it. Cosmo shot everything in the clip at the tank. At least one found its mark, spiraling into the belly of the tank. At that exact moment a Shocker shell attempted to punch through the gunge. It failed to penetrate, dispersing its charge through the tank itself. Anyone who was touching a control pad got enough of a jolt to knock them unconscious for at least a minute.

Stefan was on the move again. He leaped high, grabbing the cannon barrel, moving inward hand over hand. Below the main gun was a secondary barrel, stubby, with an adjustable nozzle. A water cannon for crowd control. Of course! Water!

Stefan swung again and again, slamming his booted feet against the stopcock. Behind that valve lay twenty thousand liters of pressurized water waiting to be unleashed. The stopcock groaned, jerked, and finally popped, allowing the water to burst forth in a powerful jet. It quickly spread across the factory floor. Troops, vehicles, and gang members were scattered before the deluge, but most important, the Parasites abandoned their prizes, scattering quickly to the upper levels.

Any that were caught in the torrent fizzed and sparked before groggily joining the rest of their kind.

Cosmo turned his empty weapon toward Mona's hideout. The sights revealed the girl poking her head out from under the track. Then, taking advantage of the complete confusion caused by Stefan, she tucked Ditto under her arm and made a run for a ventilation shaft on the nearest wall. None of the Myishi troops saw her go. The pair scampered inside, disappearing into the blackness. There was nothing more Cosmo could do for them now.

Meanwhile, Stefan had released his grip on the cannon barrel, dropping to the factory floor. He was unarmed now, and in the open. His antics had drawn the attention of several Myishi paralegals, who surrounded him like jackals, rods trained on the teenager.

Stefan raised his arms, fingers spread, but the paralegals were not about to let him come quietly, not after all the destruction he'd wreaked. They hit him with at least a dozen cellophane slugs, each one spreading across his frame like an oil slick. Cosmo saw the Supernaturalist go down, fingers clearly clawing the gunk that threatened to squeeze the life from him. On the wall, several Parasites sensed his pain, and took hesitant steps in his direction. But there was too much water.

Cosmo pounded clenched fists on the railing. There was nothing he could do except watch.

"Nice shooting, kid," said a voice.

Cosmo turned. A Myishi paralegal was standing farther down the walkway, his rod trained on Cosmo's chest. Red crosshairs flickered on Cosmo's jacket. At this range, there was no need to aim high.

"Do you have any idea how many dinars it's going to cost to repair that assault tank?"

Cosmo shook his head. He didn't speak because he was holding his breath, inflating his chest as far as possible. This would make it easier to breathe if he got wrapped.

The lawyer noticed the tactic. "Hey, kid. Don't worry, I'm not going to wrap you. You're going to come peacefully, right?"

"Right," said Cosmo warily.

"Well, okay, then," said the paralegal, pulling the trigger on his rod. A cellophane slug arced along the walkway, hitting Cosmo's chest. He watched helplessly as the virus spread across his torso. In seconds he was inside a malevolent cocoon that squeezed every bone in his body to groaning point.

Through the silver tint of the cellophane, he saw the lawyer lean over him.

"Oops," said the man, his voice dulled by the wrap. "My finger slipped."

CHAPTER 6
UN-SPEC 4

Myishi Tower

COSMO DIDN'T REMEMBER MUCH about the trip to the Myishi Corporation HQ on Journey Avenue. Cellophane slugs had some sort of mild sedative in the sealant, which was just as well, because if a person got too excited in there, he could break his own ribs with deep breaths.

Cosmo was lifted from the back of an assault truck and dumped bodily into an enormous plasti-glass vat full of viscous yellow dissolving agent. Cosmo had been in a vat before at the institute. The agent would have him puking for hours once it got into his system. Cosmo's nose and mouth were kept above the liquid by a plungerlike device attached to the top of his head. If that was removed before the dissolving agent did its work, he could get plunger burn and end up with a large circular bald patch. But there was no point worrying about that now. There wasn't anything he could do, even if the sedative allowed him to summon some willpower. The best thing to do was to float here and keep his breathing regular. Short, even breaths that put no pressure on his ribcage.

In a way, it was a relief to have nothing to do. No crazy missions, no death-defying midnight antics, and no supernatural creatures staring at him through round eyes.

Then a Parasite did attach itself to the outside of the vat, staring through the plasti-glass. But Cosmo was safe in here. The creatures could not brave the liquid.

Any other time, it would have been unnerving to have the creature so close. The sparkling blue pads of its four-fingered hands stuck to the plasti-glass. They stared at each other, boy and creature, through a yellow haze. In Cosmo's mind, the Parasite's eyes spoke volumes. *There is no escape from me*, they said.

After several minutes of implacable staring, the Parasite detached itself from the plasti-glass. Doubtless there was life to be siphoned elsewhere.

Cosmo sank into a near trancelike state. The events of the past few days bounced around his head like blobs of oil in a lava lamp. Who was he now? Cosmo Hill fugitive no-sponsor, or Cosmo Hill Supernaturalist? Who was Cosmo Hill anyhow? A product of Clarissa Frayne, with no personality to speak of. Fourteen years old and he had never kissed a girl.

Mona Vasquez. What was it about her that made his stomach lurch? Cosmo had once been injected with a mild strain of malaria as part of a vaccine test. The malaria had had pretty much the same effect on him as Mona had now. It was a pity really. His feelings were pointless. What girl in her right mind would notice Cosmo even if he were standing on a birthday cake wearing a neon heart?

Nevertheless, Mona's image grew in Cosmo's mind until it displaced all others. Her smile, the black hair curling over her collar. Those dark eyes like two chocolate buttons. She seemed to float in the liquid before him, reaching out a hand to stroke his cheek.

The sedative made Cosmo speak. Might as well, he reasoned. It's just an hallucination. "Mona," he said, and strangely there was no cellophane covering his face anymore. "I really like you."

"Is that so?" said the large bearded vat man, who was winching Cosmo's plunger. "I really like you too, sweetie."

The bearded man hosed Cosmo down, snickering the entire time, then tossed him shivering into a padded holding cell. As he left, he threw a kiss over his shoulder.

"Adieu, my prince, until we meet again."

Cosmo was too busy throwing up into the aluminium trough to respond. Not that he would say anything even if he could. In Clarissa Frayne you learned to keep your mouth shut. Every one of the no-sponsors had known that, except Ziplock.

When he had recovered sufficiently, Cosmo tore some paper from a wall-mounted roll and wiped himself down. Then he dragged a steel cot across the room until it was directly beneath the warm air vent, and lay down.

His orphanage habits were returning, as if he'd never been away. After all, what was a few days in fourteen years? Not even one percent. Nowhere close. And yet, he felt he had lived more in the past few days than in all those years combined.

When they threw you in the hole in Clarissa Frayne, there were certain survival methods the no-sponsors all knew. First of all, sleep as much as possible. That took your mind off food and your situation in general. A seasoned orphan could sleep for as much as sixteen hours a day.

Secondly, don't think about freedom. Wishing the days away just made them seem longer. And finally, try not to want anything, especially parents. That just broke your heart.

Cosmo lay on his back, staring at the ceiling. Sleep would not come. There was too much happening inside his head. Supernaturalists, Parasites, Sweethearts, Bulldogs, a Bartoli baby, and, of course, Mona.

Thank goodness he had only declared his affection for a vat man. Mona would probably laugh in his face. Not that he would ever see her again. Cosmo had no doubt that once they DNA typed him and found out who he was, he'd be on the first tube back to Clarissa Frayne and Marshal Redwood.

Sometime later, the vat man returned, still grinning hugely. A man happy in his work.

"Okay, sweetheart," he said, scratching a patch of stubble between two drooping chins. "On your feet. Someone wants to talk to you."

"Who?" asked Cosmo swinging his damp boots to the floor.

The vat man lifted Cosmo's chin with a baton. "What did you say? Did you just ask me a question?"

"No," said Cosmo hurriedly. "I mean; no, sir."

"Better," said the jailer, turning his back. "Follow me, and stay between the yellow lines, or one of the guards will wrap you again."

The vat man led him down a long corridor to a bank of elevators. There were two solid yellow lines on the floor, with scuffed linoleum between.

Cosmo stopped before the first elevator.

"No, no sweetheart," said the vat man. "You're going to the *observatory*." He said it reverently. Like it was a big deal. Cosmo followed him to the last elevator in the bank, a gold block with no call button, just a video intercom.

The vat attendant stood before the camera, smoothing his hair with one licked hand. "I got the kid here. The one who junked the tank."

There was no reply, but the door slid open noiselessly. "In you go, sweetheart," said the man pushing Cosmo inside.

"Miss you already," said Cosmo as the door closed. Why not? It was unlikely he would see the man again.

The elevator rose so quickly that it appeared to stay absolutely still. Cosmo didn't realize he was moving until one wall slid back to reveal a crystal window. The elevator was on the outside of the building and was shooting upward like a projectile from a cannon. Outside, the city flashed past in speed-blurred lines of light. Soon the golden box had outstripped the other buildings and was sailing upward toward the heavens. Cosmo felt that if the elevator stopped now, he would continue upward, losing himself in the universe.

There was no time to consider escape, and nowhere to escape to. You might as well talk about escaping from a parachute. Before the notion had even occurred to him, the elevator began decelerating, eventually coming to a halt somewhere near the edge of the atmosphere. It seemed to Cosmo that if he reached up a hand, he would be able to touch the Myishi Satellite.

The door slid open and a very large hand reached in, grabbing Cosmo by the throat. He was dragged into the most opulent room he had ever seen in his life. Illegal stuffed animal heads were mounted on the walls. Elephants, bears, a gorilla, and hundreds of birds. Even an extinct dolphin, flapping robotically in a vat of blue preservative. Low couches lined the walls, draped with luxurious throws. Expensive-looking art vied for attention, including a mime hologram in a suspended cube.

"Welcome to the Myishi Corporation," said a female voice.

Cosmo looked across the huge room to a sunken lounge area. A slender woman was reclining on a fur-lined sofa, running a finger around the rim of a crystal flute. There were at least half a dozen bodyguards within six feet of her. Cosmo could feel their eyes through the black lenses of their sunglasses. Sunglasses at night. Weirder and weirder.

One of the bodyguards adjusted a tiny dial on the arm of his glasses. "He's clean," he said in tones that could have sanded wood. "No weaponry."

Not just ordinary sunglasses then.

The woman stood. She was tall and slim. No surgery, though. This woman looked as if she could bench-press a couple of the security men. Her features were tanned and strong. The tan must have been painted on, because no one in their right minds stayed out in the sun anymore. Her hair was cropped short, blond with gray streaks at the temples. She was dressed in a loose linen suit, almost like pajamas, and wore flat leather thong sandals with a gold ring on the second toe of one foot. "So you're the one who took out an assault tank," she said. Her voice was musical, almost mesmeric. "Do you know how much one of those tanks costs?"

Cosmo shook his head.

"An absolute fortune. Never mind, we're insured. The point is that there is a seal on the tank's barrel to stop this kind of thing happening. It only opens for one hundredth of a second before each shell is fired. You managed to put a cellophane slug down there in that time. Impressive, if you meant it. We had you DNA typed, Master Cosmo Hill, nosponsor. You're supposed to be dead."

Cosmo decided that this would be a good time to change the subject. "Are you Miss Myishi?"

The woman laughed, soft peals that made Cosmo want to laugh with her. "Miss Myishi? No. There hasn't been a Myishi at the corporation's helm for nearly a hundred years. We just keep the name for public-recognition purposes. The Myishi *zaibatsu* wasn't suited to the modern business world. Too many Eastern morals. My name is . . ."

At that precise moment, the elevator door opened and Stefan stepped out. His brow was creased in its customary frown, until he noticed the blond lady. "Professor Faustino?" he said uncertainly. "What are you doing here? Did they get you too?"

Stefan shrugged off a pair of security men at his elbows and strode across the room. With a flick of a single finger, Faustino directed the security men back into the elevator. Stefan caught the gesture. He stopped short. "You work here, Professor Faustino? For Myishi?"

"It's President Faustino now, Stefan."

Confusion was written all over Stefan's face. Was this woman an old friend or a new foe? "President? I never thought you would go to work for the corporations, especially Myishi."

"Fight from the inside, Stefan. Attack from the rear."

"Well, you certainly are on the inside."

Faustino reached up, laying a hand on each of Stefan's shoulders. "Well, well, well. Little Stefan Bashkir. You have grown up."

Cosmo blinked. Little Stefan Bashkir? Who was this woman?

Stefan looked embarassed by the attention. Was he actually blushing? "It's been more than two years since I got out of the widows and orphans home. The last time I saw you,

you were still with the city police. Now you've gone over to the other side."

Ellen Faustino plucked a wafer-thin remote control from the coffee table. "Don't believe everything you hear about Myishi, Stefan. We do more good than harm." She brushed an elegant finger against a button, and the suite's entire roof slid back, revealing the stars above, and, of course, the Satellite. "The Satellite that saved . . ."

"That saved the world," completed Stefan. "We've all seen it on TV. Every twenty seconds it seems."

Faustino smiled. "Not like this, you haven't. Come over here, Stefan. And you too, Master Hill. Sit down, the view is splendid."

Cosmo crossed the plush carpet, weaving between growling bodyguards. The men probably hadn't messed anybody up yet today and were just looking for an excuse. He took a seat between Stefan and Faustino on a low sofa. Her perfume wafted over him like something he'd smelled once in a dream, but couldn't quite remember. "Comfortable?" she asked.

Cosmo nodded hesitantly. He'd never been asked that question before. The marshals in Clarissa Frayne weren't inclined to get blubbery if an orphan was uncomfortable. Often the marshals were the cause of the discomfort.

Faustino pressed a second button on the remote, and the sofa tilted backward, speakers slid out from behind the headrests. They were now looking directly through the transparent ceiling at the Satellite above. The ceiling flexed slightly, and suddenly everything was magnified by a thousand. It seemed as though the Satellite was about to crash onto the building.

Cosmo jumped in his seat.

"Relax, boy," said Ellen, placing two slim fingers on his wrist. "The observatory often has that effect on first timers."

The detail was amazing. Cosmo could pick out individual solar panels on the satellite's wings. He could see bursts of gas from its stabilizers and dish jockeys floating across the concave surface of the great dish. It was immense, mind-boggling.

Stefan was not so easily impressed. "What are we doing here, Professor Faustino? What is this all about?"

"Be patient, Stefan. That was always your failing. Sometimes a story is too big to tell in one breath."

Faustino pressed a combination of buttons, and several screens appeared on the giant lense. The screens were running old news footage from the beginning of the millennium. Scenes from war-torn Europe and the Middle East, African famine, and South American earthquakes. Wrap-around sound erupted from the speakers.

Faustino supplied the commentary. "Not so long ago, the world was tearing itself apart. There simply wasn't enough room on the planet for us all. The Myishi Satellite has gone some way to solving that problem."

Stefan folded his arms, crossing his boots loudly. International body language for *pull the other leg*.

"I know your opinion on Myishi, Stefan," said Faustino.

"But just give me a chance, and I think you'll find we're fighting the same enemy."

"I doubt that," muttered Stefan.

"The problem was that countries were not being run as businesses. Decisions were being made on the basis of religion or history, notoriously unsound motives for doing anything. States fell apart because of bigotry and centuries-old squabbles. The Myishi Corporation has taken on all these problems, and I think we're winning."

"How can you say that?" interjected Stefan. "Parts of the city are in chaos. People are starving."

"I'm not saying things are perfect, Stefan. There have been wrinkles. But this is a new system. Satellite cities could solve the world's population problem. Storage in outer space is the future, Stefan, and that's the truth. Every household has an average of ten computer-driven appliances. Do you realize how much memory space that occupies? In a city this size, that's ten blocks, just for household appliances. Then you have administration, entertainment, travel, communications. We store all that in a satellite in geostationary orbit above the city, constantly updating, constantly self-repairing."

Cosmo was first to twig to where this was leading. "Self-repairing until now," he said. "Lately the Satellite has been messing up, big-time."

Faustino switched off the news footage. "That's right. It's getting worse and worse. As you can see, we have squads of dish jockeys working around the clock. Some things we've been able to cover up, but word is getting out. Myishi stock is taking a real hammering."

"Sick and homeless people don't care much about stock," said Stefan.

A flash of annoyance curled Ellen Faustino's lip for an instant, then disappeared. "These things are being addressed, Stefan. We have long-term projects in development. Shelters, employment schemes, rehabilitation clinics. I'm doing my best to raise the money from Myishi International in Berlin. In fact, Central had signed on for a forty-billion-dinar welfare grant for the city until this latest problem came along."

"What problem?" asked Stefan, trying to fake only a casual interest.

"Oh, I think we both know what the problem is." Ellen Faustino rose from the couch, straightening her linen suit.

Stefan was out of the sofa, staring down into the woman's eyes. "I said, What problem, Professor?"

Faustino stared right back at him, not in the least cowed. "Don't talk to me that way, Stefan. Your mother would not approve. Answers, that's why I brought you here. That's why you and your little vigilante helper aren't in the interrogation block right now."

Ellen Faustino ran some more footage on the ceiling screens. "Look up, Stefan. They're playing your song."

Stefan settled back into the couch. Overhead a familiar scene played out digitally. It showed the Supernaturalists blasting Parasites, on top of the Stromberg Building, in glorious true-tone color.

Stefan winked at Cosmo. "That doesn't prove anything. Those people are wearing fuzz plates, so you can't see who they are. And even if you could, they're not hurting anybody."

Faustino looked around dramatically. "This is not a courtroom, Stefan. I don't see any lawyers in here. If I wanted you on charges, I'd have had you two years ago."

Stefan's surprise broke through his mask of indifference. "You what?"

"That's right, young man. I've had my electronic eye on you for a long time now. A special scope on the satellite, dedicated to your nightly activities. Well, you insist on running around on rooftops. And believe me, I have plenty of footage of your smiling face without a fuzz plate. Not to mention Miss Mona Vasquez and a certain Lucien Bonn, aka Ditto. I have enough evidence on your little group to have you buried deeper than a core-ore tunnel."

Stefan clenched his fists so tightly the knuckles popped. "What's going on?"

"Don't you want to know why I've never had you pulled in?"

"Until tonight," corrected Stefan.

Faustino waved her hands. "Tonight was a mistake. You got mixed up in another department's operation. If you knew the favors I had to call in to get you two released into my custody . . . That said, I have been trying to find you for the past few weeks."

"I thought you were the president. Surely you could track us with your all-seeing Satellite."

"I'm just the president of Developmental Projects. Mayor Ray Shine is the big cheese. He doesn't even know we're working together."

Again Stefan was stunned. "Now we're working together?"

"Of course, you didn't know it. You've been taking care of the city's infestation problem, or so we thought."

Aha, thought Cosmo. Here comes the reason why we're not in pain right now.

"Infestation?" said Stefan innocently.

Faustino smiled. "Oh, come on now, Stefan. Don't play dumb with me. I see them too, you know."

"See who? See what?"

Ellie Faustino crossed to her desk and activated a 3D projector set on the floor. She transferred the Stromberg footage from the ceiling screen, and a 3D high-resolution rendering of the Supernaturalists sprang into life in the center of the room. Shot from above, they resembled characters in a video game. A single Parasite crawled along an adjacent wall. Faustino froze the footage, manipulating the video until only the Parasite remained.

"I see them, Stefan. Un-spec four. The life-eaters."

For the third time in as many minutes Stefan was stunned. "You see them? Unspeck what?"

Faustino enlarged the Parasite's image. "Un-spec four. Uncategorized species four. The other three are deep-sea creatures that we're pretty sure exist, but haven't been able to capture yet. A species is not considered to be categorized until it can be captured and examined. Of course, not everyone can see this. To a normal person, we're looking at a blank projection, but to a select few, your little group included, the truth is all too clear."

Faustino turned to the security guards. "Out. All of you."

The team leader took a step forward. "President Faustino, that's against regulations."

Ellen said nothing, just stared into the man's lenses. The two-hundred-plus-pound gorilla backed down in less than five seconds.

"Very well, Madam President. We'll be in the elevator."

Ellen perched on the desktop, remaining silent until the elevator door slid shut. "When I joined the force, before I began teaching, Booshka was my beat. Back then there was still a semblance of order down there. One night I took a knife in the ribs, breaking up a domestic. I nearly died; out of body, into the light, the whole thing. The paramedics brought me back. But I saw something that night. Something I've been able to see ever since . . ."

Cosmo sat bolt upright. "You're a Spotter. Like me."

Stefan sighed through his nose. "Why don't you just sign a confession, Cosmo?"

"I kept it to myself," continued Ellie. "These sightings, convinced that I was crazy. But then I heard about someone else who raved about blue creatures. You, Stefan, after the accident. You were quite a joke in the police academy for a while. Section eight, everybody said. As your personal tutor, and a family friend, I tried to help you through the trauma. I hoped you would open up to me."

Stefan's eyes widened. "All those therapy sessions. All those questions about post-traumatic stress and hallucinations."

Ellie sighed. "But you wouldn't open up to me. Apparently you had realized that nobody wanted to listen."

"All that time in the academy together, and we both had the same problem. Why didn't you just tell me?"

"I should have, I know, but I was afraid that it would get out, and my career would be finished." She lowered her eyes. "I didn't trust you, I'm sorry. After you left the academy to set up your vigilante squad, I finished my second doctorate and came to work for Myishi, in research and development. One of my jobs was a low-budget project to trace tiny power surges that were striking on the Satellite's dish from the planet's surface. Nothing serious. Small charges, not enough to cause interference. I figured out in about ten minutes where the charges were coming from. Un-spec four were venting them. Naturally I never revealed my findings. I had a career to think of. Eventually the charges were attributed to industrial discharge from Satellite City. I went on with my work, trying to make things better in my own small way. But then, a few years ago the charges began to increase. Slowly at first, but then at an alarming rate, so much so that they began to damage the dish plates. Now the discharge is so great that it's a constant stream. We're losing links with the surface. People are dying. It's a red-light crisis for the corporation."

"People have been dying in Satellite City for years, and Myishi has done nothing about it. Now, when there's money involved, suddenly they're interested."

For the first time Ellen Faustino's voice took on a hard quality. "Don't be so naive, Stefan. Money gets things done. As soon as the Satellite lost its first linkup, all developmental projects were frozen. I had two hospitals and a rehab center in the pipeline. Gone now, unless we can sort out our Unspec problem." Faustino's temper disappeared just as quickly as it had appeared. "You've been handling the creatures for years. Destroying them very efficiently. There was no need to start up a team, or so I thought."

Stefan sat up. "What does that mean?"

"The lightning rods. Very clever, the residual charge itself gets the creature."

"Parasites," interrupted Cosmo. "We call them Parasites."

Ellen nodded. "Parasites. That's good. You were wiping out the Parasites with a single-mindedness that Myishi employees could never match, so I kept an eye on you and left you alone to do your work—*our* work. But after the recent increase in charges, I put together a small team to investigate. There are the two factors that bring on the second sight, in my opinion: near-death experiences, coupled with a lifelong exposure to Satellite City's chemical smog. The computer ran a search in the Myishi personnel files, and I interviewed everyone on the list. I found three other Spotters, all under twenty-five. I am the only one over forty. We began an in-depth study of the Parasites, especially what happens to them after you shoot them. And we found out something you might like to know. . . ."

Faustino crossed to the elevator door, checking to see that

it was closed. She then ran a bug sweeper over the walls and phones, looking for surveillance devices. When she was certain that nobody had an eye or ear on the observatory, she took a crystal video chip from her wallet, pressing it into the 3D projector. "Next-generation technology," she explained. "We can get two hundred hours of video on one crystal chip. Myishi will kick Phonetix's butt next quarter."

A life-size 3D representation of a Parasite materialized in the room. Stefan automatically reached inside his jacket for a lightning rod.

Faustino laughed. "Relax, Stefan. Amazing quality, I know. These are the first generation of lenses that can even photograph Un-spec four. What I'm about to show you is the result of months of surveillance. I'd say it was classified, but who are you going to tell?"

The Parasite began its curious lope along a projected wall. "Un-spec four seems to made of pure energy, which it obviously expends through activity. We observe the Parasite's luminosity fades the farther it travels." Faustino switched on a laser pointer. "This glowing center here is Un-spec four's equivalent of a heart. As it runs out of energy the heart pulsates more slowly. Eventually the heart will feed on the creature's body, absorbing it in order to keep beating."

The 3D Parasite faded to a pastel blue. Its skin lost coherence, and shortly after that, the heart itself did not have enough energy to keep itself intact. It disappeared in a blue flash.

"That flash," said Cosmo. "Is that what Myishi is worried about?"

Faustino shook her head. "I wish. Those flashes barely register on our meters. No, Un-spec four only lets real sparks fly after absorbing energy."

The picture changed. This time a Parasite was crouched on the chest of a fallen fireman. A stream of white-gold energy flowed into the creature's palms. The Parasite glowed like a bag of stars, then drifted up a nearby wall. The camera followed the creature to a windowsill, where it rested briefly. The absorbed energy ran through its organs with increasing speed and agitation. After several seconds of unrest, an energy discharge burst through the pores of the creature's skin, spiraling skyward.

"Now, that, I've never seen before," said Stefan.

"We believe that the Parasite's organs scrub the energy, then release completely clean power."

Cosmo's adolescent mind got it first. "So, you're saying all this trouble is being caused by Parasite poop?"

Ellen smiled. "Exactly. People have tried to say it better, and couldn't. It's a bit like trees taking in carbon dioxide and releasing oxygen. Nature's filters. This next clip is the part you'll be really interested in. We only got it last month. Since then I've been trying to track you down."

A new clip appeared in the projector ray. This one showed an obsessed-looking Stefan Bashkir in the middle of a disaster zone. Emergency vehicles were converging from all sides, and Parasites were feeding on the victims of a riot. "I remember that," said the Russian. "Food riot in Booshka, near the blockade. Nasty."

In the projection, Stefan was letting fly with his lightning rod, blasting Parasites from their perches. The camera caught one Parasite at the moment it exploded into a dozen shimmering spheres. The satellite camera tracked a single sphere for several minutes, following its rise into the atmosphere.

"Have you any idea how much it cost to get this footage? I had to buy camera time for an entire day."

Stefan didn't even hear the complaint, too focused on the sphere. It stopped rising after more than a mile, drifting slightly in the prevailing wind. The camera zoomed in until the sphere was the size of a basketball, hovering between land and space.

"In order to photograph the Parasites, our new lenses are coated with a chemical compound," said Faustino. "It took my team months to find the right solution. We told head office it was antiglare spray."

Stefan did not respond. His eyes were glued to the projection.

The sphere's surface began to ripple slightly, as inside the energy coiled itself into a rope, chasing its tail into intricate knots.

"What's happening?" asked Cosmo.

Stefan reached out his hands, sinking them into the projection. "No," he breathed.

The ropes solidified, becoming more complex. A silver star shone at their center. "It can't be. Not after all this." Two round eyes appeared. Then blue fingers, pushing against the sphere's surface, forcing the skin. "What have I done?"

The sphere's surface split, and a brand new Parasite

appeared, fully formed, and ready to siphon life from a human in pain. It spread its arms and drifted earthward on the wind.

Stefan's face was a mask of anguish. "All this time! All this time, I've been helping them. Not destroying them. Helping them to reproduce."

Faustino switched off the projector. "It's not your fault, Stefan. How could you know? All you saw were creatures who had destroyed your life. You fought them the same way I would have." She helped Stefan onto the sofa. "What we need to decide now is how to continue the fight."

"There is no fight," said Stefan glumly. "They win. It's over. How can I go on? It would take me ten lifetimes just to undo the damage I've done."

"Not necessarily," said Faustino. "To defeat Un-spec four you have to understand them. Let me fill you in on what my team has learned after hundreds of hours of satellite surveillance. Un-spec four are a parasitic species that feed on energy, preferably human life force, hiding their activities by feeding on the sick and injured. They absorb energy by osmosis, scrubbing it through bodily filters, then venting the clean energy. These ventings have grown to dangerous proportions because of the increased number of Parasites. Generally the Parasites split into two entities after several years, when they have accumulated enough energy, but due to your efforts, they are reproducing instantaneously and in huge numbers. Thus contributing to the energy-burst problem. It's a vicious circle."

Stefan's scar stretched his mouth into the cruel facsimile of a grin. "You forgot to mention that there's no way to kill them."

Faustino couldn't resist a little smile of her own. "Oh, I didn't say that."

She reactivated the projector, fast-forwarding to a different file. Another Parasite appeared in the light beams. This one was colorless and almost completely transparent, its starburst heart reduced to a flickering ember. "This one is dying."

Stefan's enthusiasm returned in a rush. "How? What caused it?"

"We did," replied Faustino. "Unintentionally. A starved Parasite will sometimes resort to electrical energy, not their meal of choice, you understand, but sometimes there isn't enough misery to go round. This one latched onto a uranium rod from a nuclear generator in one of our disassembling plants. There was too much contaminated energy. The creature couldn't recycle it and it clogged up its system. This is security-camera footage; we only got it by accident. Nobody objected—after all, to them there's nothing on the screen except old equipment. Luckily for us a new lens had been installed during a routine upgrade."

"So all we have to do . . ." said Stefan, thinking aloud.

"Is pump them full of contaminated energy," completed Cosmo.

"Exactly," said Faustino, clapping her hands. She took an aluminium briefcase from under the sofa, laying it carefully on the coffee table. "This is our proposed solution." She flipped open the case, revealing a metallic cuboid cradled in a gel coolant pack. The cuboid was connected to a digital timer. "Not very pretty, I know. But we're not trying to sell it on the mass market."

Stefan studied the device. "Some kind of pulse device. The police riot squad use these to knock out power in the buildings they're raiding. They take out mains and local generators."

Faustino nodded. "Energy pulse. Effective up to five hundred meters. The battery has been radioactively charged. Nothing serious. Safe for humans, but lethal for Un-spec four. If you could set one of these off where they live, you could do some major damage to our invisible friends."

"Have you tracked them to their lair?" asked Stefan.

"No such luck," sighed Faustino. "They disperse faster than we can track them. That's what we're working on."

"Then we're back where we started."

Ellen closed the case, sliding it across the table to Stefan. "No, Stefan, we're a long way from where we started. From this night on, you and your band have a new mission. Find out where they live, and when you do, give them a little present from me."

Stefan took the case. "I'll hunt them down, Professor. From now on that's all we do. But it won't be easy, and it will take time."

Ellen Faustino came around the table, embracing Stefan tightly. "I've missed you, my young student. And I miss your mother, every day. She brought light to this city."

Stefan returned the hug. "I miss her too," he said.

CHAPTER 7
HALO

Abracadabra Street

DITTO WAS TORN BY GUILT. He was the closest thing to an adult the group had, and yet he had fled the old factory, leaving Stefan and Cosmo to make their own way out. Stefan would never have abandoned him if the situation were reversed, he was sure of it. Maybe there wasn't much someone of his size could have done against Myishi tanks, but that didn't make him feel any better. If anything, it made him feel worse, because Stefan had gone up against a tank to save him and Mona.

But there was another reason for Ditto's guilt. There were things Stefan needed to know about him. Certain talents that he had. He should have confessed to his friend years ago, but the time had never been right. And he had become so accustomed to keeping his gifts a secret. In comic books, people with gifts became superheroes; in real life they became outcasts. And Ditto did not want to be an outcast from the only group of people who had ever cared for him.

Lucien Bonn had been christened Ditto by a sharp-tongued girl in the Bartoli institute. It wasn't a very smart nickname. Obvious, really. Ditto had a habit of repeating whatever people said to him. This gave him a moment to think of a reply. Not that he was slow—quite the opposite in fact. He just wanted to be sure that whatever he said didn't give anything away about his special talents. It was bad enough being a Bartoli baby without everyone thinking you were crazy too. *Hey, did you hear? The midget thinks he can see ghosts.* No, thank you.

Ditto's suspicions that he was abnormal were confirmed on his ninth birthday. Until then he had hoped that he was merely short for his age. But by nine years of age it was getting pretty obvious that the arrested physical development mutation so common among Bartoli babies was beginning to affect him.

Doctor Bartoli himself had called Ditto into his office for his monthly measurements. Ditto stood inside the great man's door, shivering in his paper jumpsuit. Doctor Bartoli liked to keep the air conditioning at forty-five degrees Farenheit. He said that cold was good for the intellect. "Well, now, Lucien," said Bartoli, opening Ditto's file on his computer. "Let's see how you are progressing. Stand on the spot."

Ditto positioned himself on a red circle in the center of the floor. Bartoli circled him with a measuring tape and cranium calipers. He hemmed and hawed as he measured each of Ditto's limbs, his trunk, and his head size.

"Another failure," he said eventually, slumping into his office chair. "Just like the rest. Where did I go wrong?"

Ditto didn't answer. The doctor was talking to himself as he always did. Eventually Bartoli addressed the small shivering boy. "Well, Lucien. I am sorry to tell you that you will in all likelihood grow no taller. Your head is one quarter the length of your person; by nine years, it should be only one fifth. The Bartoli bug has bitten."

Ditto felt his heart sink. He had been so hoping for a normal life outside the Institute.

"But all is not lost. Perhaps you have other gifts. Something to elevate you above us normal humans. Perhaps Dr. Bartoli opened a door somewhere in your mind? Eh, Lucien? Do you have other gifts?"

Bartoli was pretending that the question was a casual one, but his entire body was tense, waiting for the boy's answer.

Ditto was only nine years old, but he was no fool. Years of smart drugs and intelligence exercises had left him quite perceptive. He knew the importance of this question. He also knew what happened to Bartoli babies who admitted to having gifts. They were moved to another wing of the Institute and observed twenty-four hours a day. They were medicated, injected, and interrogated for as long as Bartoli could hold on to them.

The doctor leaned forward in his chair. "Do you see things, Lucien? Some of the other children claim to see strange beings. Do you see beings, Lucien?"

Ditto could have told the truth then. *Yes, Doctor, I see them all around us. The blue creatures. They can see me too. Sometimes they visit. And that's not all. I can help people. Make them feel better just by touching them.*

He could have said all of that, but he didn't, for to reveal his talents would have meant spending the rest of his life as an experiment.

So Ditto looked Bartoli straight in the eye and said: "Do I see things? Well, I saw a werewolf once, outside my window. I thought it was a dream."

The doctor sighed. "Very well, Lucien. There is nothing special about you. As a special favor I will personally see to it that you are sent to a state school and not to Clarissa Frayne. You can go."

And that was it. No apology. No compensation for being born a mutant. Within six months, Ditto had been moved out of the Institute into a state school, where he stayed until the age of sixteen. In all that time he never told anybody about any of his gifts. His secrets stayed secret until Stefan came into his life. And even Stefan did not know everything. But soon he would, and there would be hell to pay when his friend found out.

Ellen Faustino sent Cosmo and Stefan home in a Myishi Prestige Stretch. The luxury ten-wheeler car was half the length of a city block, and boasted a TV window, fully stocked fridge, and sofa bed. Stefan was not impressed. He hunched forward in his seat, kneading his forehead as if that could make the ideas come faster.

"Miss Faustino was right, you know," said Cosmo tentatively. "It isn't your fault, Stefan. You were just doing your best. How could you possibly know that the electricity was making them reproduce?"

Stefan did not respond. After saying good-bye to his old tutor, guilt and helplessness had dealt him a double blow. It was a combination that would be hard to shake.

So Cosmo did what any teenager would do. He raided the fridge, stuffing his pockets with as many snacks as he could cram in. Whatever wouldn't fit, he ate. Fourteen years in Clarissa Frayne had taught him never to leave food behind. It was quite possible that the combination of the acid vat and the junk food would have him throwing up for the next day or two, but if he left any food behind, he would regret it for years.

Stefan broke his silence six streets west of Abracadabra Street. "Anywhere here is fine."

"President Faustino said I was to drop you at your door," objected the driver.

"Maybe she did," said Stefan. "But I'm not ready to give up the location of my headquarters just yet."

The driver laughed. "1405 Abracadabra Street. I've already sent the coordinates to the Satellite."

Stefan sank even deeper into his foul mood. The Supernaturalists were no longer a secret organization. There were adults involved now. The corporations were involving them in their schemes. The next thing you knew, they'd all have dental plans and pensions.

Mona and Ditto were waiting anxiously when Cosmo and Stefan emerged from the elevator. Mona ran to greet them, but Ditto hung back, uncharacteristically quiet, without so much as a sarcastic crack to welcome the returning pair. His secret was fermenting inside him, bursting to be released.

"Where have you been?" demanded Mona, wrapping one arm around Stefan's shoulders and the other around Cosmo. "We thought you two were in jail for sure."

Stefan shrugged her off. "Set up the Parabola on the roof. I want it running twenty-four-seven."

Mona stepped back from the pair as though she had been slapped. "We were worried, Stefan, about the two of you. Don't we deserve an explanation? Aren't we supposed to be a team?"

Stefan almost talked then. He nearly shared his burden, but the guilt and the helplessness were still too strong. "Not now, Mona. Okay? Just set up the dish."

"The Parabola?" said Mona. "That never worked before. I don't even know if it's charged."

"Just set it up, Mona," said Stefan, his voice barely more than a whisper. "Please."

The youth stumbled toward his cubicle without another word. With each step he seemed shorter. The group watched him go in silence.

"What happened to him?" asked Mona, when the echo of Stefan's footfalls had faded. "I've seen him upset before, but not like this. It's like his life is over."

"Not over," Cosmo replied. "He just has to start it again." He explained what had happened at Myishi Tower. How blasting Parasites just speeded up their reproduction process. Three years of helping your enemies to populate the planet. The words seemed to hang in the warehouse air. Damning their actions. How many people had had their life force drained because of the Supernaturalists?

"I don't believe it," gasped Ditto. "Those blue bubbles are baby Parasites?"

"Not babies. They come out all grown up and thirsty for life force."

Ditto climbed up on a stool beside the table. "It's the energy-scrubbing part that interests me. These creatures are part of nature. Like us. Maybe we should think about what helping them to reproduce means to the ecology."

Mona rounded on him. "The ecology! These monsters are sucking the life out of people! You wouldn't be worried about nature if you'd ever had one sitting on your chest."

"Hey, come on, Mona; don't blow a valve. I'm only saying that we have to find another way. Speeding up the Parasites' reproduction process is not good for anyone."

Mona took several breaths, then punched Ditto gently on the shoulder. "You're right, of course. It's a shock, that's all. I thought we were doing the right thing. Actually saving people. Now I don't know, and Stefan, well, he won't even talk to us. . . ."

Ditto walked across the table, wrapping his short arms around Mona's shoulders. "He's supposed to be our leader.

But sometimes we forget how young he is. Stefan will be okay in the morning, you'll see. Now, you set up the dish. Take your time. We won't be going hunting tonight."

Mona sniffed. "Okay." She turned to Cosmo. "Sorry about the dramatics. I am glad to see you back safely. Let's go up on the roof, and I'll show you how to operate the Parabola."

Cosmo nodded, smiling, but Ditto slapped a thermo-strip on his head. "Absolutely not. Cosmo needs to get some sleep. Oh, I'm sure you two youngsters would love to spend the day discussing circuit breakers beneath the smog. But this young man is not properly healed from his adventure on the rooftop. If he doesn't rest, we could be looking at a fever or even rejection. He must be dead on his feet."

As soon as Ditto said it, Cosmo began to feel tired. Suddenly his forehead ached and his knee sent twinges of pain from ankle to hip. "Actually, I am a bit tired. Maybe I could come up later. . . ."

"That's okay," said Mona. "You sleep as long as you need to. Ditto is right, you've been through a lot. I can show you the Parabola tomorrow."

Cosmo nodded. He would sleep now, even though he would love to spend the day discussing circuit breakers with Mona Vasquez.

After his time in the vat, Cosmo barely had the energy to crawl to his bed. Already the narrow cot seemed like home to him. Something of his own. Although his body was in Abracadabra Street, his dreams roamed abroad, stopping off in Clarissa Frayne and Myishi Tower. The vat man and Redwood morphed into one person, shaking a fist at him. A fist dripping with cellophane sludge. *Come back to us*, the mixed-up man said. *Come back, Cosmo, we've got a dark room waiting for you. A dark room full of sharp things.*

Cosmo woke with a start, tumbling from his bed onto the pig-iron floor. The military green blanket was tangled around his legs, and for a moment, Redwood's insane face hovered before his eyes.

Cosmo sat, letting consciousness get a grip on his vision. Gradually, reality overpowered his dreams. The sleep, however troubled, had done him good. The swelling had gone down on his forehead, and his knee barely hurt at all.

Once my hair grows back, I'll almost pass for human, he thought with a wry smile.

Cosmo stood, pulling on the army-style fatigues provided by Bashkir. You could never have too many pockets, apparently. The warehouse was quiet, apart from a croaking snore from Ditto's cubicle. To look at him, you wouldn't think the Bartoli baby's lungs were big enough to produce a noise like that. Stefan's curtain was still pulled across, but Mona's bed was empty and made. Either she was up already, or she hadn't been to bed.

There was something else unusual. An absence of a noise that was as much a part of the Abracadabra Street warehouse as the curtains. The computer off-line. Of course it was. There would be no more midnight jaunts. No more lightning rods and no more blue spheres. People would just have to lose their life force, as they had probably been doing for thousands of years.

Cosmo poured a cup of sim-coffee from the pot. More for the warmth of the mug in his hands than the actual taste. There was another cup on the table; its chrome handle fashioned to resemble an exhaust pipe. *Mech-lube* said the letters on its face. Cosmo filled the mug and headed for the elevator.

Walking onto the roof was like jumping out of a plane. A mere building did not seem sturdy enough to stop a person plummeting earthward. Just breathe, Cosmo told himself, and don't look down. The sun was setting now, made purple by the chemical smog. That's why we can see the Parasites, thought Cosmo. Chemicals and near-death experiences. The trauma awakens the sixth sense, and the chemicals in our bloodstream keep it awake, in certain cases.

There was a small breezeblock hut on the roof. Squat and basic, with no luxuries except for power lines twisted through a foam-insulation-stuffed hole in the wall. On the low roof stood a mic-and-dish apparatus. It looked like an old-fashioned digital TV antennae, but closer inspection revealed three modern chip boxes soldered to its base. Obviously this was the Parabola Stefan had referred to.

Mona was inside on a plastic bench, wrapped in a foil sleeping bag. Lightweight and superinsulated, the bags had been pioneered by astronauts and made popular by homeless people the world over. Mona's head lolled back against a large cushion with Styrofoam balls leaking from one corner.

Cosmo took a moment to study her. She was pretty, as far as he could tell, but not like the girls on TV. Pretty in a real-person kind of way, as if there were feelings behind the face.

"Are you coming in, or are you just going to stand there?" said Mona, without opening her eyes.

Cosmo tried to speak. Say something clever, he ordered his brain.

It's not going to happen, replied his brain. You have enough spare cells for one word. Make it a good one. "Coffee," blurted Cosmo. It could have been a lot worse under the circumstances.

Mona stretched like a cat, her wiggling toes peeking out from under the unzipped sleeping bags.

"Little piggies," said Cosmo's mouth before he could stop it.

Mona opened her eyes, swiveling them to spear the unfortunate youth. "Excuse me, Cosmo?"

"This little piggie went to the market. It's a rhyme . . . for babies."

Mona drew her toes beneath the foil. "I'm not a baby, Cosmo."

"Sorry. There was this boy in the orphanage. He used to say that every time he saw a piggie."

"So now I'm a piggie."

"Exactly. No, no. Not you, your toes. How could you be a piggie? You're too . . ." He prayed silently that Mona would cut him off before he could finish the sentence, but she had no intention of doing so.

She sat back, tilting her head to one side. "I'm too what?"

Cosmo felt as though his brain were expanding. Surely the plate in his head would pop right off. "Too . . . eh . . . human."

Mona stared at him. "Have you ever had, like, a conversation with another person before?"

Cosmo shrugged. "Not really, unless you count *Yes, Marshal. No, Marshal. Whatever you say, Marshal, sir.*"

Mona accepted the mug of sim-coffee and thankfully let the subject drop. "Thanks, Cosmo. What time is it?"

"Sunset," said Cosmo.

Mona peered through the hut's window. "Purple tonight. People with allergies are going to suffer. Did you ever see a movie sunset, Cosmo? All orange and pretty. Do you think sunsets were really like that?"

Cosmo shrugged. "Maybe. I doubt it. They can do anything with special effects these days."

Mona took a sip of the sim-coffee. "You're probably right." She shrugged off the sleeping bag, leaning forward to a control box balanced on two blocks and a plank. A green light winked on the display. "Excellent," she said. "Fully charged. Now we can spot any Parasite within a mile of Abracadabra Street."

Cosmo studied the box. It didn't look sophisticated enough to make toast, never mind tracking ghostly creatures.

"If this thing can track the Parasites, surely we can find out where they live."

"It can spot them," corrected Mona. "Not track them. As soon as they leave the dish's footprint, they're gone. The Parabola was invented by the big power companies to pinpoint power leaks, not to track Parasites. It operates on the same principal as a platypus's beak. They use sensors in their bills to hone in on electrical charges generated by living beings. I saw that on one of those nature vids that Stefan makes us watch as part of our *education*."

The Parabola control box was plugged into an ancient laptop computer. Mona booted it up, opening a 3D-grid program.

"Whenever the Parabola dish picks up a Parasite's spectrum, it logs its position, speed, and direction. Over time we get a buildup of information."

"Could this lead us to where the Parasites live?"

"No," said Mona. "It's a complete waste of time. They can come from anywhere, at anytime. Their direction depends on what disaster they're heading for. And the dish only has a footprint of one square mile."

"So why are we doing it?"

Mona checked behind her to make sure they were alone. "Desperate measures. We ran this program for over a year with nothing to show for it. We should be out there, hunting them."

"But even if we find them, what can we do? The lightning rods just help them to breed."

Mona ran her fingers through tousled hair. "I don't know. What about water? Maybe we could spray them down. There must be something."

A blue blip appeared on the screen.

"There's one, look! A hundred yards northeast. Traveling at sixty miles per hour."

Cosmo hurried to the window. In the distance a lone Parasite disappeared over the lip of a building.

"So what good is that to us?" asked Mona. "None, unless we can catch him." She leaned back on the cushion, hugging the foil blanket tight. "What we need is a miracle."

Cosmo smiled. "Well, we're in the right place."

"You got that right, Cosmo. Abracadabra Street. You know why it's called that?"

Cosmo sat beside her on the bench, shaking his head.

"Years ago, the geniuses who designed Satellite City decided that there would be specific sections for the artisans. That's why you have Van Gogh Arcade and Whitman Heights. All the painters were supposed to live in Van Gogh, and all the poets in Whitman. Abracadabra Street was for Vegas people. Magicians, lounge singers, and dancers. It was a stupid idea. You can't put art in a box. Nobody with real talent is going to be told where to live. Stefan picked this place up for a song. He doesn't even pay taxes. Smart guy, most of the time."

"Most of the time," said Stefan's voice behind them. His tone did not resonate with cheer. Nobody would be asking Stefan to play Santa in the Christmas pageant, even if there were more than a couple million people still celebrating that holiday.

"Mind if I take over? I need to talk to our new Spotter."

Mona got to her feet, holding the blanket around her shoulders. "Sure. I could do with a few hours in a real bed. Who knows? I might even go out in the daylight, now that we have the nights off."

Mona bent low so her face was level with Cosmo's. "That was nice shooting with the tank. You saved me again." She kissed him on the cheek. "Thanks."

"Welcome," mumbled Cosmo. His face felt as though someone had plugged it in to a wall socket.

Mona laughed. "You keep this up, and you'll spend your whole day getting kissed."

Cosmo got a sentence together. "Maybe next time you'll save me. Then I'll owe you a kiss." It was a grammatical masterpiece, given the circumstances.

"Maybe," said Mona, her eyes twinkling. She walked up to Stefan. "Are you talking to me now?"

Stefan didn't look any happier than he had the previous night. "Listen, Mona. Last night, I was in a bad way. My work got trashed."

Mona poked his chest with a knuckle. "Our work. We're the Supernaturalists. A team."

"You're right. A team. I'll keep it in mind from now on."

She squeezed his forearm gently. "You do that, Stefan."

Mona ran across the cold rooftop, taking tiny steps inside the silver cocoon of her sleeping bag. Stefan stepped inside the hut, closing the concertina door. He sat beside Cosmo. "So, Cosmo, how are you feeling?"

Cosmo shrugged. "I don't know. I feel like a TV screen with

nothing on it. Blank. I haven't had time to become a person."

"Satellite City can do that to you. This place has no respect for individuals. Fit in, do what you're told, and don't ask questions." He twiddled a dial on the Parabola box. "You have time now, Cosmo. Time to be part of the group."

"Am I really? Part of the group?"

Stefan sighed. "That's what I wanted to talk to you about. I've been in bad temper lately, Cosmo. But that's not you, it's me."

Cosmo did not answer immediately, staring intently at the computer screen. "If I'm ever to be a real part of this group, you need to tell me."

"Tell you what?" asked Stefan, though he already knew.

"Why we're doing this? What happened to you?"

Stefan's face was grim for several seconds, then it softened. He had made up his mind. "Okay, Cosmo. You deserve the truth. But take my word for it, sometimes knowing everything doesn't make it any easier to sleep at night. . . ."

Stefan leaned forward, resting his face in his hands, and began speaking. Hesitantly at first, but soon the words rolled out like pebbles from a sack.

"Three years ago I was a hotshot cadet. Fifteen years old, and at the top of my class. Professor Faustino, my tutor and a close family friend, had put my name forward for officer school. Then one day it all went horribly wrong. My mother called me at the academy. She needed a lift home from the clinic where she worked, and I had just passed my cruiser jockey test. So I picked her up in the police cruiser. I figured

I would swing by our apartment, then drop the cruiser off at police HQ."

Stefan kneaded his eye sockets with his fists. "Stupid. A police cruiser is always a target. Always. Innocent civilians are never supposed to be taken in the car. I knew that. What was I thinking?"

"What happened?" asked Cosmo.

"We were halfway home when the car exploded. The techies said it was a camouflaged mine in the chassis. They never found out who planted it."

Stefan ran a finger along the scar at the edge of his mouth. "I was pretty broken up. Mother was badly injured too. Very badly. But she would have lived, I'm certain of it. I've seen plenty of wounds, and she would have lived."

"If it hadn't been for the Parasites?" guessed Cosmo.

"Those blue devils swarmed down on us like bees on honey. And I couldn't move, I couldn't save her. I just lay there pinned by the cab. Watching while they sucked my mother dry. Three of them landed on me. Arms and chest. With those big eyes staring down."

Stefan took a break, dragging a sleeve across his eyes. "The paramedics were there in seconds. There happened to be a unit close by. Ditto saved me with a defibrillator. But for my mother, it was too late. I was too late. I failed her."

Cosmo thought long and hard before speaking. "You didn't fail her," he said. "The Parasites are natural. You can't fight nature."

Stefan draped an arm around Cosmo's shoulder. "Thanks,

Cosmo," he said. "That's a nice thing to say, but whales were natural, and we sure got rid of them."

Compared to the preceeding week, the following days were extremely quiet. Mona monitored the Parabola closely, but the computer could not convert the sightings into a pattern.

Finally Stefan called a meeting after a trip to see his mother's ashes. He had visited her almost every day since the meeting with Ellen Faustino. More than ever now, he missed her strength and guidance.

"I've been thinking about all this," he said, gesturing at the warehouse and its array of equipment. "It's madness, all of it. What did I think we could do against . . . nature? Every time we blasted a Parasite, we created a dozen new ones to prey on our kind. How many lives did that cost?"

"But we have the energy pulse now," objected Mona. "All we need to do is find a nest, and we can undo all that."

"No, you were right, Mona," sighed Stefan. "The Parabola never worked. I have no right to put you in danger." He paused, looking each one of the group in the eye in turn. There was something big coming. Mona reached across under the table, squeezing Cosmo's hand. Whatever Stefan said next would affect all of them.

The Supernaturalist leader took a deep breath. "I have made a decision. From today on, we're officially normal people."

The statement echoed through the warehouse. Normal people? Was there any such thing?

"You never put me in danger," said Cosmo. "No one forced

me to do anything. I did what I thought was right. All you did for me was to save my life."

"Me too," said Mona. "If it hadn't been for the Supernaturalists, I'd be an oil slick by the side of a racetrack somewhere."

Stefan shook his head. "The time has come for me to wake up. My mother has gone, I have to accept that."

Mona jumped to her feet. "We can't just give in, Stefan. You know what our destiny is. We fight these things until we can't fight anymore. Tell him, Ditto."

The Bartoli baby's eyes were downcast. "Maybe the boss is right," he said. "Maybe we should call it a day."

Mona threw her hands in the air. "I don't believe this. One operation goes bad and everybody falls apart."

"Falls apart? That's not it, Mona. That's not it at all. We gave it our best shot, but it's like trying to mop up the ocean with a tissue. Who says we can't be happy like ordinary people for a while?"

Mona's face was red with anger. "Normal people are being sucked dry by these creatures, only they don't know it. You want to watch and do nothing while the Parasites go about their business?"

Stefan caught Mona gently by the shoulders. "It's not what I want. But we're beaten. We're a bunch of kids. What can we do?"

"Myishi is with us now," whispered Mona. "We have the energy pulse and the Parabola."

"It doesn't work. It's never worked. It took me a long time to see it, but I see now."

"A pity about that Parabola," said Cosmo thoughtfully, almost to himself.

Mona turned from Stefan. "What do you mean, Cosmo?"

"Something Professor Faustino said. The Parasites often feed on electrical energy. I bet if we found energy leaks, we'd find Parasites." He rested his chin on one hand. "If only we had a bigger dish."

Mona ran to the nearest window, tearing back the heavy curtains. "Myishi has a pretty big dish," she said, pointing to the stars. "One more shot, Stefan. One more try."

Stefan's resignation cracked like a mud pack, revealing the old determination underneath. "Ditto," he said. "Where's my phone?"

"Absolutely not," said Ellen Faustino.

Stefan couldn't believe what he was hearing. "Professor Faustino, all I'm asking for is a data port on the Satellite. One plug-in, what can that hurt?"

Faustino's face was grim on the phone screen. "The Satellite is off-limits, Stefan, even to me. I'm only president of research. I couldn't get a job scrubbing the floor on the Satellite."

The phone's handset almost cracked in Stefan's hand. "Fine, you run the scan. A concentration of energy leaks in the city center, that's all I'm looking for."

Faustino consulted a digital diary on her desk. "That's a much better idea. I can get a slot in a couple of months."

"A couple of months! Do you have any idea how many

people will be sucked dry in a couple of months?"

"I can't help it," protested Faustino, swiveling her digital diary so Stefan could see the screen. "Look at the clients we have waiting. Nike, Disney, Krom. The Satellite costs millions per uplink. Do you realize the advertising power of a single broadcast? There's a five-year waiting list for Satellite time. A couple of months is the absolute earliest I can get in, and even then I'll be calling in every favor I owe."

Stefan struggled to stay calm. "How am I supposed to deploy your energy pulse if I can't locate the Parasites?"

Faustino was unfazed. "Stefan, this entire operation is clandestine. Un-spec four does not exist. Neither does the modified energy pulse. Neither, for that matter, do you or your vigilante band. What do you want me to do? Go to Head Office with a story about spooky blue creatures that are scrubbing energy?"

"No," admitted Stefan, scowling into the phone's screen. "I suppose not. But what do you want *me* to do?"

"I want you to find another way," said Ellen Faustino.

Stefan closed the handset. "Don't worry," he said. "I will."

Booshka Region, past the blockade; Satellite City

Mona steered the Pigmobile through the teeming life of Booshka. Technically she shouldn't have been driving manually at all, but there wouldn't be any police down here to check her license, or lack of it. The nighttime gangs had been replaced by throngs of ordinary peaceful people. In the pale blue daylight, life went on as it did all over the world. Whatever their circumstances, people still had to eat, live, and love.

Stalls sprang up along the side of the road like magicians' tables. African tailors rubbed elbows with Asian hackers and European shoemakers. Trade was brisk and haggling was lively.

Cosmo watched the world go by from his seat in the Pigmobile. "It's not a bad place to live."

"In the daytime," said Stefan. "And will be a lot better if Professor Faustino can get her welfare grants back online."

Ditto was checking his chin in a small mirror. Hoping for some bristles. "Sure. Which is why we're doing this behind her back."

"Professor Faustino is on the inside," said Stefan. "She has to follow the rules; we don't. If the Supernaturalists can take care of the Parasite problem, the Satellite stabilizes and the welfare grants will flow. Everybody's happy."

"Especially Myishi," said Ditto, pocketing the mirror. "I think it's very nice of us to do their job for them, especially since they've been trying to kill us for years."

Mona yelled back from the driving seat. "Do you have any better ideas, Ditto? Do you?" She gave him a full five seconds to reply. "No? I thought not. You never do."

"I never do? It's just healthy skepticism," said the Bartoli baby. "We can't all be sheep. This entire situation stinks. Suddenly we're working for the corporation. I don't like it."

"I don't like it much either," said Stefan. "But Professor Faustino is my friend first, and corporation second. We can trust her."

"Are you sure? Would you bet all our lives on it?"

"The only life I'm betting from now on is my own. Once we track the Parasites to their lair, I'll be the one setting the energy pulse. From today on, you kids are computer jockeys."

Mona nearly crashed the mobile. "Kids? Who are you calling a kid? You're only a couple of years older than us. If I'm old enough to run around on rooftops, I'm old enough to set energy pulses. I'm not here to watch things on a monitor."

"You will be involved, from a safe distance. And if you don't like the new arrangement, stop the van and get out. I'm sure the Sweethearts would be really happy to welcome you back."

Mona jammed her foot on the accelerator. "You know something, Stefan? Sometimes you can be a real pig."

They drove for more than three hours until the Pigmobile was skirting Satellite City's beltway. Next stop, the desert. Cosmo could see the end of the city and it fascinated him. There was an end to the city? For some reason, he had always imagined the entire city to be a giant prison. And even if you did leave, how did people survive out here in the countryside?

This was not like the countryside you saw in old videos. There were no horses galloping in slow motion, and no swings hanging from the trees. In fact there weren't many trees. Most plant life this close to the city had been killed off by chemical smog or factory overspill.

Here, the people existed outside the Satellite's footprint and free from its influences. Most of the countrysiders lived in small one-story dwellings cobbled together from whatever material was likely to stay upright for the longest time. To Cosmo the houses seemed wildly exotic. After a lifetime of pig iron, it was refreshing to see walls constructed from chunks of reinforced highway bridges, and roofs made from old billboards.

Ditto shuddered. "This place gives me the creeps. You know they don't have Satellite TV here? Some houses only have ten or fifteen illegal stations. What do they do all day?"

"Stay alive," said Stefan, pointing at a mountain of junk in the distance. "Over there, Mona. That's where we're going."

As they drew closer, Cosmo realized that the junk mountain was actually a fenced-in yard filled to overflowing with discarded rubbish from the city. Two armed guards stood in the shade of a covered tower, their weapons as ancient as everything they were guarding.

Mona stopped the Pigmobile before decorated iron gates that had, in a previous life, been the entrance to a theme-park ride called Dino Doom.

Stefan opened the side door, stepping into the heat and dust. There were two rifles trained on him from above.

"You'd better keep on truckin', kid," said one of the guards, an emaciated specimen with no more than three teeth. "'Less you got sumfin' worth tradin'. Never mind what the gate says, this ain't no fun park."

"Shut up and listen," said Stefan, with his usual tact. "I need to see Lincoln. Tell him it's Bashkir. And if this gate is not open in two minutes, then I'm holding you responsible."

The guard thought about arguing, until Stefan glanced pointedly at his watch. Then he decided to go and get Lincoln. If this tall, armed youth wanted someone to be mad at, the guard would prefer that it wasn't him. There was something about those piercing eyes, and the twisted scar stretching his mouth.

The second guard spat after his workmate. "Run like a rabbit, chicken boy. You ain't got the spine of a lug worm." Obviously the man was fond of animal imagery.

Stefan climbed back into the car. "I think we're in."

"Must be your charming personality," muttered Mona, still sore over the "stop the van and get out" comment.

"Now, when we get in here," Stefan went on, "I want everybody to be extremely careful. Did you ever see those movies about the Wild West, where gunfights get started over the least little thing?"

Cosmo nodded.

"Well the Junkyard is like that, except with real bullets. Ditto, you're a kid until I say so."

Ditto groaned. "Aw, Stefan. I hate being a kid."

"We might need an ace up our sleeves. You're it."

Considerably less than two minutes later the Dino gates swung open, manned on each side by one of the strange guards. Seeing them at close range, Cosmo realized that the men were much better seen at a distance.

"Bring that sucker in, Mistuh *Bashkeer*. Park 'er in front of the lobby."

"Whooeee," said the other. "You sure are one hog-ugly critter."

Cosmo didn't know if the man was talking to the Pigmobile or his own reflection. Then again, he was in no position to sneer at other people. His own head was no oil painting since Ditto had patched it up, although at least now he had some stubble to cover the lumps on his skull.

Mona steered through an assault course of automobile skeletons, parking in front of a porch constructed from rusting satellite dishes. The lobby, apparently.

"Remember," said Stefan to Ditto. "Act immature."

Mona laughed. "Act? Just be yourself, Ditto. Nobody will notice the difference."

The ugly twins escorted them through a curtain of nuts and bolts threaded onto copper wire. Inside was even dirtier than outside. Every inch of surface was coated with a pungent mixture of oil, dirt, and rust. Millions of rust mites flourished in the ceiling, their activities sending rust flakes fluttering down like robot moths.

Behind a desk constructed from storage pallets sat a man, clearly at ease in the filth. His feet were propped on the desk, bare toes being licked by an obese ginger cat.

"Nice cat," noted Stefan. "What's his name?"

"Camouflage," answered the man. "When this cat shuts his eyes, you couldn't find him in here with a pack of bloodhounds."

Stefan swiped the man's feet from the desk, sitting opposite him. The cat hissed, running along the man's leg to his stomach.

"I see you don't believe in manners."

"Manners won't buy you much in the Big Pig, or beyond it, Lincoln."

Lincoln's face was gaunt, with bags under his eyes like melted flesh. He could have been any age and of any race, though his accent was decidedly upper class. He wore a three-piece pinstriped suit; unfortunately it was at least twenty years old. "You know my name, boy, but I don't know who you are. You used the name of a friend of mine to get in here, but you certainly are not Dr. Aeriel Bashkir."

"I'm her son, Stefan. She told me about you."

Lincoln studied him for a moment. "Yes, you have her eyes. How is your mother?"

Stefan dropped his gaze. "She died. Three years ago."

Lincoln was silent for several moments. "I'm sorry to hear that. She was a good woman."

"She was. From what she told me, you owe her a favor."

Lincoln laughed. His teeth were the same color as the rest of him. "Perhaps. But I certainly don't owe *you* any favors, dear boy. Favors are nontransferrable."

Stefan put his elbows on the desk. "Lincoln, five years ago my mother traveled out of the city and took out your ruptured appendix. No other doctor in the city would have done that. While she was here, she saw a HALO going up. She told me all about it. We both know that you're the one who has been sending up pirate HALOs for years, without any permits, safety or otherwise. One call from me and the Myishi privates would be cutting this place into cubes with space lasers. And the ugly twins here would be absolutely no help."

Lincoln was unimpressed. "You've met Floyd and Bruce. They're my boys. I took them in off the street when they were barely out of nappies. I believe they were twenty-six at the time. Stupid as rocks, poor fellows, but they certainly can shoot. As a matter of fact they have big old bolt guns pointed at your head right now.'

"Oh, really?" said Stefan. "Well, I'd advise them to look down."

"Look down?" said Floyd. "You wouldn't be tryin' to take our eyes offa the target, would you?"

"You must think we were born last Tuesday," added Bruce, his voice whistling slightly through the gaps in his teeth. "We got you all covered. You and the two juvies."

"What about the baby?" asked Stefan.

Floyd snickered. "What about him? What's he gonna do? Spit up all over us?"

Floyd and Bruce felt two lightning rods being jammed painfully into their kneecaps. Ditto was grinning up at them. "You're the one's who'll be spitting up, if I empty a full charge into you."

Lincoln had to laugh. "Bartoli?"

Ditto nodded. "One of the last."

"Okay, dimwits," said Lincoln. "Put away the bolt guns before the little one makes your hair curl."

Floyd and Bruce grudgingly did what they were told.

"A genuine Bartoli," said Lincoln, "what are your mutes?"

Ditto scowled. "I prefer the term *special talents.*"

"Mutations, special talents, whatever term you wish. What can you do?"

"I'm the medic in our group."

"Healing hands. I've heard of that. Are you sensitive too?"

"To what?"

"The spirit world. The TV scientists say that Bartoli woke parts of the brain that have lain dormant for millennia."

"I know what the brainers say," snapped Ditto with unusual ferocity. "No, I'm not sensitive. Good looks—that's it."

Lincoln lay back in his threadbare chair. "It looks like you got the drop on me, Stefan. So let's get down to business. What can I do for you?"

"I need a High-Altitude Low-Orbit ship," said Stefan bluntly.

Lincoln laughed. Rust flakes fluttered from the creases in his face.

"A HALO, just like that. No schmoozing first?"

"I don't have time for schmoozing. I need a HALO, now. Today."

"What would I be doing with a HALO? That would be illegal. I'd have public and private police trying to lock me up. Your mother must have been mistaken. A desert hallucination, perhaps."

Stefan brought his fist down on the desk. "My mother was

a spaceship nut. It was her hobby. She used to bring me down to the Cape to watch the rockets take off. She knew every model ever made. She was not mistaken. You're the space pirate the privates are all looking for."

"And if I am?" said Lincoln. "Not that I'm admitting anything, mind. Who else would clean up space? Who else would salvage all those junked satellites? In my humble opinion, whoever is sending up those rogue HALOs is doing Earth a favor. The world's first cosmic trash man. The occasional pirate TV broadcast is a small price to pay for clean space."

"Yeah, yeah, you deserve a medal. Now, where's the ship?"

Lincoln's face was suddenly deadly serious. "Why would I give a ship to you people? A bunch of children? You're not old enough to drive that heap of junk outside, not to mention a HALO."

"You grow up quickly in the Big Pig," retorted Stefan bitterly. "We've survived on our own for years. The only thing adults have done for us in the recent past is try to kill us. You can program the HALO from here. She'll go up and back without us having to touch an instrument. All we want to do is be on board."

"You still haven't told me why I would want to give you my ship, if I had one. What's in it for me?"

Stefan drew a computer panel wallet from inside his new overcoat. He laid it on the table.

"And what is that?" asked Lincoln, trying to appear disinterested. "The latest 3D video game?"

"No, Lincoln, it's a piggyback panel. With a Lockheed Martin solar panel face and a two-million-gigabyte memory capacity. I acquired it recently from a friend."

Lincoln nudged the panel. "Piggyback panel. Oh, really. What's on the memory?"

"Nothing, at the moment. Plenty of memory there to run a pirate TV station."

Lincoln weighed the panel on his palm. "In theory. But you need a big dish to hook into."

"We have a dish. The biggest."

"Don't kid a kidder, Stefan. Nobody gets near the Satellite without corporate access codes. You go within a mile without codes, and they blast you into space."

Stefan slid the panel inside his pocket. "You leave the codes to me. This is the opportunity of a lifetime, Lincoln. I can hook you up with a panel on the Satellite. You'll be broadcasting for months before they trace the panel."

Lincoln scratched a clean patch on his chin. "And all I have to do is?"

"Give me the starter card for the HALO I know you have parked out back."

"Two million gigabytes, you say?"

"All yours. I give you a linkup chip and you're set."

Lincoln was sold, but he fought against it. "You know how much one of those chips costs, Stefan?"

"About one tenth of what you'll make from the independent TV companies."

"This could be all lies, Stefan. Maybe you just need my ship, and you don't have any codes."

Stefan's glare cut through the particle heavy air. "You have my word, Lincoln. I swear it on my mother's grave."

Lincoln waved his hands. "No need to get all morbid, swearing on graves. That kind of thing is bad form."

"Well, do we have a deal?"

Lincoln stood, rust fell from his clothes like dry snakeskin. "Yes, young Bashkir. We have a deal."

Stefan extended a hand. "Let's shake on it."

Lincoln ignored the gesture. "We can shake when you bring my ship back in one piece."

Lincoln led the Supernaturalists around the rear of the junkyard, to what appeared to be a solid wall of salvaged cars. He fished a garage-door remote from a string around his neck and hit the button. The wall split down the middle, rolling apart on rickety tracks. Immediately half a dozen stocky dogs lunged forward on bungee chains. Their lips were drawn back to reveal yellowed teeth, and dribbles of slobber swung from their jaws like jump ropes.

Lincoln hit another button on the remote, and the bungee-chains were coiled in.

"I don't care how hi-tech things get, you can't beat a hungry mutt for security."

The dogs were a curious breed, with blunt snouts and red pelts.

Lincoln threw them a handful of bones from a bucket. "You like my babies? They cost me a pretty penny. I ordered them test-tubed from Cuba. Mostly pit-bull genes. Some bear too, and a few strands of chameleon for color."

The HALO sat on a grille surrounded by a cage of ice. Refrigerator pumps spewed subzero crystals onto the glossy surface. The ship's hull shimmered inside the frozen panes.

"You are a very fortunate young man, Stefan," said Lincoln. "We had a launch planned for tonight. Nothing special, just a routine trawl to see what we could pick up. Otherwise it would take a few days to ice up the frame."

Cosmo shuffled close to Mona. "What's the ice for?"

"Camouflage, Cosmo. The HALO needs a couple of liquid-fueled boosters to shoot her the first half mile before the solar band kicks in. That kind of heat is going to show up on Myishi scanners. They don't have any patience for pirates messing about in space. The ice stops the launch site showing up on-screen. Pirates have been using ice boxes for decades."

Floyd and Bruce hauled one of the ice panels across with bailing hooks. The HALO sat on four blocks like a car that's had its wheels boosted.

The Supernaturalists stepped inside the icy sheath. Cosmo touched the ship's cold paneling. "This thing flies?"

Lincoln clipped him on the ear. "Of course she flies, cheeky boy. She flies, she soars, she glides. But most important, she lands." He handed over the starter card with a flourish. "I don't suppose you'll be sharing the purpose of your voyage."

Stefan pocketed the card, handing over the Lockheed Martin solar panel.

"You suppose right, Lincoln, old bean. We leave at dusk, so you have three hours to transfer whatever software you need onto the panel."

"Do you have a mechanic?"

Mona was already busy with a screwdriver at one of the access panels. "We have a mechanic. Gimme an hour and I'll tell you if we have a ship."

Mona reported twenty-four electronic, computer, and mechanical glitches on her HALO checklist.

"Twenty-four," said Stefan, rubbing his chin. "Anything critical?"

Mona consulted her list. "Mostly comfort stuff. The air filters are due for a change, but if it's a quick run we should be okay. I did pressure tests on the space suits. They all need patching, except one. So you'll be going out alone, Stefan."

"Good. No more unnecessary risk for anybody from now on."

"The flaps barely move, so no sharp turns. Most of the circuits are held together with tape from the last century, and the windscreen is filthy."

"Wipers?"

"No."

"Okay. Get a sponge and some hot water. We blast off in an hour."

The HALO weighed fourteen tons and was roughly

conical in shape. The craft was steered by tail flaps and a dozen gas jets, six of which were actually working. At some stage the hull had been painted European Union blue, but most of the color had been scraped off during various salvage missions. At the ship's base were two fixed boosters that would provide the propulsion for the initial gravity break, at which point the "wedding band" would take over.

The wedding band was a gold-plated ring of solar panels that oscillated continuously as the ship moved. Each panel charged in turn, then moved back to make contact with a magnetic ring on the hull, to deposit its charge and make room for the next cell. In outer space, the HALO resembled nothing so much as a surfer girl twirling a Hula Hoop.

"How far into outer space are we going?" Cosmo asked Mona.

Mona was running a final system's check, with a little help from a dog-eared manual.

"Technically, we're were not going as far as outer space, just past the edge of the atmosphere. What's the difference, Cosmo? A fall from anything over fifty feet will kill you. In any case we're far more likely to die from a pressure leak than a fall."

"Thanks," said Cosmo. "I feel better now."

"Good, because you're my copilot."

Cosmo pulled his combat jacket closer against the chill from the ice sheets. "Copilot? Mona, I can't even send automobile coordinates to the Satellite."

"Don't worry, Cosmo. The computer does most of the

work, and when we get close enough, the Satellite will guide us in."

"If we get the access codes," Cosmo reminded her.

Mona frowned at a red light on the console. She rapped it with a knuckle, and it turned green. "If Stefan isn't worried about that, then I won't worry either."

Lincoln poked his head through the hatch. "The Lockheed," he said, handing Mona the piggyback panel. "Make sure you get a solid contact. Liftoff in ten."

Mona didn't take orders well. "Liftoff in ten? Is there a mission control somewhere that I didn't notice?"

Lincoln smiled sweetly. "No, my sarcastic little munchkin, there is no mission control. But my fridge pumps are out of gas, so you go in ten or the ice frame melts, and if that melts, then you don't go at all. I'll let you explain that to Stefan, shall I?"

Mona returned to her final check. "Good point. Ten minutes it is."

Nine minutes later the Supernaturalists were strapped in gyro chairs, their ribs protected from g-force by armored vests. Above them the ice plates shimmered in the twilight.

"That ice will break, won't it?" asked Cosmo. "It looks pretty thick."

Mona's finger hovered over the ignition button. "It should, in theory. The prow has been fitted with an icebreaker."

Ditto and Stefan sat in the rear. In fact there were only three proper seats, so Ditto sat on Stefan's knee, secured by an extended harness. The Bartoli baby was not pleased. "Of all the humiliations my condition has forced me to endure, this is the worst."

Stefan patted him on the head. "There there, little fellow. Shall I tell you a story?"

"Stefan. This is not the time. I may be small, but I can still do some damage."

Mona twisted in her gyro chair. "You seem a bit cranky, Ditto. Maybe you have gas."

Ditto lunged forward, but the harness held him fast.

"Let's go, Mona," said Stefan. "Before he gets loose."

Mona flipped the ignition's safety cap. "We're gone," she said, pressing the red button.

With a massive roar, the boosters sparked, turning the ice to steam in seconds. The container melted around them. Steam billowed around the HALO, obscuring the view screen.

The craft left the launch pad slowly, struggling against the gravity that weighed it down. Power gauges fluttered into the red as the computer upped the thrust. The ice-cutter nose-piece cracked the overhead ice pane, then punched through. Below them water boiled and recondensed to form a thick mist.

Cosmo felt as though he were being shaken to pieces. This was not flying the way it was depicted in the TV holiday vids. Then again, this was not a Satellite-controled executive leisure craft. The HALO was a twenty-year-old twin booster pirate craft with barely enough memory to power an entertainment system.

The nose dipped slightly.

"This is the dangerous time," said Mona, through chattering teeth. "If the initial burn is too strong, the stern goes up faster than the nose."

"Then what?"

"Then we pinwheel."

"Pinwheeling doesn't sound good."

"It isn't."

The computer throttled back a fraction, straightening the ship.

"Okay, we're vertical. Now for the fun part."

Cosmo, the novice, was going to ask yet another question. *The fun part*, he wanted to say. *What's the fun part?*

Then the wedding band deployed, adding the power of superefficient solar cells to the fading boosters and the HALO's own lithium batteries. The ship took off at fifteen hundred miles per hour through a bank of green-tinged cloud, like a stone from a sling. G-force stuffed Cosmo's words back down his throat.

Mona managed to speak, though the cords in her neck stood out like bridge struts. "The fun part," she said.

Blue sky, thought Cosmo, when the shuddering stopped. The sky really is blue. Strands of viscous smog still clung to the windscreen, but beyond that was an azure sky dotted with stars. It was an amazing sight. Blue, just like old postcards. The view from the Myishi observatory had been impressive, but this was even better, because the sky was all around them.

Cosmo even saw a white cloud hovering on the edge of space.

A message droned from a computer speaker. *Gravity one fifth Earth's norm. Activating artificial gravity.*

"Good," said Mona. "This floating around is not doing my stomach any good."

Then the computer said, *Artificial gravity failed.*

Mona banged the gravity switch several times, without success.

"Oh, great," she muttered. "Vomit comet."

"What?" asked Cosmo, then he felt the contents of his stomach rising.

"Stay very still," warned Mona. "Reduced gravity takes a bit of getting used to. Don't take off your harness." She glanced over her shoulder. "No gravity. Try not to move about."

"Too late," said Stefan.

Ditto was hanging forward in his harness. His face was green, and there was a brownish pool floating in the air before him.

"I shouldn't have had that pazza this morning," he moaned.

Stefan pulled a miniature vacuum cleaner from below the seat and cleaned up the vomit. "Thanks, Ditto. This is just the kind of job I like. You can be sure I'll be bringing this up again, if you'll pardon the pun."

The computer applied the brakes, or more accurately the forward jets, slowing the HALO to four hundred miles per hour. The Satellite hung on the edge of space like an alien mother ship. The stylized Myishi logo pulsed gently across the dish's concave belly.

"I read that it takes as much power to run that logo as it takes to light twenty city blocks," said Mona.

As they drew closer, the Satellite filled their field of vision, and they could make out hundreds of maintenance dish jockeys working on repairs across the dish's surface. They wore magnetic boots and were tethered to the dish's gantry by bungee cords and climbing rings. Their movements were skilled and graceful, as they launched themselves into space, then snapped back to exactly the point where they needed to be.

"I bet that's not as easy as it looks," said Ditto, wiping his mouth. "I'm glad it's not me going out there."

The consol radio beeped three times.

"Incoming," said Mona, opening a channel. A voice issued through the speakers. The voice was as cold as space itself.

Unidentified HALO, this is Satellite Command, you are in Myishi space.

Stefan removed his harness, pulling himself and Ditto along the floor railing.

"We read you, Satellite," he said into the reed mike. "Just fishing out the access code."

"Thirty seconds," said the voice. "Then we will initiate targeting."

Stefan pulled his vid-phone from his pocket and searched the menu for outgoing calls. He selected the last call he had made to Ellen Faustino at Myishi Tower, and ran the video. On the phone's tiny screen Ellen appeared, explaining to Stefan why she could not get a spot on the Satellite. To illustrate her point, she swiveled her computer screen to show him the backlog. The company list was clearly visible on the screen. And beside each company, its access code and timetable.

"Okay, Satellite. We're a maintenance team from Krom Automobiles."

"You're from Krom?" said the security man. "In that bucket of bolts?"

"Hey, we're maintenance, not royalty," said Stefan, trying to sound injured. "The five P.M. advertisement is skipping, so they sent us up to clip on a new panel."

"We could have fixed that from up here. Seems an awful long way to come."

"No offense, but you guys charge an arm and a leg just to polish the solar panels, and we were in the neighborhood. We have the code, so just light up the port for us."

"Punch in the code first. Then we'll talk about your maintenance port."

Stefan handed his phone to Mona, who punched in the relevant ten-digit code twice, the second time to verify.

"Okay," said security grudgingly. "You're in. Port seventy-five. Follow the landing lights, and don't leave your port."

"Roger that, Satellite. You have a nice day now."

The order to follow the landing lights was unnecessary, since the computer locked onto the red beacons' frequency and directed the HALO to port seventy-five. The beacon lights were arranged in concentric circles that acted like a target, pulling them closer to a steel walkway that extended from the dish, one of several hundred that were attached in this quarter. The Krom logo was painted on the walkway. The ship docked with a grating thud, and two dish jockeys rushed to secure forward and aft cables.

"We're in," said Stefan, unhooking Ditto. "Get the cables ready while I put on my suit." He grabbed a suitcase from the overhead locker and disappeared into the latrine.

Ditto unwound a snaky conduit from the loading bay. Inside were two cables: a power cable and a modem lead. The ancient ship was not equipped with wireless capability for this volume of information. "As far as Myishi knows, we're just charging the batteries and replacing the Krom video chip, but while he's out there, the bossman slips in the modem lead and we hijack the Satellite for a sneaky search."

"How long will that take?"

"Not long, Cosmo. About a minute should do it. Any longer, and Myishi will realize what we're doing. There's also the fact that the real Krom team is due here soon."

Stefan emerged from the latrine. He was not wearing the suit.

"It's off," he said. "We'll have to find another way."

Mona swiveled her chair to face him. "What? Another way? Why?"

Stefan held out the suit. The name *Floyd* was scrawled on the nametag in red paint. "This suit. It's too small."

"No," said Mona. "Spacesuits are *one size fits all*. The arms and legs are concertina design."

Stefan sighed. "Generally, yes. But this suit is last-century. Tailored for an individual. A short individual. It's not going to work. Cast off, before we're found out."

Mona popped the clips on her G-Vest. "I'll go then, Stefan."

"Even if I liked the idea, it's not practical. You're the pilot, Mona. If the computer goes down, which it very well could in this flying junkyard, then it's up to you to get us home, or within a hundred miles of it."

Mona chewed her lip. Stefan was right. "Ditto. You've been around computers. You go."

The Bartoli baby folded his arms across his chest. The body language was clear for everybody to see. But just in case there was some uncertainty, he said, "In your dreams, Vasquez. A case full of growth hormones couldn't tempt me into that suit. In any case, like Stefan said, the suit isn't adjustable. You put me in that thing, and I'll look like a baby playing dress up."

Cosmo's throat dried up suddenly. No one would ask him to go. He was the rookie. It was up to him to volunteer. "I'll do it," he blurted.

Stefan pointed a stiff finger at him. "No,"' he said. "Shut up, Cosmo. You don't know what you're saying."

Cosmo's brain agreed. He had no idea what he was saying, but he was part of the team, and this job needed to be done. "I'll go. The suit will fit me. I just have to plug in a few wires, right?"

Mona was not as ecstatic as he thought she would be. "I don't know, Cosmo. It could get dangerous. Maybe we *should* forget it."

Ditto floated to head height. "Listen to Vasquez, kid. It's not the job I'd worry about, it's the drifting off into space for all eternity."

Cosmo pointed out the windscreen. The walkway was barely twenty feet long. "I can see the port from here. I'll be tied on all the way. What could go wrong?"

Ditto slapped his own forehead. "You had to say it, didn't you? You're jinxed now, for sure."

"I know how important this is," argued Cosmo. "If we go back to Satellite City without the scan, then how long will it be before we get another chance? I don't see what the problem is. This is far less dangerous than running around rooftops, and you had no problem with that."

"I know, Cosmo," said Stefan. "But I've learned a lot in the past week. I've come to my senses."

Cosmo held out his hands for the suit. "Five minutes and we have a map of every Parasite nest in the city."

Stefan gave it to him. "Five minutes, Cosmo. Then we're pulling you in."

Cosmo had the world at his feet. Looking down through the walkway's wire mesh, he could see Earth more than fifty miles below. From up here it seemed damaged. Through gaps in the multicolored smog banks, Cosmo could clearly make out the Los Angeles brush fires that had been world-wide news for over a month now.

The Satellite dish loomed overhead like a frozen tidal wave, poised to crash down on him and all the shuttles docked at the various ports. There were at least forty other ships anchored along this level alone. Dozens of dish jockeys were doing exactly what he was doing now, linking their HALO computer with the Satellite.

There was no intercom in Floyd's helmet, so the only thing Cosmo could hear was his own breathing amplified by the bubble helmet. At least, the visor had been coated with an antifog spray, so his vision remained clear, apart from several scratches and pockmarks.

Cosmo began to talk to himself, for some company. "Okay, Cosmo. Nothing to it. Collect the conduit and plug it in to the port. Attach the piggyback, wait for the thumbs-up, then reel the conduit back in. Easy."

Floyd's boots were not magnetic, so Cosmo had to drag himself along the ship's hull inch by inch. Space seemed to suck him gently, willing him to let go. But even if he did, there was a bungee cord securing him to the HALO. "Nothing can go wrong. Get to work."

Stefan and Mona were at the porthole, watching him anxiously. Cosmo gave them the thumbs-up, then bent low to retrieve the conduit from the air-locked tube through which Ditto was feeding it. He dragged the ribbed white tubing out, attaching it to a Velcro strip on his chest. His movements were slow and awkward in the low gravity.

Cosmo headed for the port, struggling to control his limbs, while all around dish jockeys bounced and pirouetted across the face of the dish.

The safety rail seemed tiny as he held it from inside his

bulky padded gloves, and he checked constantly to make sure that he actually had a grip on it. Inch by inch he hauled himself along the walkway, his boots floating behind him, the bungee umbilical undulating like a slow-motion jump rope.

At last, Cosmo reached the Satellite dish. His first job was to attach Lincoln's pirate plate. He slipped the Lockheed panel from a flapped pocket and clamped it directly onto another one. The panels were so thin that from a distance it would be almost impossible to spot. Only ten more feet to the uplink ports. Handrails crisscrossed the dish's surface, and Cosmo pulled himself upward, trailing both cables behind him. Five feet now, almost within reach.

The modem and power sockets had a flip-up safety cover. All Cosmo had to do was open it up, and plug in both cables. Simple, except that he couldn't reach. With the dish's curve, the safety cover was farther away than the solar panels, and Floyd's bungee cable was a couple of feet too short. Cosmo stretched the cable to the limit of its elasticity, but it was still too short. It seemed incredible to come this far, only to be foiled by the last few feet.

He turned slowly toward the shuttle. Inside, Mona was beckoning him back. "What can I do?" he asked himself, his voice bouncing around the helmet. "There's no other way."

Except to untie the bungee cord. Just for a second.

The idea popped into his head from nowhere. Untie the cord? Madness?

Just for a second. Clip it to the rails and plug in. Two steps and you're there.

Maybe, but one false move and you're lost in space.

Two steps.

"Idiot," said Cosmo to himself, unclipping the cord.

He saw Stefan from the corner of his eye. Basic lipreading told him the Supernaturalist heartily agreed with Cosmo's opinion of himself. Mona was slapping her palms against the plasti-glass screen. She wasn't too impressed with him either.

Cosmo used one hand to clip his bungee cord onto the handrail, being extremely careful not to let go with the other. It wasn't as if he were going to make a habit of this. A one-time-only deal. Providing he didn't allow his concentration to lapse, he should be fine.

A mere two steps later he was at the uplink port. Cosmo threaded his arm through the handrail, locking his elbow. Two rhinos tugging at his boots couldn't force him to let go now. He ripped the conduit from the patch on his suit and screwed it into the port. Inside the conduit a power lead and modem cable locked into place. A light flashed green on a panel beside the portal. Contact. Now all he had to do was count to sixty.

Stefan was hunched over the laptop that he had wired into the onboard computer.

"Is it running?" asked Mona, hands and face pressed against the glass.

Stefan raised a finger. *Wait!*

"I can't believe he actually untied himself. *Estúpido*. I hope he doesn't think this will impress me, because it won't. Is it running?"

Stefan clapped his hands. "It's running. Now all we need are sixty seconds."

Whereas Mona was pretending to be unimpressed, Ditto actually was. "There goes another Spotter. We're going to have to take out an advertisement on TV. Wanted: crazy kid with a death wish. Robotix plates supplied."

"Think positive," snapped Mona. "All he has to do is hold on for sixty seconds."

Ditto chuckled. "Sixty seconds. The way his luck's been going lately, it may as well be a lifetime. I wouldn't be surprised if a meteor picked this exact moment to strike the dish."

Which of course, wasn't what happened at all.

Cosmo was counting.

". . . Fifty-eight elephant, fifty-nine elephant, sixty . . . elephant."

An extra elephant, just in case. Time to head back to the bungee cord. He was unscrewing the conduit when a tiny tremor shuddered through the entire Satellite.

Cosmo glanced upward. Overhead, a residential unit seemed a little askew. Inside, people were tumbling past the windows. Another tremor. This time much larger. Around him, dish jockeys were dislodged and floated out to the end of their tethers. The residential unit was definitely not right.

Two of its corners had come completely away from the main structure. A third tremor, a monster compared to the other two. The residential cube came away completely, and so did Cosmo.

With a surprised shout that only he could hear, the teenager's fingers were wrenched from the handrail, and he floated off into space.

All around him, emergency lights began to flash on the helmets of every dish jockey, alerting them to the danger. The residential unit drifted farther from the main structure, driven by the gas venting from its torn life-support tubes. Cosmo could only watch and try not to panic. Panic would mean deeper breathing, and his oxygen readout was already edging toward the red.

The rescue was fantastic. Dozens of dish jockeys hurled themselves into the void, latching on to the unit before it was out of range. They wrapped their limbs around any protuberances, clinging on like human anchors. Several more jumped repeatedly on one end of the unit, spinning it around, so the gas jets propelled it back to the Satellite. It was stupendous. These people were space cowboys. Cosmo wanted to applaud. Then he remembered his own plight.

Something collided with his chest. Cosmo's first thought was fleeting and ridiculous. *Alien!* But no, it was a dish jockey. The man's face was red, and he shouted spittle onto the inside of his visor.

Cosmo pointed to his ears, shaking his head.

The jockey took a sonic sucker from his belt, sticking the

little speaker onto Cosmo's helmet. Contact was immediate.

". . . the hell are you doing, boy? Untying yourself like that! Are you soft in the head?"

"Eh . . . sorry."

"Haven't you read the company mail? The Satellite is unstable. We've been having more and more of these breakaways lately. Lucky for you I saw you. What company are you with?"

Cosmo racked his brain. "Eh . . . Krom. I'm with Krom."

The jockey rolled his eyes. "Krom. Typical. I bet you haven't had more than a couple of hours space time. Employ amateurs, save money, that's the Krom way. You can't be much more than a boy. How old are you?"

"Twenty-two," mumbled Cosmo hopefully. "I drink a lot of water. It keeps me young looking."

"Twenty-two," repeated the jockey, casually reeling them back to the dish. "I must be getting old."

The jockey completed a space roll, depositing them back on the platform. He clipped Cosmo back onto his bungee.

"I'm going to have to write this up," he said, stripping a pad from a computer on his wrist. "What's your name?"

Just in time, Cosmo remembered the name on his suit. "Eh . . . Floyd. Floyd Faustino."

"Well, Floyd," said the jockey, typing on the computer's keyboard. "This is going to mean a fine for Krom, and probably for you."

He printed off a card, stuffing it in Cosmo's spacesuit pocket.

"You have fourteen days to pay that fine, or else your dish-jockey license will be revoked."

"Yes, sir," said Cosmo humbly. "I'm sorry, sir."

The jockey was unimpressed. "Never mind the *sorry sir*, just pay the fine."

And with that, the jockey propeled himself across the dish to help secure the residential unit. Cosmo dragged himself shakily to the shuttle.

Mona was waiting inside the airlock. "Moron," she said, punching him on the shoulder.

"I know," said Cosmo miserably, his legs wobbling inside the suit. "Can we please go back to Earth? Please?"

Stefan was reading the results of the scan. "I don't know, Cosmo. When you hear the results of this scan, you might want to stay up here."

Cosmo took off his helmet. "What is it? he said, laughing. "It's not as if the Parasite nest is under Clarissa Frayne?"

No one else laughed. Not so much as a smile.

CHAPTER 8
PULSE

Abracadabra Street

COSMO HADN'T SPOKEN MUCH ALL the way back from space. He wasn't sulking exactly, because there was no one to be angry with. He was just wondering when it was all going to end? How many times did one person have to escape death in a week? And now he was being asked to go back to the place of his nightmares. The place that he had spent the past fourteen miserable years trying to get away from.

"Will you do it?" asked Stefan, when they were gathered around the table.

Cosmo studied the faces looking back at him. The Supernaturalists. He was one of them now—after all, he'd gone into space for them. But it wasn't all about him, or even the group. This energy pulse had to be detonated for every human on the planet. When you grew up an orphan, sometimes it was difficult to think about anyone besides yourself. But now he had Mona to think about, and Stefan and Ditto.

"It's a simple plan," continued Stefan.

"Oh, like the last simple plan," said Cosmo.

"That was a simple plan, until you began improvising. This time you will simply be pointing the way."

"You make it *sound* simple, but something will happen, it always does. I've noticed that my new knee starts to itch when trouble is near, and it's itching like crazy now."

"Trust the knee, Cosmo," said Ditto in a spooky voice.

"Shut up, Ditto," snapped Mona. "This is important."

"Sure, it's real important that we plant Myishi's bomb for them."

"It's a pulse. An energy pulse."

"So they say. Who knows what this thing really does?"

Stefan opened the briefcase, swiveling it to face the Bartoli baby. "It's a pulse, Ditto, okay? I checked it myself."

Ditto ignored the device. "Yeah, whatever. Did Myishi give you stock options too?"

Mona lost her temper. "Can't you say anything positive? I'm beginning to wonder whose side you're on."

Ditto jumped to his feet, which didn't make much difference. "What's that supposed to mean?"

Stefan put a hand on Mona's arm. "Leave it."

"No. I'm starting to think that you don't want us to catch the Parasites."

Ditto's face was crimson. "Maybe I don't want us to catch them for Myishi."

"Well, then, maybe you should find some other line of work."

They stared at each other for several seconds, then Ditto broke eye contact, storming off to the elevator.

"You were out of line, Mona," said Stefan, when the echoes of the argument had faded.

Mona folded her arms stubbornly. "So was he."

Stefan stood, selecting a suit from a hanging rail. "You're going to have to apologize before I get back."

"Before *we* get back," said Cosmo. "You'll never get under there without me."

Stefan threw him a smaller suit from the rack. "Well done, Cosmo. I need you to lead me into the lion's den. You're going back to Clarissa Frayne, one last time."

The Clarissa Frayne Institute for the Parentally Challenged

Marshall Redwood wasn't unduly concerned when the two suits came in the front door. The men were probably medical reps looking to test some new product. They looked a bit like a comedy double act. One tall one and one short one. They could have been slave traders as far as Redwood was concerned. If they wanted to kidnap the orphans, Redwood would help them load the truck. He didn't owe the Clarissa Frayne Institute a single thing. Especially not since they'd stuck him behind a desk in the security booth, pending an investigation. And all because of that slippery no-sponsor Cosmo Hill. Apparently Cosmo had survived the dive he took from that rooftop and was now listed as a fugitive. If Cosmo had just been a good little boy and died when he was supposed to, then Redwood would not have to sit here with the other lame idiots, watching TV eight hours a day.

Fred Allescanti, possibly the biggest idiot in Satellite City, was drinking sim-coffee in the security booth's only decent chair.

"Hey, Fred. You want to give me a turn in the swivel chair?"

Fred took another annoying slurp of brown liquid. "No can do, Redwood. My back plays up something terrible if I don't support it right."

Redwood frowned. "What if I just take the chair? Let's say I just go crazy and throw you straight through the window, and just occupy the chair while you're getting your sutures?"

"Go ahead, big shot," grinned Fred. "I could use the compensation money."

Maybe Allescanti wasn't as dumb as he looked.

"Well, at least stop slurping that sim-coffee. I swear, Fred, you're driving me demented. Who knows what I might do?"

Fred pointed at the camera over their heads. "Make sure you do it on camera, Redwood, I can use the footage in my court case."

Redwood's face burned red. Even Fred Allescanti was getting lippy since he'd been demoted. He needed to get back on the streets, back where he had some power. If only he could somehow recover Cosmo Hill.

A red alert began to bip softly on a security computer. The icon was in the shape of a running man. One of the no-sponsors was on the move outside a designated area. At last, someone to vent his frustration on. Redwood activated the tracker-pattern program, running a match on the pattern. One by one the orphans were eliminated, as they were located in their beds or designated leisure areas. Who was on the move? Who was left? The signal was very faint, as if most of the electronegative micro beads used to track the orphans had been removed, or shorted out.

Shorted out? Redwood's heart rate speeded up. Only two orphans could have shorted out their micro beads. One was dead, and the other was Cosmo Hill.

Redwood called up Cosmo's pattern. It was very faint, only the faintest pulse, but definitely active. The marshal doubted if the scanners would have picked him up at all if he weren't close by. Very close by. On his way down to the basement by the looks of it.

Redwood consulted the security screens, checking the two suits he'd mistaken for medical researchers. The short one must be Cosmo. For some insane reason, Hill had actually returned. Redwood didn't know why, and he didn't care. This was his chance to redeem himself. He could bring in Hill and his accomplice. Of course, he would need to talk to Hill alone first, to make sure they had their stories straight about the night of the crash. Redwood stood, taking a rod from the gun cabinet.

"Hey, Redwood," said Fred. "What are you doing with a rod? You're not a floor marshal anymore."

Redwood didn't even look at him. "I'm going on my rounds."

"Rounds? What are you, a doctor? We're security, we don't do rounds here. That's why we have cameras."

"Not in the basement, we don't. It's about time someone checked down there. You want to come?"

Allescanti lolled back in the swivel chair, wrapping his hands around a warm coffee mug. "No thanks, Redwood. It's all yours."

"That's what I thought," said Redwood, holstering the rod.

Cosmo and Stefan walked straight in through the front door. Cosmo's knees almost buckled as soon as the smell of the institute's cheap disinfectant hit his nostrils. He stood still for a moment, allowing the memories to wash over him. Ziplock, Redwood, and years of medical experiments. He took several deep breaths, steeling himself. Stefan peered at him from under the brim of a felt hat.

"Are you okay, Cosmo?" he said, the bristles of his false moustache waving slightly.

"I'm okay. Let's go."

"Are you sure?"

Cosmo nodded. "Ten minutes, and we're in and out."

They approached the admissions booth, and Stefan flashed two laminated fake IDs at a guard playing a handheld video cube. Cosmo kept his head down, in the shadows of his own hat.

"Komposite," said the guard, trying to look as though he cared. "You guys had quite a fire over there last week."

205

Stefan nodded. "Yeah. Took out the entire canteen, worse luck."

The guard shook his head sympathetically. "What are you testing today?"

Stefan patted the attaché case under his arm. "I could tell you, but then I'd have to kill you."

The guard gave him two visitors' passes. "Yeah, sure. Good one. You can collect these ID cards on your way out."

Stefan clipped a pass to his lapel, handing the other to Cosmo. The guard was back playing his video game before they had taken half a dozen steps.

"He never even looked at me," whispered Cosmo.

Stefan smiled. "They don't pay these guards enough to pay attention."

Cosmo led them through a vaulted reception area lined with 3D photos of a long-dead Clarissa Frayne doing noble things with youngsters. Hiking, reading, digging holes, among various other outdoor activities. There was nothing noble about the Frayne Institute. The authorities were more inclined to dip the no-sponsors in experimental vats than take them mountaineering.

They passed several guards, but no one questioned them. They were simply two more suits from some medical company. And anyway, who would possibly have a motive to break into an orphanage? Cosmo kept his eyes down and his collar up, hoping that people would think he was a short man and not a tall kid.

"In here," said Cosmo, shouldering a flimsy plastic door

hidden behind a statue of Clarissa Frayne. In this particular statue, the institute's founder was cradling an abandoned infant. Every orphan in the orphanage had heard stories about Miss Frayne. Apparently the woman had hated children, and she was the one who had coined the term *no-sponsors*.

The doorway opened onto a claustrophobic corridor, devoid of decoration and with only emergency lighting.

"Charming," said Stefan.

"You should see the dormitories."

The corridor became colder as it sank below sea level. The emergency lights grew more and more ancient, until eventually their path was illuminated by wall-mounted coil bulbs.

"Lightbulbs," chuckled Stefan. "You don't see those anymore, outside a movie theater."

"All the power is leeched from the main power lines. Clarissa Frayne has been doing it for as long as I remember. For some reason, down here is the only place no-sponsors can go without being detected."

Stefan nodded. "Of course. The energy leak would white out your scanner patterns."

The corridor sank down and down, until finally they came to a dead end, flanked by two overflow pipes.

"Back in the early days, when the city used to flood, these made sure the basement drained."

"And now?"

Cosmo hauled back a maintenance hatch. It opened surprisingly easily. "Now the orphans use them to hang out."

Inside the pipe were several levels, constructed from cardboard and waste pig iron. Rickety ladders connected each level, descending farther into the darkness.

Stefan tested a ladder with his weight. It collapsed beneath him. "I'm not twelve years old anymore," he said, opening his jacket. Strapped to his chest was the one of the vests that Ditto had stolen from the lawyers on the roof of the Stromberg Building. He tore open the Velcro pad covering the rappelling kit and wrapped the cord around a solid handle.

Stefan slapped his own back. "Okay, Cosmo. Climb on."

Cosmo did as he was told. "Next time, promise me that we'll use the stairs. Just for once."

Stefan winked. "I'll see what I can do," he said, swinging down into the blackness of the pipe.

They seemed to drop forever, right down into the center of the earth. In fact the cord ran out before the pipe. Stefan took a lumi-light from one of his pockets. He snapped it to activate the luminous crystals before dropping it to the ground. The bottom of the pipe was inches away.

"Maybe tonight is our lucky night," he said.

"It's about time."

They disengaged from the rappelling cord, dropping to the floor with a thump. The pipe was almost entirely corroded, so they felt their way out onto a hard rock floor. Cosmo stubbed his toe against a thick cable. He dropped to his knees, tracing it back to a junction box.

"I've got something here. A switch."

"Makes sense," said Stefan. "If the Clarissa Frayne people are stealing power, they would have to be able to see what they're doing. Turn it on, Cosmo."

Cosmo wrapped his fingers around the thick switch and pulled until he heard a sharp click. The cavern was instantly illuminated by a dozen halogen spotlights. They were in a vast tunnel, originally blasted by Satellite City's sandhog crews almost a century ago to accommodate gas, water, and electricity pipes. The hundred-foot-high power conduits had been stripped back to bare wire in places and were feeding several small generators. A bass hum emanated from the naked wires.

The wires weren't exactly naked. They were clothed in a luminous blue carpet. Sleeping Parasites. Millions of them. Each creature's silver heart pulsed in time with the alternating current.

Stefan tightened his grip on the energy pulse.

"This must be the place," he whispered.

Cosmo's first thought was to run. It was his second thought too.

Stefan placed a hand on his shoulder. "Don't worry, Cosmo. We're not dying or in pain. If we were, they'd be all over us. All we have to do is tread carefully, and there's no reason for the Parasites to take any notice. Hell, we could sing an opera now, and it wouldn't wake them up. They don't respond to sound, just pain."

"You're sure about that? You have actual evidence?"

"Not as such, no. But I feel it in my gut."

Cosmo giggled with more than a touch of hysteria. "I'm feeling something in my gut too."

"All you have to do is stay here. I'll plant the energy pulse, then we go out the way we came in. Two minutes. That's it."

Stefan walked carefully through the maze of piping and cable, stepping over sleeping Parasites as he went. His aim was to plant the pulse as close to the heart of the group as he could, where it would do the most damage. They could remote detonate it from the street, unleashing an electrical storm on the creatures. If Ellie Faustino's theory was correct, the dirty energy should rip the hearts right out of the Parasites, but not affect the humans at all, so long as they weren't too close to the blast.

Stefan climbed an ancient stepladder, gently wedging the attaché case beneath the main pipe's lower curve. There were Parasites all around him, breathing, glowing, living.

He climbed down the ladder, turning to give Cosmo the thumbs-up. He never completed the gesture, because Cosmo was not alone. A large man had him pinned by the neck from behind, with a rod pressed into the skin of his cheek.

"Hi," said the man. "Nice of you to drop in and plant a bomb under us all."

Stefan was accustomed to acting under pressure. If it had been just him and the stranger, he would have gone for his rod, but now somebody else's life was in danger.

"Do it," said the man, grinning. "Reach for your weapon,

and this kid will be sucking plastic faster than you can blink."

"Take it easy, Redwood," said Cosmo. "You don't know what's going on here."

"I know, all right," said Redwood. "You're trying to blow up the Institute and put me out of a job. Agnes would love that."

Stefan took a slow step closer. "Redwood? I've heard of you. You like to beat up children. You want to take a chance on someone your own size?"

Redwood laughed. "My own size? Kid, you're half a foot taller than me. I'm not stupid. Just take out your weapon and slide it over."

Stefan felt a bead of sweat slide down his backbone. They were safe from the creatures, unless someone got hurt—then the Parasites would awaken. "Okay, Redwood, take it easy. Here's my lightning rod."

Stefan lifted his weapon from its holster with two fingers. He set the rod down, kicking it across the floor. "There, you see. I'm unarmed."

"And the detonator," ordered Redwood. "Don't tell me you were going to blow yourself up with the building. You have a detonator there somewhere, so hand it over."

Stefan ground his teeth in frustration. "Redwood, this is not what you think. Just listen for a minute . . ."

Redwood jammed the rod under Cosmo's chin. "*You* listen, moron. It's simple enough. Give me the detonator or I wrap the boy, for starters."

"Okay, okay. Here it comes."

Stefan unbuttoned a flap on his suit pants, drawing out a metal cylinder with a red button on top. The red button was protected by a plasti-glass cap. Idiot-proof. No timer, just flick and press.

Stefan gave diplomacy one last shot. "Redwood . . . Marshal Redwood. This is not a bomb. It's an energy pulse. There are creatures all around us . . ."

"Shut up!" commanded Redwood, jamming the shrink wrapper painfully into Cosmo's neck. Painfully. Pain.

The Parasites began to sit up. Electricity was all very well, but if there was pain to be had . . .

"Slide over the detonator now!"

A wave of Parasites popped up like falling dominoes in reverse, their soulful eyes searching for the source of the pain. A million eyes landed on Cosmo. A million and counting.

"Redwood," stammered Cosmo. "We have to get out of here now. They're coming."

The Parasites sprang from their perches, advancing in waves across the rock floor. They ignored Stefan completely, focusing on Cosmo.

Stefan flicked the detonator's lid. "Let him go, Redwood, or we all go up."

"You're bluffing!" spat Redwood. "You won't do it. You're no fanatic."

Stefan's thumb hovered over the button. "You know something, you're right. We're not fanatics. In fact we're really *grounded*."

The parasites flowed around him, leaping over his head. Stefan was barely visible in a sea of blue.

Grounded? thought Cosmo. What does he mean?

Then he got it. *Grounded*, of course. Cosmo made sure his rubber-soled boots made solid contact with the tunnel floor, and closed his eyes. This was going to sting.

Stefan's thumb settled on the button. "Last chance, Marshal. What are you going to do?"

The Parasites were inches from Cosmo's neck.

"I'm going to wrap the kid first, then you," said Redwood.

"Wrong answer," said Stefan, and pressed the button.

The energy pulse detonated, releasing a blue mushroom cloud of tainted power into the tunnel. With the howl of a hurricane, the mushroom grew to fill the space, then sank into the rock. The halogen spotlights blew out immediately, sending sparks showering down like neon snow. Lightning bolts sparked from the center of the blast, targeting the Parasite's silver hearts. They were skewered, dozens on each bolt, vibrating as the dirty energy passed through their organic filters. The lightning bolts split like a spider's web, spearing Parasite after Parasite in turn. The creatures attempted to deal with the sudden influx of power, but it was too much for their systems. One by one they flashed blue, then collapsed to the rock floor, their silver hearts cold and black.

The humans fared slightly better, especially Cosmo and Stefan. Their rubber-soled boots conducted the worst of the shock away from their bodies. Nevertheless, they were given a severe rattling by the power surge. Cosmo felt his eyes roll back in his head, and the legs of his trousers began to smoke. Stefan's hair stood tall on his head, and his jacket caught fire. He whipped it off, slapping it against the rocks.

Redwood was not so lucky. He had stupidly released his grip on Cosmo when he realized that Stefan was not bluffing. If he'd only held on for a few more seconds, the energy surge would have passed right through him into the boy. As it was he felt the full brunt of the charge. The effect, while not as spectacular as what happened to the Parasites, was no less permanent. The electricity ignited the viscous hair oil he liked to slather on his precious locks, and burnt every follicle of hair from his head. Not only that, but it scorched the pores so the hairs could not grow again. Then the electricity picked the marshal up as if in a giant fist and slammed him into the tunnel wall. As he lay there, his clothes singed and dropped off, until the man was left wearing nothing more than Bugs Bunny long-johns.

Cosmo shook the shock from his system. "What is that?"

The room was lit by lightning bolts.

Stefan picked up his lightning rod. "Bugs Bunny. A 2D rabbit. " 'What's up, Doc?' That was his catchphrase."

The light faded as the Parasites dropped to the ground. Their hearts were black and shriveled like lumps of coal.

"We did it," said Stefan, his smile grim in the fading light.

"Yes. We got them."

Stefan snapped a lumi-light. "Not all of them, but it's a start. We know it can be done. Now, we need to get out of here, or we'll be blamed for this, and not the good marshal."

Cosmo nodded. Redwood would take the blame for the power cut. It was a nice bonus.

One of the marshal's eyes flickered open.

Cosmo leaned in close. "That was for Ziplock, Bugs," he said.

The Clarissa Frayne Institute for the Parentally Challenged was in total chaos. Not only was the main generator gone, but the emergency power too. The dormitory gates had been deactivated, and the tracker program was dead. The no-sponsors were running riot. Most of the guards were on transfer duty, so it was left to a single squad to maintain order.

Fred Allescanti had taken charge with disastrous results. So far he had managed to wrap two of his own men, and allowed several orphans to slip through the main doors. Lucky for the security team, the fire doors locked automatically in the event of a power cut. It had finally occurred to Allescanti to construct a barricade at the foot of the main stairs. They would hold the orphans there until power was restored.

Cosmo and Stefan approached the madness from behind. Fred Allescanti was firing cellophane slugs at anyone who poked his head around the corner. So far he had only hit things he wasn't aiming at. The stairwell was covered with so many globs of cellophane that it resembled the inside of a handkerchief.

"You no-sponsors had better get back to bed," he roared. "Or you'll spend tomorrow in a vat, I'm not kidding you."

Cosmo felt his temper rising. "Those kids will suffer," he told Stefan. "Every time something goes wrong, the guards blame us."

Stefan handed his charred jacket to Cosmo. "Not this time," he said.

The tall Russian youth drew his lightning rod and loaded a clip of gum balls. He slimed three of the guards from behind, and disabled the other three with well-placed blows. In all it took about four seconds.

The orphans came down the stairs like a tide, crashing the barricade and pooling around Stefan's boots.

"Any of you ever been outside on your own?" asked Stefan.

A little kid shuffled forward, his eyes barely visible behind a hank of black hair. "I escaped to the streets for a couple of weeks before they bagged me."

"What's your name?"

"My street name is Fence, on account of that's what I do."

Stefan took his hand, then wrote a number on the boy's palm. "Run south, boys, past the blockade. Fence knows the way. When you get to the canal, call this number."

Fence raised his free hand.

"Yes, Fence?"

"They got some kind of trackers on us. Last time, the marshals bagged me as soon as I set one foot outside Booshka."

"Did you feel a shock just now, before the lights went out?"

The boys nodded. Some of them still had socket hair.

"That was an energy pulse. It shorted out the power and the tracker micro beads in your pores. You're free to go."

The orphans were silent for a moment, digesting this momentous news. Then they burst into spontaneous cheers, clambering up Stefan's tall frame like squirrels.

"Hold it, now," said Stefan. "You have to move before reinforcements show up. Call this number. The man on the other end is a friend of mine. He's always on the lookout for market boys. He'll give you work and a place to stay. The wages aren't huge, but they're fair."

Fence squinted. "This could be another trick. How do we know we can trust you?"

Cosmo stepped forward. "Remember me, Fence?"

Fence swept the hair from his eyes. "Cosmo Hill. Wrap me if it isn't. We all thought you were dead. What happened to your face?"

Cosmo rubbed the bulging robotix plate in his forehead. "It's a long story, Fence, maybe later. Just do what Stefan says. You can trust him. He saved my life, and anyway, life outside has got to be better than in here. This is the only chance you will ever have to make a clean break."

The word spread along the stairway. Cosmo was alive, and this man was his friend. If Cosmo could survive on the outside, they all could.

"Okay," said Fence. "I'll call the number, but if you're setting us up, I will hunt you down."

The little boy stuck out his hand. Stefan shook it. "Fair enough."

A siren sounded in the distance. Obviously, news of the breakout had spread to the authorities.

"Time to go," said Cosmo. "Now or never."

"Now," decided the diminutive Fence, leading the no-sponsors into the night, like a modern-day Pied Piper.

Abracadabra Street

Mona knew she would have to apologize to Ditto; she was just putting it off for as long as possible. Crunch time came when Stefan called to say they were on the way home. The mission had been a total success, and they'd be pulling into the garage in ten minutes. If she didn't shake off her sulk right now and apologize, Stefan would drag her up onto the roof.

"Oh, all right," she moaned to no one in particular. "I'll apologize, but only because I'm the bigger person, in more ways than one."

The elevator was on the roof level, so to save time, Mona took the fire escape. The elevator was so old that it still had ropes and pulleys instead of a magnetic field. By the time it reached her floor, she could have finished apologizing and cooked a five-course meal.

Mona climbed the outside of 1405 Abracadabra Street, keeping close to the wall to avoid the acid mist that shimmered earthward. Pretty soon that mist would turn to mothball-size raindrops, and the sound of car alarms would reverberate through Satellite City.

She arrived on the rooftop just as Ditto was leaving it. The Bartoli baby had laid down a ladder and was crossing to an adjacent building.

"Hey, Ditto, what are you doing?"

But the wind snatched her words away, and Ditto did not turn around. Very strange. What did he think he was playing at? Mona knew what she should do was come back later. But she also knew she wouldn't. This entire situation was too intriguing. So, moving with catlike grace and silence, Mona followed her fellow Supernaturalist across to the next building.

Ditto had left the ladder down, so that meant he intended on coming back. Mona would have to be careful. If she didn't return before Ditto, she could be stranded on this rooftop with the rain coming.

Ditto hurried across the pig-iron surface, skirting the oily puddles that had been eating through the roof over the years. Mona clambered on top of the roof box. From there she could see everything; but from his low vantage point, Ditto could not see her.

The diminutive Supernaturalist crossed to the northern corner of the building. The Statue of Endeavor punctuated the skyline beyond him, its red light winking in his hand. There was a blue light too. Closer. On the rooftop itself. Mona drew a sharp breath. A single Parasite lay in the shadow of the roof's edge. That explained it. Ditto must have seen the creature on the Parabola and had come to investigate.

What would he do now? He never carried a weapon, and

Stefan had already detonated their only energy surge. Mona was about to leap down from the roof box and join her companion when Ditto did a strange thing. He knelt down before the creature and held out his hand. The Parasite, weak from lack of energy, its pulsating heart a dull blue, reached out its four-fingered hand toward Ditto's. They were acknowledging each other. Communicating.

Mona nearly fell off the roof. This was incredible. Who was Ditto? What was he? All this time, had he been a traitor in their midst? She fumbled her phone from her pocket, calling up Stefan's number on the speed dial. But no. That wasn't enough. It would still be her word against Ditto's. She needed more.

Mona's phone was a pretty old one, without much in the way of technology. But it did have picture capabilities. Sixty seconds of video or a hundred stills. Mona selected video, and pointed the phone's fish-eye lense toward Ditto and his blue friend. Just in time to see Ditto deliberately cut his finger with a penknife and offer the wound to the Parasite. The creature wrapped four fingers around the wound, draining a silver stream of life force. In seconds its natural bright blue color had been restored. It released Ditto, and floated to its feet.

Mona checked the video to make sure she had seen what she thought she'd seen. Ditto had healed the Parasite. It all made sense now. Of course Ditto never carried a rod, of course he had argued against the energy pulse. He was in league with the Parasites.

Ditto was sucking the wound on his finger when the elevator

door opened. Stefan and Cosmo were back. They were gathered around Mona in a tight group, looking at something. Her phone screen.

"Hey, what is that?" asked the Bartoli baby. "One of those comedy e-mails? Some of those things are hilarious."

Stefan took the phone in trembling hands. His face was tight and pale. "Yes, Ditto. Do you want to take a look? It's a real scream. By the way, what happened to your finger?"

Pins and needles erupted all over Ditto's back. "I caught it on that panel, on the elevator door. You know the one that sticks out."

"I know the one. Here, have a look."

Ditto took the phone, pressing the *play* triangle. For a moment he didn't realize what he was looking at, but then it became terrifyingly clear. He had been caught. Rumbled. Finally. After all this time, the moment of truth had come. Or, the moment *for* truth.

"Okay," he said, handing back the phone. "This looks bad, I know, but I can explain."

Stefan looked straight ahead, avoiding Ditto's eyes. "Pack your gear and get out. I want you gone by morning."

"Wait a minute. Hear me out."

Mona advanced on the Bartoli baby. "All this time, why didn't I see it? No wonder you wouldn't shoot the Parasites. No wonder you argued against anything that might actually work."

Ditto backed up a step. "Anything that might actually work? It wasn't like that."

"What was it like then, Ditto? Every day, stabbing us in the

221

back. Stabbing humans everywhere in the back. Why don't you go over to Clarissa Frayne and heal all those Parasites Cosmo just blew up?"

Ditto hung his head. "I wish I could," he mumbled.

The comment enraged Stefan. He picked Ditto up by the collar, standing him on a workbench. "You wish you could! How long have you been betraying us, Ditto? From the very beginning? Three years?"

The accusations beat down on Ditto like hammer blows. The little man seemed to shrink even further, hunching in on himself.

Stefan poked him in the chest. "If I see you again, I will treat you like an enemy, and believe me, you don't want that."

"You don't understand, Stefan," protested the Bartoli baby. "You don't see what's happening."

Stefan laughed in his face. "Oh, let me guess, another conspiracy theory. Myishi is running us for their own ends. Ellie Faustino has been lying through her teeth."

The truth burst out of Ditto like a missile. "They take pain!" he blurted.

Cosmo felt that something big was coming. Whatever Ditto said next would change all of their lives forever.

"The Parasites take pain. Not life force, just pain. They help us. They have always helped us."

Stefan turned his back on Ditto. He didn't want to hear this. "Rubbish. You'll say anything to save your skin."

"Do you remember what Lincoln asked me at the junkyard?"

Mona remembered. "Your mutes. He asked if you were sensitive."

Ditto sat on the bench. "Bartoli babies often have certain gifts. I have healing hands. I can take your pain away."

"I knew it," said Cosmo. "After my accident, you took my headache. You said it was the medicine, but it was you."

Ditto nodded. "This gift is something I have in common with the Parasites. We do the same thing; maybe that's why I'm sensitive to them. I feel the supernatural, and they feel me. People call it second sight."

Cosmo remembered something. "Back in the junkyard, Lincoln said you had healing hands. I thought he was talking about you being a medic, but he knew taking pain was a Bartoli mutation."

Ditto examined his own palms. "They're not actually healing hands. Nothing heals the body faster than the body itself. I just take away pain."

Stefan absolutely refused to believe it. "This is junk. All junk."

"Parasites are nature!" Ditto persisted. "They are energy converters, just like me. Just like every other being on the planet in one way or another. All my life I've been able to see them. To feel them. I was afraid of them at first, until I realized they were just doing what I did. They aren't some malignant species. They're attracted to pain. They take it and convert it to energy. The cycle of all life."

Stefan whirled. His face was red with barely suppressed anger. "And what about my mother? I saw what the Parasites did to her."

"She was dying," said Ditto softly. "They helped her. They eased her passing. The Parasites take the pain away, when it's too late for the body to heal itself. That used to be the case before they began multiplying out of control. Before we upset the natural order."

"One reason. Give us one good reason to believe you now, when you have lied to us for so long."

Ditto sat at the table, rubbing his eyes with the heels of his hands. "For as long as I can remember, the creatures have been there. We don't communicate exactly. Not like humans, but we sense each other. I know when they're agitated or sleepy. There was one other Bartoli baby with the same ability. Number eighty-two. But the second sight terrified him, drove him insane. Now he lives in Booshka and wears a blindfold. Never takes it off. I didn't go crazy, because I suspected the creatures were there to help us: make the pain bearable, prepare us for the next life."

Cosmo interrupted. "There's a next life?"

"Yes. I catch glimpses of it every now and then."

Even Mona was interested. "What's it like?"

Ditto thought about it. "Different."

"Quiet!" yelled Stefan. "All of you. If this is true, why didn't you tell me years ago?"

Ditto lifted his eyes. "I almost told you a million times, but I had no real proof except what I felt. For the first time ever I was part of a family and saying what I felt would have destroyed that. And for what? You would never have believed me then without proof. If anything, you were more fanatical in the beginning. Time is beginning to mellow you, Stefan. Recently you've even started to worry about the troops. That's a new development."

"You could have tried!"

"I know I should have, but I decided to do what I could from within. You weren't actually destroying the Parasites—I felt that all along—and I was able to do whatever I could for the accident victims. I didn't know we were helping the creatures reproduce."

"Fight from the inside," muttered Cosmo.

Ditto nodded. "Exactly, and it would have been just fine if Myishi hadn't got involved. Do you realize what you did tonight, Stefan? If what you say is true, you killed a huge number of the creatures. I wish I'd had the courage to tell you the truth earlier, but I never thought this energy pulse scheme would work. Scientifically it shouldn't. How many humans are in pain right now because I stayed quiet? Humans like your mother?"

Stefan began to shake. "Shut up!"

"You don't want to listen, Stefan, because for years you've had someone to blame for your mother's death. This is the truth, Stefan. Accept it."

"I don't know what it is, but it's not the truth. Nothing you've ever told us was the truth. You wouldn't know the truth if it popped out of a manhole and took a bite out of your Bartoli backside."

Ditto took out his phone. "Just call Faustino. Tell her you have reservations. Ask her team of scientists to study the possibility that these creatures do not drain life force, just pain. Natural anesthesia."

"Why should I?"

"Because if I'm right, thousands of people are crippled with pain who shouldn't be. Just as your mother wasn't, at the end. Just as you weren't, if you let yourself remember."

Cosmo remembered how, after his rooftop fall, his pain had disappeared the moment the creature had touched him. He remembered how all he'd felt was calm. No fear.

"And if you're wrong?" asked Stefan.

Ditto stood on the bench, drawing himself up to his full height. "If I'm wrong, I'll pop out of a manhole and take a bite out of my own Bartoli backside."

Ellen Faustino was in the car when Stefan called. "I thought I might be hearing from you, Stefan," she said, a smile tugging at one corner of her lips. "That was you at the Satellite, wasn't it? Floyd Faustino indeed. However did you get those access codes? Surely I didn't accidentally allow you to glimpse my computer screen."

"I don't know what you're talking about," said Stefan innocently.

"I thought you might take matters into your own hands," continued Ellen. "In fact I hoped you might. Sometimes the red tape just takes too long to unravel."

"It's starting to sound like I'm working for you, Professor Faustino."

Faustino's smile widened. "Yes, it does, doesn't it? That

was you at Clarissa Frayne, too, I presume. The Supernatur-alists don't waste any time, do they?"

Stefan chose his words carefully. "If that was us, and I'm not for one second admitting that it might have been, then we may have a problem."

Ellie frowned. "A problem? But the energy pulse worked perfectly. I would have preferred if you hadn't knocked out the power in ten city blocks, but it was short term, and my team has been gathering Un-spec four bodies all morning."

It was Stefan's turn to frown. "Gathering bodies? What for? Why?"

Ellie held a finger to her lips. "I don't want to say any more on a company line, I've already said too much. Just excited, I suppose. You can see for yourself on your next visit."

"To pick up my paycheck?" said Stefan wryly.

"I'm a busy woman, Stefan. What's this problem that has you so worried?"

"One of my team, a soon to be ex-member, feels that the Parasites, Un-spec four that is, may not be as malignant as we thought. He believes that they simply ease our suffering. Take our pain, as it were. If that's true, then there's no need to fight them."

"What?" Faustino paused. "I can't imagine how that would be possible, but I'll put my entire team on it immediately. No more energy pulses until we determine the truth. Just stand down for the time being, until we can put some trials together. It shouldn't take more than a couple of weeks to get results. Can you wait that long?"

"I've waited three years," replied Stefan. "I can wait a couple of weeks."

Faustino's eyes were downcast. "I know that this must be hard for you to accept, Stefan. But, remember, nothing has been proven yet. We may still be on the right track."

"Two weeks," said Stefan, closing the phone.

Ditto released a breath he'd been holding for almost the entire call. "Two weeks. I'm right, you'll see."

Stefan threw his phone to him. "I don't want to hear it, Ditto. Whatever the results of Professor Faustino's trials, you've been lying to us for years. We put our faith and our lives in your hands, and they never were your priority."

"I never did anything to hurt anybody or anything. I won't apologize for that."

"It's too late for apologies, Ditto. You deceived us all. We can't trust you anymore. At first light, I want you out of here."

Ditto looked up into Stefan's eyes. They were hard and hurt. "Very well. If that's how you want it, that's how it will be."

Stefan turned his back on the Bartoli baby. "That's how I want it," he said.

Cosmo lay on his bunk, watching a cluster of rust mites eating into a bolt head on the ceiling. It seemed that as soon as the Supernaturalists came out of one crisis, another one dropped from the sky on their heads. Cosmo felt like a rat in a maze, never knowing what seemingly innocent course of action would lead to disaster. And for what? So they could persecute a group of supernatural creatures who were just trying to help mankind? If what Ditto said was true.

Look on the bright side, he told himself. At least your hair is growing. In a couple of months, you won't look like the back end of a troll anymore.

Mona appeared in the doorway to his cubicle. "*Oye*, you awake?"

Cosmo sat up on the bunk. "Yes. I got a couple of hours sleep, but I dreamed about Ditto."

Mona perched on the end of the bunk. "I know what you mean. I don't think Stefan can cope with this. First he's helping the Parasites multiply, then it seems they were only trying to take our pain."

"If Ditto is right."

"Yes, if Ditto is right."

Mona pulled her hair back into a ponytail, wrapping a band around it. "I've been thinking about moving on, Cosmo. Maybe getting a job with Jean-Pierre in Booshka—he's been trying to rope me in for years. Anyway, if he's not going to be around much longer, someone has to keep the gangs' cars on the road."

Cosmo felt his stomach churn. The idea of Mona actually leaving had never occurred to him. "Are you sure? You seem like such an action girl."

Mona smiled. "Yeah, I love the shoot-'em-up. It's like a vid game. Blast the evil blue aliens. But they're not aliens, and maybe they're not even evil. I don't think I could point a rod at something unless I was one-hundred-percent certain."

Cosmo nodded. He felt the same.

"So I was thinking. I'm going to need a grease monkey. Someone who learns quick. You think you could do a sim-oil change?"

Cosmo grinned, his teeth shining in the darkness. "Me? You want me to come with you?"

Mona punched his shoulder. "Why not? We make a good team. You're always saving me . . ."

Cosmo opened his mouth to say yes, but the word stuck in his throat. "I'd love to, Mona. There's nothing I'd like more, but Stefan took me in."

Mona's eyes were sad, but not surprised. "I understand, Cosmo. Don't worry, I'm not going anywhere until Ellen Faustino has finished her tests. Maybe you'll change your mind."

"Maybe," said Cosmo gloomily. Just him and Stefan. What a laugh riot that would be.

Myishi paralegals were very good at being quiet. An entire squadron could run past a deer, and the animal would never even cock its head. They also had a lot of high-tech gadgetry that helped them to be even more sneaky. Each paralegal carried a total of thirty pounds of equipment to help them climb, cut, burn, and capture.

The paralegals and their thirty pounds were transported through the air by Myishi Whisper Copters, a combination helicopter and glider with vertical liftoff capability and rigid glider wings. Not to mention, enough armament to obliterate anything stupid enough to point more than a finger at it.

The paralegals had several methods of entry in their manual, but their all-time favorite was *ghostlike*. They liked their quarry to wake up in a cellophane wrap, with no idea how he got there. No fatalities. Less paperwork.

Abracadabra Street was no great challenge for a squadron that had broken into several foreign banks, two crime lords' strongholds, and a private kindergarten. They simply rappelled down the walls, set radio jammers to cancel out the motion sensors, and adhered large squares of glass solvent to the windows.

When the squadron leader gave the command, the paralegals passed a current through the solvent squares and suckered the windows out of their panes. The entire procedure was covered by the building's heavy curtains.

Two dozen paralegals entered the premises through various entrances, and set their goggles for body heat. When the command was given they split into four groups and went after their specified targets.

In truth, many of the paralegals felt slightly disappointed. They had heard a lot about the vigilante Stefan Bashkir, and were hoping he would make a real fight of it. But it looked as though this would be done the easy way. Nobody would resist them here. It didn't even look like anyone was awake.

Cosmo opened his eyes to find three Myishi paralegals in his cubicle. One was jacking a cartridge into his rod. Cosmo took a deep breath to inflate his chest.

"You've done this before," said the paralegal, pulling the trigger.

* * *

Mona, always a light sleeper, actually made it out of the bed before they got her. Amazingly, for a girl with no formal combat training, she managed to incapacitate two paralegals before the third tagged her with a Shocker. They waited until she had stopped shaking to hit her with a cellophane slug.

Stefan heard the struggle in Mona's cubicle. He burst through his own cubicle door, straight into the arms of half a dozen paralegals. Several more were packing up the Supernaturalists' weaponry and computers. For the first time in his life, Stefan Bashkir went without a fight.

"You're making a mistake," he said, lacing his fingers behind his head. "We are working with Myishi. Just contact President Faustino at the R&D department. I'm telling you, this is all a mistake."

A paralegal wrapped him at close range. "That's what they all say," he said.

Ditto was lying awake on his cot, fully clothed. His duffel bag sat on the floor, ready for the morning.

"Pazza delivery?" he said to the first paralegal through the door.

"No one likes a smart-ass," said the man, and wrapped him.

CHAPTER 9
LAB RATS

Myishi Research and Development Facility,
Mayor Ray Shine Industrial Park, Satellite City

THE MYISHI PARALEGALS READ the Supernaturalists their rights, then winched them up to a waiting Whisper Copter on the roof. They took a ten-minute hop north to the Ray Shine Industrial Park, landing on a helipad on the roof of a Myishi facility. Cosmo's favorite vat man was waiting for them beside the plasti-glass vat in the building's detention area.

"Hiya, sweetie," he said, attaching the suction cup to Cosmo's head. "I had a feeling we'd be seeing each other again. They flew me over here especially for this job. I'm on double overtime."

The Supernaturalists were tossed unceremoniously into the vat of yellow acid, dangling from a series of suction cups. The sedative in the cellophane had seeped into their systems by then, so they offered no resistance, relaxing in their liquid prison. The acid solution immediately went to work on the cellophane wraps, eating through the virus coating. It was a slow process and it would be at least an hour before they had any mobility. Until that time, they had no choice but to hang there and think nice thoughts. Any struggle would only tighten the cellophane's grip on their chests.

Once the vat man had finished tying off the last Supernaturalist, he made a call on the building intercom. Within minutes, Ellen Faustino arrived, flanked by two bodyguards. When she saw the Supernaturalists suspended in the vat, she actually slapped the vat man on the chest.

"What do you think you are doing?" she demanded. "These people are supposed to be dead! All I wanted to see was four bodies to be sure they were dead. These are clearly very much alive."

Inside the vat, Faustino's words cut through Stefan's daze. *Dead!* There must be a mistake. What was happening here? Why would Professor Faustino want them dead? Ellen Faustino wouldn't want anybody dead. She was a scientist.

The vat man didn't exactly bow, but he came close. "Sorry, President Faustino. Nobody told me. I'll lower them immediately. In twelve hours there'll be nothing left but molecules."

Stefan tried to speak, but his breath barely rippled the cellophane. He thrashed weakly in the acid vat, but the wrap held him tightly.

"So you're awake, Stefan," said Faustino, resting her palms against the plasti-glass.

Stefan's mouth couldn't ask why, so his eyes did it for him.

"Are you confused?" asked Faustino. "Don't you understand what's happening here?"

They were all listening, fighting the sedative.

"It's as I told you, Stefan, you were working for me. All of you. The Supernaturalists were cutting corners that I couldn't. Getting jobs done that would take me months to get clearance for. And I don't have that kind of time."

She paused in her narrative, ordering the vat man to the other side of the facility.

"This is top-secret stuff," she explained. "If he hears any more, I'll have to kill him, and good vat men are hard to find. Things were going fine until you developed a conscience. You found Un-spec four, just as I knew you would, and you set off the energy pulse. If I had tried to do either of those sneaky things, I would surely have been found out."

Stefan didn't feel very sneaky at the moment. He felt gullible and naive.

"It could have been perfect; the Supernaturalists knock out the Parasites, and my team collects them. I would have developed a clean power source and saved the Satellite. But now, suddenly, after three years, the obsessed Stefan Bashkir changes his mind and doesn't want to fight Parasites anymore. Now the Supernaturalists are no longer assets, they are loose ends. And we all know what happens to loose ends. They get cut. In a few hours there will be no trace of you or your little group. I even had my boys confiscate your equipment from Abracadabra Street. There won't be so much as a computer file or a fingerprint left by the time I'm finished."

Stefan swung his lower body at the tank wall, but his rubber-soled boots bounced harmlessly off the plasti-glass.

Faustino laughed. "Still the same little Stefan. Fighting all the way. Just like your mother." She leaned closer to the tank. "There are two more things you should know, just to punish you for slowing down my plan. First, your teammate is correct. Of course Un-spec four do not suck life force. Only an obsessive like you could believe that. We conducted tests on lab rats. Several rats were injured. Those kept in an underwater environment, away from Un-spec four, survived no longer than the ones helped by the Parasites. We also conducted human trials, on . . . ah . . . volunteers. The results were the same. Intervention by Un-spec four actually lowered the subjects' stress levels. They take pain only. To cap it all off, their energy emissions actually seem to be repairing the ozone layer. That bit about them destabilizing the Satellite was just another lie to get you hooked. If it makes you feel any better, the Pulse did not kill them. Energy cannot be destroyed—basic science. The Pulse does seem to have rendered them sterile, so levels will quickly drop to normal."

Cosmo felt his eyelids droop. Stay awake, he told himself. Or you may never wake again. Beside him, Mona was already unconscious. But Stefan's eyes grew brighter by the minute. Hate kept him going, as it had for three years.

"You're really going to love this second piece of information, Stefan," continued Faustino. "If you ever bothered to check my academy record, Stefan, you might have seen that several other cadets suffered near-death experiences."

Faustino watched Stefan intently, waiting for him to get it. Suddenly he did, jerking violently inside his cellophane cocoon.

Ellen clapped her hands. "Well done. The penny drops. That's right, Stefan. I was already working for Myishi, even back then, and you were part of an experiment. I became a Spotter through a genuine accident, but you were created. I realized how Spotters were made, and decided to make a few more. Did you never think it strange that the ambulance just happened to be around the corner? All arranged. Eventually I would have recruited you to my group, but you quit the force and started up a little group of your own. It was unfortunate about your mother, but it is against regulations to carry passengers in a police cruiser, so you have only yourself to blame."

Stefan stopped struggling abruptly, hanging from his suction cup. Bitter tears coursed down his cheeks, pooling inside the cellophane.

"Aw," crooned Faustino. "Have I broken your spirit? What a shame."

She snapped her fingers, summoning the vat man. "Dunk them," she ordered. "I don't want as much as a back tooth left to trace them back to R&D."

"No problem, Madam President," said the man. "Consider them out of your life." He climbed the steps to the suction-cup winches, freeing the ratchets on each one. The cogs spun freely, submerging the Supernaturalists' heads in the giant vat of acidic compound.

"Nicely done," said Ellen Faustino. "Expect a little bonus in your paycheck."

"Thank you, Madam President, always a pleasure."

But the vat man was talking to himself; Ellen Faustino was already gone. There was work to be done, and she did not have a few hours to watch Supernaturalists dissolve in acid.

Of course, dissolving was the least of the Supernaturalists' problems. They would suffocate long before the acidic compound could get to work on their skin and bone. The cellophane had relaxed its grip slightly, but not enough to allow them to climb out of the vat. By the time their limbs were free, any pockets of air trapped in the cellophane would have long since leaked out.

Cosmo struggled against sleep. The rest of the group had already succumbed to the cellophane's sedative. He could only guess that his own system was building a resistance to the chemical because he had been wrapped three times now.

Think, he told himself. It's up to you. There must be a good idea in your head somewhere. There must be something in that patched-up head . . . Wait a minute. Something in his head.

A memory flashed across Cosmo's vision. In the warehouse, after his accident. Mona had said something to him: *Lucky for you Ditto had a couple of robotix plates lying around. He used one to patch your fractured skull. Those robotix plates are made of the same material used to armor assault tanks. When your skin heals up, Ditto says you'll be able to head-butt your way through a brick wall.*

The robotix plate.

Cosmo wiggled his way across to the vat wall, drawing his head back as far as possible. Struggling against sleep, breathlessness, and thick liquid, he butted the plasti-glass with all his strength. The tank wall flexed slightly, and a bolt of pain shot through Cosmo's forehead.

The vat man wandered over curiously. "Hey, sweetie," he said, grinning. "Are you trying to escape? I'm afraid skin and bone are not going to do it." He rapped on the tank. "Plasti-glass. Nothing short of an assault tank is going to get you out of here."

Of course, Cosmo didn't hear any of that. All he could hear was the shrill whine of his own headache. There was no option but to try once more. Gritting his teeth, he butted the plasti-glass again. When the pain receded, he noticed a tiny crack in the tank.

"Stop that," said the vat man, rubbing the crack with his thumb. "I have to clean this thing."

One more, thought Cosmo. I have breath for one more.

Cosmo pulled back his head, and with the all the strength in his head, neck, chest, and spine, butted the plasti-glass in precisely the same spot. A clang reverberated around the vat walls.

The crack widened, spreading to the outside of the tank.

One drop. Just one drop.

"Give it up, kiddo," chortled vat man. "Just go to sleep. Make it easy on yourself."

The crack spread some more, like the web of a silver orb-weaving spider. A single drop of yellow acid wormed through the gap, eating into the untreated interior of the plasti-glass pane.

Vat man frowned. "How did you—"

The plasti-glass blew. It probably took the cracks a few seconds to decimate the front of the tank, but it seemed instantaneous. The vat man's jaw had just enough time to drop open in disbelief before his mouth was filled to overflow with acidic compound. Several thousand gallons of acid followed the first spurt, careering across the facility floor into various corners. The Supernaturalists and their harnesses were borne along with the deluge, dashed onto the tiles like fish in a fish box.

The vat man fared worst. His slight frame met the liquid hammer blow head-on, not to mention several sections of plasti-glass that battered him halfway up an adjacent wall. He slid back down to the submerged floor, a lump already rising on his head.

I may as well go to sleep now, thought Cosmo. Everybody else has.

Of course, the Supernaturalists were not in the clear yet, hampered, as they were, by unconsciousness and cellophane wraps. At any moment another member of Myishi personnel could stroll into the vat department and discover the disaster, or security could switch on the monitor and realize that things were far from dandy in the basement. But at least the

Supernaturalists were alive for the moment, something no betting man would have put money on.

Minutes passed slowly, ticking by to the tune of yellow grunge dripping from the shattered vat. As time moved on, the acid did its work, slowly eating through the cellophane wraps. Forty minutes it took, but finally Stefan was free. As untainted air flushed the sedative from his lungs, consciousness returned. He punched his way free of the final cellophane strands, like a butterfly shaking off its cocoon. He struggled to his knees, coughing up an acrid mixture of cellophane and acidic liquid. Slowly his dreams were replaced by recent memories.

"Faustino," he breathed, gingerly releasing the vacuum cup on his head.

Ditto was next to wake. "What did I tell you? Who's the traitor now?"

Stefan ripped the remaining cellophane from the Bartoli baby's frame. "Seems like all my friends are lying to me these days."

Ditto cleared his lungs loudly. "The ambulance that picked you up. You have to believe me. I didn't know."

Stefan patted his shoulder. "Of course you didn't. She used all of us."

Bashkir pulled Mona from beneath a plasti-glass pane. "How did we get out of there anyway?" he asked. "I thought we were dead for sure."

Ditto turned Cosmo over. A sliver of metal was visible through the torn skin of his forehead. "Believe it or not, I think the rookie saved us again. He used his head."

Ditto placed a hand on Cosmo's forehead. A slight silver shimmering played around the contact.

"I can take some of his pain, for a while. The healing, he'll have to do on his own."

Stefan sat Mona up. "You should have told me, Ditto."

"You're right, I should have. But now that you do know, what are you going to do about it?"

Stefan pulled a capsule of smelling salts from the medi-kit on his belt. He snapped it under Mona's nostrils. "I'm going to find out why Ellie Faustino is collecting Parasites."

Mona woke up shouting. "No way, *Mamá*!" she cried. "No way am I going to wear that dress!"

Stefan picked her up, laying her on a surgical table. "Okay, Mona. It's okay. You're with friends."

Mona squinted suspiciously. "No dresses?"

"No. No dresses. Just relax. Try not to move."

Mona's face was decidedly green. "Okay if I throw up?"

"Be my guest," said Stefan, taking two steps back.

Cosmo flapped on the floor like a fish, fighting off a nightmare enemy.

"The kid has been through a lot in the past few weeks," said Ditto.

Stefan hoisted Cosmo onto another surgical table. "After tonight, it's over. Normal lives all around."

Ditto shook ropes of melted cellophane and acidic compound from his hands. "Really? Where have I heard that before?"

The vat man was not overly eager to share any information, but one look at the Supernaturalists' faces weakened his resolve.

"I don't even work here full-time. Sometimes I do some special work for President Faustino. Off the books, you understand."

"I understand," said Stefan. "We were very nearly off the books ourselves."

"Nothing personal, just doing my job."

"Yeah, yeah, nothing personal. Anything for a little something extra in the paycheck."

The vat man was lying in a pool of acidic compound. The yellow liquid was beginning to burn the folds in his flesh.

"Two questions," said Stefan. "And you'd better answer me straightaway, because if you do not, the consequences will be dire."

Vat man nodded so fast his chin was a blur. "Okay, ask away."

"One, where's our gear?"

"Gear? Gear? You mean equipment, rods, and computers?"

"Rods are the priority right now. Where are they?"

Vat man raised a finger. "Is that the second question?"

Stefan closed one eye, the other bulged dangerously. The scar stretching his lips twitched. "No, idiot. That is still the first question. Tell me where our stuff is. Now!"

"Okay, okay. Over there, in the blue bins. I was supposed to incinerate it after I had flushed your molecules down the drain. No offense."

Stefan nodded at his teammates. They rifled through the blue bins, selecting rods, clips, holsters, and phones.

"Better take the fuzz plates too," said Mona. "We don't want to be caught by surveillance cameras."

They hosed each other down, then strapped on their gear, feeling very much like foxes in a bolt-hole, surrounded by baying hounds. Well-armed foxes.

"Second question," said Stefan, hoisting the vat man upright by the collar. "Where's Faustino?"

The anguish in the vat man's eyes showed that he didn't really want to answer the question. "I wish I could tell you, I really do. But . . ."

"This had better be a really good *but*," warned Stefan. "Your immediate future depends on it."

Vat man's Adam's apple bobbed in his throat like a tiny alien trying to get out. "It's a big facility. President Faustino could be in her office, or the conference room, or on her rounds. I don't know."

"At this time of night? Rubbish."

The vat man checked the wall clock. "When President Faustino comes in this late, it's usually for off-the-books work, a bit like my own. Usually, she concentrates on the Unspec project, whatever that is."

"That's the one. Where?"

The vat man sighed. This was going to cost him his job. "Lab one. At the end of the corridor, turn right. You'll know it by the two guards on the door. They're the only security on at night."

Stefan dropped the man into a pool of acidic compound. "Good. Now look into my eyes and promise me you won't sound the alarm the second we're out the door."

"Me," said vat man. "Sound the alarm? Absolutely not. You have my word."

"Hands up who believes him," said Stefan.

No hands went up.

"That's what I thought," said Stefan, checking his lightning rod for cellophane slugs.

Ditto was being a real baby. He stumbled down the corridor, bawling his little eyes out. The two guards outside Lab one couldn't help but notice.

"Hey, look," said Guard A, a strapping female with muscle implants all over her upper body and night-vision eyeballs. "A kid. How did a kid get in here?"

"Search me," said Guard B, an equally strapping male, with a thick beard that grew almost to his eyes. "But you know the rules. He's gotta be wrapped."

Guard A punched him on the shoulder. The punch would have shattered most people's collarbones. "Hey, have a heart. You're not afraid of a little kid are you?"

Ditto was beside them now, wiping the tears from his eyes.

"Of course not," said Guard B. "I'm not afraid of some kid."

The kid grinned a grin, nasty beyond his apparent years. "You should be," he said, pulling a lightning rod from inside his shirt.

Guards A and B were wrapped before they had a chance to say, *Where's your mommy?*

The Supernaturalists crouched outside the laboratory door, fuzz plates pulled over their faces. There were two frosted-glass panels in the door. The light emanating from the lab was blue.

"I hate being a kid," sniffled Ditto.

"Focus," said Stefan. "This is a dangerous situation."

"A couple of midnight scientists? Very dangerous. The security people are already wrapped."

"Don't forget Ellie. I never met anyone who could hit harder or shoot straighter. She was one of the head combat coaches in the academy."

"Point taken. The usual plan?"

Stefan put his hand on the door handle. "No. Cosmo and Mona stay at the door. There may be more security in the building. Ditto, you come with me into the lab. We take a quick look around, without wrapping anyone if possible, shoot a few seconds of video, then back to Abracadabra Street to plan our next move. We will have to take care of this situation, but not today. We're not ready."

"But, Stefan!" complained Mona.

"Another day," said Stefan firmly. "Today we look around only."

Cosmo felt that it wouldn't be that simple. Something unexpected would happen, and before he knew where he was, the Supernaturalists would be up to their necks in trouble once more.

The lab door was unlocked. Stefan and Ditto slipped through soundlessly. Mona stuck her foot in the frame, keeping it open a crack.

"You never know," she whispered to Cosmo. "They might need us."

The door opened to an elevated walkway, overlooking a huge laboratory. The walls were painted sterile white, and fifty-foot strip lights lined the ceiling. Lab technicians scurried across the white tiles like albino ants, and in the middle of it all was a giant sunken construction which resembled nothing more than an enormous spirit level. Solid machinery on both ends with a transparent blue section in the middle.

"So just to confirm, we're going to take a few frames of video, then hightail it back to Abracadabra Street?" said Ditto.

"That was for the benefit of the other two," said Stefan. "You and I both know we'll never get a chance like this again. As soon as Ellie finds out we've escaped, this place will be sealed up tighter than a camel's nostrils in a sandstorm. We have to find out what's going on now."

Ditto nodded. "That's what I thought. What do you make of that thing down there?"

"A generator of some kind. Nuclear, I'd say."

"But nuclear power is banned on every continent."

Stefan nodded thoughtfully. "Maybe, but not in space."

Ditto and Stefan drew their weapons and proceeded slowly down the stairs. Ditto opened his phone and shot some video of the lab. "In case Mona is watching," he whispered.

A sudden crack splintered the air. A flat noise like bamboo striking wood. Ditto recognized it immediately. A gunshot. A real gunpowder slug being fired. Booshka gangs often modified lightning rods to accommodate actual projectiles. The bullets were subsonic, but coated with Teflon to make up for their slowness. Stefan clutched his chest, stumbling backward against the wall. Then he bounced forward again, toppling over the railing. His tall frame plummeted twenty feet, straight down.

"Stefan!" screamed Ditto, his juvenile voice rent with anguish. Bashkir lay face down on the tiling, a pool of blood spreading from beneath his torso. He wasn't moving.

Below on the laboratory main level, Ellen Faustino looked up from the readout panel she had been inspecting. "Why am I not surprised?" she muttered, shaking her head.

Ditto pulled his lightning rod. "Faustino!" he shouted.

"Take a moment, Mr. Bonn, or should I say Ditto, to study your chest."

Ditto looked down. There was a bright red dot jittering across the material of his shirt.

Faustino approached the steps. "My little voice told me to take precautions. You Supernaturalists have proved slippery in the past. So I left a just-in-case man covering the door. Seems like I made the right decision. He will shoot you too, Ditto. There are no cameras in this room. Nothing to incriminate us later. Now, drop your weapon."

Ditto did so, watching it clatter through the bars onto the floor.

Faustino raised her voice. "Now, tell the other two to join us, or my man in the shadows will be forced to pull his trigger one more time."

Ditto tensed. "Go ahead and give the order. At least two of us will live to talk."

Cosmo and Mona tumbled through the access door. "No!" said Cosmo. "We're here. Don't shoot."

"Morons," hissed Ditto. "Now we're all dead."

Mona raised her hands. "Just trying to buy us some time."

Ditto descended the stairwell slowly. The laser dot stayed on his chest. "What are you doing here, Faustino? What is this madness?"

Faustino pointed to Stefan. "Check your leader first. If I must explain this machine, I don't want to have to go through it all twice. You two children, get down here where I can see you. Remember, at the teeniest sign of heroics, you inherit the laser dot from Mr. Ditto."

Ditto hurried to Stefan's aid. With considerable effort, he flipped the Russian and checked his heartbeat. It was faint, but there.

Stefan clasped Ditto's hand, placing it on the chest wound.

"I see now," he whispered, his voice ragged. "I see it all. Things are different here."

Ditto supported his head. "No, Stefan. Not yet. We have things to do."

"Take the pain away," grunted Stefan through blood bubbles. "It's holding me down."

Ditto concentrated, seeking the pain out with his sixth sense, pulling the energy into himself. He felt the buzz of electricity pulse through his small frame. "Better?"

Stefan's eyes were clear. "Better. Much."

The wound was bad. Very bad.

"You're not cured, Stefan. I can't cure you."

"I know, Ditto," said Stefan after a coughing fit. "I know."

Several scientists scuttled off to other parts of the facility. They had no desire to witness whatever happened next. Faustino was left with a single bodyguard and, of course, a hidden sniper.

"Down here, you two," she said to Cosmo and Mona. "I want you all together."

Stefan lifted himself onto one elbow. "Tell me this isn't what I think it is, Faustino? Not even you could be this heartless."

Faustino laughed her delighted little-girl laugh. "Oh, Stefan, still a spark of decency left in you. I remember you in the academy, always so naive. You actually joined the police to help people, and you're still doing it."

"But a nuclear reactor? After all the disasters the world has seen? There isn't a government alive that would buy into nuclear power. How could Myishi do this?"

Speaking was not easy for Stefan now. Even staying conscious took concentration.

Faustino drummed her fingers on her chin. "My work

here is officially unofficial. Oh, Ray Shine knows what I'm doing well enough, but he pretends not to. That way if anything goes wrong, I'll be the only one taking the fall. That's what business is all about; finding someone to take the blame. Except this time, there will be no blame, only profits."

Stefan stumbled toward the generator. Both ends were traditional enough, but the center was a double-glazed plasti-glass cuboid insulated with hydro-gel. The surface plate was the size of a football field. Inside the cuboid, at least a million Parasites jerked and bucked as radiation passed through their biological filters.

"We collected the Un-spec four, which you so kindly knocked out for us, with an electromagnet, and keep them imprisoned with hydro-gel. This entire lab has hydro-gel in the cavity walls. That's why there's not a Parasite on your chest right now."

The reactor was a vision of torment. The creatures that should be fulfilling their natural role as painkillers were writhing in the bowels of a nuclear reactor.

Faustino was unaffected by her own cruelty. "It's quite clever, really. The reactor itself is a water model, but we have replaced the water with living creatures, Un-spec four."

Stefan locked his knees, to keep them from folding. "You're deranged, Faustino. Completely insane."

Ellen Faustino wiggled both eyebrows at her bodyguard, as if this was the daftest statement she had ever heard. "Insane? Do you have any idea what I have accomplished here?"

"No," said Ditto, eager to buy time. "Do tell us."

"Ah yes, Mr. Lucien Bonn, the Bartoli baby. People called Bartoli insane too, you know." Faustino walked onto the floor level plasti-glass pane that sealed the reactor's central section. Below her feet, hundreds of thousands of Parasites shuddered. "The problem with the boiling water reactor was that it contaminated the water, and eventually the turbine blades. Un-spec four take care of that problem. Not only that, but they are much more effective at slowing down neutrons and sending them back into the uranium core. They keep the reactor completely clean, and one-hundred-percent efficient, and use one tenth the amount of uranium. Un-spec four are a natural miracle."

"But people are suffering without them," gasped Stefan.

"Oh, grow up, Stefan," snapped Faustino, her true savage nature flashing through the sophisticated image. "People suffer all the time. I don't cause suffering. With the Faustino NuSun, I may actually help people. I might even initiate some of those fictitious welfare projects I told you about, though the helping thing would be incidental. I'm mainly doing this for the money."

"The Faustino NuSun," said Stefan bitterly. He staggered to the edge of the generator. Giant turbines whirred beneath Faustino's feet, sparks of pure energy playing around their layered blades.

"Why, Professor? All those *accidents*? Risking all those lives. My mother is dead."

The last vestiges of civility dropped from Faustino's eyes like scales.

"The Satellite is falling, you idiot!" she yelled. "Falling out of the sky, because it is too heavy and too low. There are too many commercial units for the original structure to support. To keep it in its present orbit, its commercially viable orbit, Myishi needs a new generator, a lighter and more efficient generator. If it doesn't get one, Myishi loses all its advertising contracts. Billions of dinars. Billions. And that's just the tip of the iceberg. Myishi is contracted for ten more satellites. Ten! It's the biggest deal the world has ever seen. And the Faustino NuSun will power every one."

Stefan waved his hands at Cosmo and Mona. They rushed to his aid, propping him up, one under each arm.

"Lift me," he whispered, his tones laden with agony. The pain was coming back. The young Supernaturalists did as they were told, helping Stefan onto the platform.

Faustino's bodyguard took a step nearer. "Close enough, boy. Don't make me dislocate a few things."

"Don't worry about it, Manuel," said Faustino, rising onto the balls of her sandaled feet. "Stefan never could beat me on the practice mat. Now I have a couple of quarts more blood than he does and no hole in my chest."

Stefan knelt on the plasti-glass. Below him was a blue hell. A hell he'd created. An ocean of Parasites undulated beneath him, their eyes dull and glazed.

Faustino knelt. "Is this how it ends, Stefan? A whimper on the floor. You should have stayed in the vat."

The bodyguard took off his sunglasses. "President Faustino, I'm nervous now. I gotta tell you. And I don't get nervous easy."

"Relax, Manuel. Cover the kids. Do you think you can manage that?"

Manuel rested the glasses on the bridge of a nose that had been broken so often it was almost flat. "Yes, Madam President. I got the kids."

Faustino kicked off her sandals, bouncing like a boxer. "Well, Stefan, do you have one more round left in you?"

Spasms racked Stefan's chest. "I'm not going to fight you, Professor."

"Really? Oh come on. I'm the one responsible for your mother's death, remember?"

Stefan did not rise to the bait. "There's a better way to get you."

Faustino stopped bouncing, her smug grin faltered. "And what's that?"

"Fight from the inside," said Stefan, his voice barely audible. "Attack from the rear. Remember?"

Stefan's hands were moving, hidden in the folds of his coat.

"What are you doing? What have you got there?"

"Nothing dangerous. Just my phone. Nothing to worry President Ellen Faustino."

"A phone? Who can you ask for help?"

"Nobody. I'm not asking anybody for help. Just sending some mail."

Faustino stepped closer. "Mail?"

"I got a friend with *V News* who would sell a couple of limbs to see the video I'm shooting right now. He's going to owe me, big-time."

It took Faustino a moment to realize what was happening, but when she did, her face twisted into a Halloween version of itself. "He's sending video! If the press gets hold of footage of our reactor before we're ready, it's over!" She dived at the injured Russian, clawlike hands digging beneath his torso. She pulled Stefan's hands out. They were empty.

"Surprise," he said, wrapping his arms around Faustino in a bear hug. She beat his chest with her fists. With no result. Stefan struggled to his feet.

"Dead man's grip," grunted Stefan, sweat collecting in his eyebrows. "The last thing I'll ever do."

Anyone with police training knows about the dead man's grip. If a suspect is dying, and knows it, stay well out of reach, because the last thing he catches on to often goes to the grave with him. It's amazing how someone with only seconds to live can find the strength to bend metal and snap bones.

The sniper in the rafters transferred the laser dot to Stefan's head.

Manuel spoke into a mike hidden in his sleeve. "No. Hold your fire. Repeat. Hold your fire. I'll handle this."

"I'm not the one shooting video," Stefan whispered. "It's Ditto."

"Get the kid!" screeched Faustino. "The blond one."

Manuel pointed his lightning rod at Ditto. "You got a phone, kid? Hand it over."

"Sure, I have a phone. Take it easy, Manuel. I'm just going to reach into my pocket and get it."

Manuel nodded. "Okay. You do that. Real slow. Don't make me wrap you."

Ditto kept one hand in the air, reaching into his pocket with the other. He took the phone out with two fingers. "Look, here it is. No problem. I'm bringing it over."

"No. Stay where you are. Toss the phone."

Ditto nodded almost imperceptibly at Cosmo. "You want me to toss it?"

"That's what I said. What are you? Short *and* stupid?"

"Okay, Manuel, don't panic. Here it comes."

Ditto tossed the phone high. Much higher than necessary. One set of eyes followed its arc. Manuel's. Cosmo and Mona pulled lightning rods out of their belts, and hit the bodyguard with at least four cellophane slugs. The virus spread across his frame, wrapping him completely in seconds.

Ditto smiled. "A thing of beauty," he said, retrieving the phone.

"Idiot!" screamed Faustino, her voice muffled by Stefan's bulk. "Half-wit!"

"You're running out of options, Professor," said Stefan weakly.

Faustino squirmed to face him. "Don't kid yourself, Stefan. I still have my sniper. He can keep your Supernaturalists off the plasti-glass until you die. That shouldn't be long now."

The sniper's laser dot hopped from target to target. The man in the rafters was uncertain who to cover.

"Give it up, Stefan. There's no way to win."

The red dot strayed onto the plasti-glass. Cosmo, Mona, and Ditto ducked behind a string of monorail coaches.

Stefan smiled. There was blood on his lips. "They're safe now. It's just you and me."

"Nothing has changed. It's still a waiting game."

Ditto's voice pierced the hum of the generator. "Don't do it, Stefan. There must be another way."

"What's he talking about?" asked Faustino.

Stefan ignored her. "Sorry, Ditto. All of you. You're on your own now."

Cosmo grabbed Ditto's shoulder. "What does he mean?"

Ditto dropped his head into his hands. "Stefan is dying. That bullet was too close to his heart. He wants his death to mean something."

"Mean something?" said Mona. "Mean what?"

Ditto poked his head over the top of the coach. "An end to pain."

With the absolute last ounce of strength in his legs, Stefan struggled to his knees, bringing the piniomed Faustino down with him.

The laser dot flashed across his vision, settling on his forehead.

"I'm going to kill her,"' he shouted at the rafters. "She killed my mother."

Faustino tried to call out, but her face was smothered in Stefan's chest.

"I mean it! I'll kill her."

The dot jittered. The sniper was uncertain.

"She's a dead woman."

The hidden gunman made his decision. A muzzle flashed high in the shadows, propeling a subsonic bullet from the rod's barrel, spinning along the length of the laser beam, shedding its coat of gel as it traveled.

Stefan saw the flash. He'd been waiting for it. Counting on it. He allowed his knees to buckle, collapsing to the floor a milisecond before the subsonic bullet buzzed past his ear, drilling straight through the twin layers of plasti-glass.

Faustino saw gel bubble through the holes. "No!' she cried.

The bullet sped into the reactor's interior, taking a chip out of one of the turbines. The chip spiraled upward, scoring the plasti-glass like a finger through sand. More and more hydro-gel dripped down, scattering any Parasites with the energy to move. Alarm lights flickered on a dozen consoles, automatically shutting and sealing the reactor's nuclear sections. But the Un-spec four area was irretrievably breached. Cracks raced along the surface, competing with each other to reach the edge. Each crack gave birth to a million more, until there wasn't a square foot of unbroken plasti-glass left. Hydro-gel dropped in waves, sparking a dozen fires on the floor beneath. Parasites crawled from its path, but they could not flee without clean energy.

Faustino's cheek rested on the plasti-glass. "Let me go," she pleaded.

Stefan did so. "It's too late, Professor," he said. "Don't worry, you won't feel a thing."

Faustino scrambled to her feet, but before she had taken half a dozen steps the transparent surface collapsed entirely, plunging them both into the belly of the reactor's central section. Every window in the facility was blown out, hydro-gel dripping from the double glazed panes.

Stefan landed on his back, but there was no pain. There was no pain because a single Parasite had draped itself across his chest. The agony flowed out of the Supernaturalist into the creature.

"Take it," said Stefan, the words rustling through his lips. "Be free."

The Parasite pulled out the pain in a rope of glistening silver. In seconds its desiccated heart pulsed vibrantly again. The Parasite's round, soulful eyes stared into Stefan's own.

"I understand now," said Stefan. And one more word after that. A word or a last breath. "Mother."

The Parasite reached out a four-fingered hand, laying it on the shoulder of a suffering brother. A burst of energy flowed through one to the other, liberating the second. And so Stefan's pain spread, rationed between a thousand Parasites, giving each one the energy to escape the nuclear reactor and find the energy to free more Parasites. They scampered up the walls, avoiding globs of hydro-gel, and scattered through the lab like leaves caught in a whirlwind.

Stefan's heart had stopped beating, but he had just

had time to watch them go. And in the middle of all that blue, there was something else. Someplace else. Somewhere different.

Cosmo and Ditto were leaning over the lip of the reactor's central section. Ditto seemed like an actual child, with tears streaming down his face.

"You had to do it, Stefan," he sobbed. "You had to be the big, stupid hero. Nothing else would do."

Cosmo, as usual, couldn't believe what was happening. "You mean he goaded that sniper?"

"Of course. A bullet was the only way through the plastiglass. He was waiting for the muzzle flash. Slow bullets, you see."

Parasites whirled all around them, hunting for energy. Already some had returned through the shattered windows, carrying energy to free the others. A single Parasite hovered by Cosmo's shoulder, its head cocked expectantly.

Cosmo stepped back. "It senses something." A red dot appeared on his chest.

"Oh, no," said Ditto. "The sniper is still up there. Don't move. I'll try to negotiate."

Ditto raised his hands, turning toward the source of the beam. "Faustino's finished!" he shouted at the shadows. "You don't have to do this. We have money."

There was no reaction for a moment, then the familiar *whup-whup* of a cellophane slug being fired and striking. Mona stepped from the blackness, high up in the rafters. "I took advantage of the confusion to wrap the sniper," she said holstering her lightening rod. "It's what Stefan taught me." She paused for a second, working up the courage to ask. "Is he gone?"

"Yes," replied Cosmo. "He's gone." And so was the hovering Parasite.

Mona was quiet for several moments. Cosmo thought he saw her slender frame shake. After that she pulled herself together. "Then we had better be gone too. There are alarms going off all over the building. The paralegals will be here any minute."

It was true. Cosmo could already hear sirens in the distance. He took one last look over the edge, then hurried toward the stairwell, and freedom.

CHAPTER 10
FALLOUT

Utopian Acres; Satellite City suburb,
two weeks later

INCREDIBLY, ELLEN FAUSTINO SURVIVED to be brought before the Myishi Chairman. As soon as her skin grafts had taken, she was choppered out to Mayor Ray Shine's estate in Utopian Acres.

Mayor Ray Shine, who also happened to be Chairman of Myishi Industries in Satellite City, cut short a golf game especially to talk to her. Ray was a flamboyant character who did not believe in dressing down for any occasion. Today's outfit was a yellow-and-pink checkered sweater with matching peaked hat, tweed breeches, and Argyle socks.

The mayor parked his massive girth behind a desk set on ivory legs, and poured a glass of purified water, leaving Faustino to squirm. He drank deeply, belched gently, and sighed. "Ellie, Ellie, Ellie, what have you been getting up to out there in R&D?" His voice was gentle, but Faustino knew him to be the most ruthless man she had ever met.

"Ray, Chairman Shine, with respect, you know exactly what was going on. I told you."

"You did?" said Shine innocently. "I can't seem to recall that conversation. And there doesn't seem to be a record of it. No, I'm afraid you're on your own this time, Ellie. A pity the press got hold of that video. Developing a nuclear reactor, what were you thinking?"

Faustino bristled. "I was thinking that I could save this company. You saw the figures, I would have done it too . . ."

"I know, if it hadn't been for the naturists running around with no clothes on."

"The Supernaturalists," said Faustino, through gritted teeth. "And they are a lot more dangerous than you give them credit for, even with their leader gone."

"Yes, well, maybe I'll keep an eye on them. Anyway, you don't need to worry about that, you being dead."

Faustino's heart jumped into her throat. "Dead? Really, Mr. Chairman, there's no need for—"

Shine silenced her with a wave of his hand. "Not *dead* dead, Ellie. Press dead. We had to give the news crews a scapegoat, so you're it. Fortunately, the body was too disfigured to identify, and I don't think there's any chance of your being recognized, not with your new face."

Faustino blushed, something she hadn't done since she was a schoolgirl. "So what does Myishi have planned for me?"

Shine leaned back in his chair, until it creaked. "The fact

is, Ellie, that your reactor was our best hope. I don't know how you did it, but somehow your test figures showed promise. Your Un-spec four creatures sure were doing the business."

Faustino perked up. "So, you're not canceling the project?"

"Of course not, but we will have to be a lot sneakier."

"How sneaky?"

Shine smiled. "The South Pole."

Faustino almost objected, but she knew all too well what happened to people who argued with Ray Shine.

"Is that okay with you?"

Ellen forced a smile. "The South Pole. Isolated. No interruptions. Fine."

Mayor Ray Shine stood, straightening his chequered sweater. "Good. There's a chopper waiting to transport you to our Antarctic facility. Have a good trip."

"Excellent. Thank you, Mr. Mayor." Faustino rose with the aid of a crutch, hobbling to the office door.

"Oh, and Ellie?"

"Yes, Mr. Mayor?"

"You only get one second chance. Mess this up, and you may need some of those Un-spec four creatures yourself. Are we clear?"

"Crystal, Mr. Mayor."

1405 Abracadabra Street

There wasn't much left of the Abracadabra Street warehouse but windows and walls. And most of the windows had holes in them, where the paralegals had cut through. For two weeks the Supernaturalists cleaned, fixed, and grieved, trying to repair the damage done by Myishi. There was still a long way to go.

"We still have our bunks," said Mona, putting a brave face on it at the end of a particularly tiring day.

Ditto kicked the ruptured remains of the refrigerator. "Well, whoop-de-doo. Bunks, thank heaven for that. No food though."

Cosmo was trying to connect a salvaged hard drive into a gutted computer. "Mona brought some pazzas back earlier. She left them on the Pigmobile's engine. Maybe you're not interested in pazzas anymore, after the HALO incident."

The Bartoli baby rubbed his hands together. "Are you kidding? I couldn't hold a perfectly good foodstuff responsible for my weak stomach," he cackled, heading for the elevator. "Pazzas and bunks. What more could a young man ask for?"

Suddenly a deep weariness settled into Cosmo's bones. He righted a chair and settled onto it. But sitting down didn't seem to help. He'd barely had four hours sleep in a row since they had lost Stefan. Sometimes it all seemed so pointless.

"What do we do now?" he asked Mona after several minutes silence. "Without him?"

265

Mona shrugged. "Day by day, like we have been, like every-body else. There are big changes coming to Satellite City. More and more people living outside the footprint. In a few more years, there may not even be a Satellite. We'll have to make our own way. At least we're alive. At least we have friends."

Cosmo wasn't ready for comfort just yet. "But he kept us together. He kept us going."

Mona cleared her throat. "You know, Cosmo, technically, back there in the laboratory, I did save your life."

Cosmo was still staring at the floor. "That's right. With the sniper. I meant to say thank you, but it all happened so . . ."

Cosmo suddenly remembered a conversation they'd had on the roof.

Maybe next time you can save me, he'd said to her. *Then I'll owe you a kiss.*

He looked up. There were tears in Mona's eyes, but she was smiling. He stood slowly, suddenly wondering if the plate in his forehead was sticking out. "I owe you a kiss."

Mona pointed to her cheek. "That's right. You do."

Cosmo's knee plate began to itch. "I've never actually . . . I mean . . ."

Mona smiled mischeviously. "Maybe we should forget the whole thing."

Cosmo nodded. "Maybe."

Then he kissed her.

Of course, Ditto chose this moment to return with an armful of pazzas. "Oh spare me," he said, throwing an empty wrapper in the recycler. "Now I'm going to have to put up with you two making doe eyes every time we go out hunting supernatural creatures."

"Creatures?" said Cosmo. "What creatures? The Parasites are friendly, remember?"

Ditto began tinkering with the back of his favorite TV. "Parasites? Who said anything about them? Let me tell you, there are a lot worse things than Parasites. Just because you two can't see them doesn't mean they aren't there. I'm sensitive, remember. A Bartoli baby. Nothing hides from me."

Ditto took a huge bite from his second pazza. "Believe me," he mumbled through a mouthful of food, "the Supernaturalists' work is far from over. But we do need some equipment. What do we have left?"

Mona pulled a starter card from her pocket.

"We have the Pigmobile."

Ditto nodded. "It's a start."